F
LEW

Lewis, Beverly.

The photograph.

$19.99

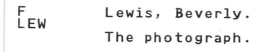

DATE			
11-30-15			

The PHOTOGRAPH

Books by Beverly Lewis

The Photograph
The Love Letters
The River

HOME TO HICKORY HOLLOW

The Fiddler
The Bridesmaid
The Guardian
The Secret Keeper
The Last Bride

THE ROSE TRILOGY

The Thorn • The Judgment
The Mercy

ABRAM'S DAUGHTERS

The Covenant • The Betrayal
The Sacrifice
The Prodigal • The Revelation

THE HERITAGE OF
LANCASTER COUNTY

The Shunning • The Confession
The Reckoning

ANNIE'S PEOPLE

The Preacher's Daughter
The Englisher • The Brethren

THE COURTSHIP
OF NELLIE FISHER

The Parting • The Forbidden
The Longing

SEASONS OF GRACE

The Secret • The Missing
The Telling

The Postcard • The Crossroad

The Redemption of Sarah Cain
Sanctuary (with David Lewis)
Child of Mine (with David Lewis)
The Sunroom • October Song

Amish Prayers
The Beverly Lewis Amish
Heritage Cookbook

www.beverlylewis.com

BEVERLY LEWIS

The PHOTOGRAPH

BETHANYHOUSE

a division of Baker Publishing Group
Minneapolis, Minnesota

© 2015 by Beverly M. Lewis, Inc.

Published by Bethany House Publishers
11400 Hampshire Avenue South
Bloomington, Minnesota 55438
www.bethanyhouse.com

Bethany House Publishers is a division of
Baker Publishing Group, Grand Rapids, Michigan

Printed in the United States of America

Library of Congress Cataloging-in-Publication Data
Lewis, Beverly.
　　The photograph / Beverly Lewis.
　　　pages ; cm
　　Summary: "In a 1980s Amish community, three sisters face a time of transition in their family, and each searches for a way to define her own future"— Provided by publisher.
　　　ISBN 978-0-7642-1728-9 (hardcover : acid-free paper)
　　　ISBN 978-0-7642-1247-5 (softcover)
　　　ISBN 978-0-7642-1729-6 (large-print)
　　　1. Amish—Fiction. 2. Sisters—Fiction. I. Title.
PS3562.E9383P48 2015
813'.54—dc23　　　　　　　　　　　　　　　　　　　　　　　2015009450

Scripture quotations are from the King James Version of the Bible.

Cover design by Dan Thornberg, Design Source Creative Services
Art direction by Paul Higdon

15　16　17　18　19　20　21　　　7　6　5　4　3　2　1

To
Carole Billingsley,
whose prayers and love
are twofold blessings.

Now and then, in this workaday world, things do happen in the delightful storybook fashion, and what a comfort that is.

—From *Little Women,* by Louisa May Alcott

Prologue

TRUTH BE TOLD, I was taught never to feel sorry for myself. *"Nothin' helpful comes from pity,"* Mamma often said, expecting me and my siblings to be grateful and cheerful, no matter what came our way. I confess to missing her and *Dat* terribly as we continue life without them. Yet I've scarcely time to dwell on the past. My youngest sister, Lily, has caused me no small amount of concern since our widowed mother succumbed to pneumonia last winter.

I recall one of those frosty January days when I stepped into Mamma's bedroom and saw her standing with eighteen-year-old Lily near the sunlit window. Our mother was swathed all in white from head to foot and had somehow managed to pull herself up from her sickbed to don her best organdy *Kapp*, matted hair all *strubblich* beneath. She was talking quietly to Lily, her untied bathrobe hanging from her frail shoulders.

"Just look at those critter tracks in the new snow." Mamma pointed out the window, then turned to face Lily, still not noticing

me. "*My dear girl, be ever so careful what tracks you make, and where they might lead those who follow.*"

It wasn't new, this sort of talk from our mother. But this time, Lily's lower lip quivered, and she looked with sad eyes through the windowpane, saying nary a word.

Little did she or any of us know that precious Mamma would leave this old world behind just three short weeks later. Leaving Lily for me to look after, trying diligently to keep her on the straight and narrow path.

Our older sister, Frona, had been fretting over Lily just as I was. She especially worried over what was to become of the three of us, since we were still unmarried and living in the farmhouse where we grew up, here in Lancaster County's Eden Valley. Living there on borrowed time, since our brother Menno had inherited the place from our parents.

"Tonight we'll have some answers," Frona informed me after breakfast this mid-May morning. "I just hope we like what we hear."

The youngest of our four older married brothers, Menno had worked the land there since Dat's passing, helping Mamma and then us to keep things going. While he was often around the farm, he didn't often set foot in the house, other than for the occasional noon meal, but he'd told Frona he was eager to drop by after supper for a talk. By the look of gloom on her face, I felt she needed assurance all would go well. "It's awful *gut* of Menno to check in on us, remember," I replied.

"Ain't sure what's up," Frona said, frowning again. "But I have my suspicions."

"Well, I guess we'll know soon enough." I set about making my delicious peanut butter balls, Menno's favorite, wanting to offer him some when he arrived.

I've learned in my twenty years that a person really has no idea how life's going to play out. Things often start out fine and then take a hard turn. Dat and Mamma, healthy as they seemed, left us in their prime. *Jah,* I knew firsthand that when hard times came, you needed something to cling to. In my parents' case, it was their trust in our heavenly Father. 'Twas the same for me.

Unfortunately, it wasn't true for pretty Lily. Mamma had always been her rock during such times, and without her around, Lily seemed lost. We all were, in our own way, just not nearly as openly, nor as desperately.

At night, when Lily curled her slender body next to mine as we huddled like spoons to keep warm in the bed we'd shared since childhood, I'd hear her talking to herself and crying softly. The words might have been prayers, but if so, they were nothing akin to the ones Mamma had taught us. Sometimes Lily could say the most senseless things, honestly, and I tried my best not to take them to heart.

"All the fun in life is passin' me by," Lily had said soon after Mamma died. *"I work hard from sunup to sundown, and for what? Just to start all over the same way tomorrow."*

"But work can be fun," I reminded her.

"Maybe for you and Frona."

I let it go, remembering what Mamma's lifelong friend Naomi Mast had once said: *"It's better not to ponder too much what folks say when they're grieving."*

"Time to go an' greet your devoted patrons, Eva," said Frona, trying to shoo me out the side door to my candy shop that morning. It was built onto one end of the house—all Dat's doing, although Mamma had been in agreement, back when I was only twelve and already creating the kinds of tasty candies a person couldn't seem to stop thinking about.

"You've found your calling, Eva," my father once said, beaming. *"And we're the happy—and hungry—receivers!"*

Even as a girl, I often lost track of time while creating new recipes, always trying to outdo myself with tantalizing confections to tempt the tongue. Some said my candies were like a riveting series of books—you couldn't wait to get your hands on the next one. And right quick, there were more orders for homemade fudge and crystal sticks than I had room for in our kitchen, large though it was. So my father had taken it on himself to build the sunny and welcoming candy shop, with its attached area for a small work kitchen. The very first time I stepped inside and looked around, I felt like I'd died and gone to Glory.

"For me, Dat?" I'd said.

My father kissed my forehead. *"All for you, little Eva."*

I smiled back at him, one of a thousand happy memories.

"You're daydreaming again." Frona was staring at me, waving in front of my face. "You have customers!"

"Soon as I wash my hands," I told her.

"Be sure to bring back the gossip, ya hear?"

"Why don't ya just come hear it for yourself?" I turned on my heel to head for the sink. "And while you're at it, you could help over there, too."

Frona snapped her long white dish towel into the air. "I've plenty to do here, believe me. Anyway, I saw Dienners' boy out there in line."

"Can't imagine why."

Frona gave me a knowing grin.

I lathered up real good, then rinsed and dried my hands. It wasn't for her to know what was or wasn't in my heart for twenty-year-old Alfred Dienner. After all, he was the first fellow to ask me to go riding, four years ago when I was but sixteen. Alfred was real nice and not bad looking, either, but he planned to farm, and I couldn't bear the thought of being a farmer's wife.

Stuck in a farmer's crowded kitchen . . .

"Best hurry," Frona said, her eyes softening. "We need every cent to pay for new gardening tools." Plain as a plate, my sister was also a worrywart.

I recalled the times Menno and our other brothers—Emmanuel, Stephen, and Rufus—had encouraged Frona to worry less and trust *Gott* more. "For goodness' sake, we'll be fine," I told Frona. "I promise."

"*You* promise?" Frona moved to the back door and looked out the window, dish towel hanging limply over her arm. The sun shone onto her smooth, round cheek. She looked as vexed as ever, despite her pretty green cape dress and matching apron, the hems nearly brushing her ankles.

"We've always managed to pay our bills on time."

Frona blinked her gray-blue eyes at me behind her thick glasses. She'd taken it upon herself to wear Mamma's old pair, saying they helped her see everything she'd been missing. "*Puh!* I've never understood why you're so *hallich*," Frona huffed, like being happy was something to be ashamed of. She leaned her plump self against the windowsill and glowered.

"Mamma loved watchin' the birds, remember? Our heavenly Father looks after even the lowly sparrow."

Frona puffed her cheeks and blew air, then plodded over to the gas-powered fridge. Opening it, she merely stared inside. After a time, she made a sound clear down in the back of her throat and looked back at me. It was as if a gray shadow passed over her.

What's she so worried about?

While Frona was prone to fret, especially over the future, I wasn't exactly immune to that sin. Dat frequently reminded us that problems were designed to strengthen our faith. *"In every-thing, give thanks,"* he would say.

So, in memory of dear Dat, I was determined to count our blessings—family, friends, and fudge. Then and there, I chose to believe that whatever was on Frona's mind just now, I needn't think twice about. Our Father in heaven would take care of us. Besides, most things a person worries over never come to pass.

CHAPTER ONE

· ❀ ·

EVA ESCH STOOD BEHIND the wooden counter greeting each of her candy customers on the warmest morning so far of this budding month of May. Sunlight filled the neat and tidy shop that Friday, and between sale transactions, she happily scurried about, arranging the taffy and the well-formed peanut butter balls in an attractive array. Her father, Vernon Esch, had purposely designed the counter to face the windows, so young Eva could see her customers arrive. *"Not too high and not too low,"* he'd said of it, having her stand just so as he pulled out his measuring tape with a flourish. At her tender age, it was important to take into consideration any growth spurt she might experience; Dat had insisted Eva just might be as tall as Mamma one day.

She realized anew how considerate their father had always been, gone now four long years. With the recollection lingering, she looked up and caught sight of tall, very blond Alfred Dienner. Heavens, he must have been staring at her.

Politely, she smiled back, and Alfred didn't look away as a more timid young man might. His warm hazel eyes held her gaze, and his face brightened, his lips parting.

Has he come to ask me out? Eva wondered.

Alfred stood waiting, turning a slip of paper over and over in his hands. His strapping frame evidenced long hours of hard work at his father's farm on Stony Hill Road. His face was already tan, his manner confident. Whoever ended up married to Alfred would surely be well cared for, raising a brood of future farmers and little dishwashers.

Directly in front of Alfred, two of Eva's kindly neighbors, sixty-year-old Sylvia Lantz and her thirty-year-old daughter-in-law, Josie, talked in *Deitsch* as they made their way up the steps beneath the plain green awning. Above the shop door was the hand-painted sign, *The Sweet Tooth*.

Josie and her husband, Sam, and their school-age children resided in Sylvia's farmhouse, where the senior Lantzes had worked the land and nurtured nine children, eight of whom had survived to adulthood. The youngest Lantz girl had drowned one summer years ago, and two others—Tilly and Ruth—had left the Plain community for the world, living somewhere in Massachusetts near the coast, according to the grapevine. Eva really didn't know all of the details.

What she *did* know was that whenever she tried her best not to look Alfred's way just now, she could still see him out of the corner of her eye. If he offered an invitation, *should* she accept?

As it turned out, both Sylvia and Josie wanted the small white chocolate fingers, as Eva liked to call them. The petite bars melted in your mouth, more than making up for their lack of size with rich flavor.

"Can't resist 'em," Sylvia said with a glance at Josie. "I'll have three dozen, please."

"I sure hope there'll be enough left," Josie said, covering her mouth to smother the laughter.

"You know me better'n that." Sylvia's plump face turned pink. "I'll be happy to share with ya if Eva runs out."

Eva smiled at the banter between them, a bit envious as she watched Josie gently touch her mother-in-law's arm.

"*Mei Mann* will be ever so grateful," Josie replied, a mischievous glint in her pale blue eyes. "Your sweets are truly the best, Eva."

"*Jah*, 'tis a gift, makin' these candies like ya do." Sylvia nodded her head, grinning at Eva. "The most delicious, *wunnerbaar-gut* treats ever, hope ya know."

Josie smiled, too. "*Ach*, I'd give almost anything to be able to make these delicious goodies. My husband would be over the moon."

Eva blushed; it was impossible to ignore Alfred next in line. Even so, she took care to bag up first Sylvia's order, then Josie's, the two women talking about their "perty springtime flowers," and Sylvia marveling aloud about her fifty-year-old rhubarb patch that had once again sprung to life.

Eva wondered if she, too, might someday enjoy a close relationship with a mother-in-law. She certainly yearned for such a connection. Fearing she might betray her private thoughts to Alfred, she purposely looked down at the counter when he stepped up, tall and straight. His voice was confident and clear as he gave his order, then waited politely.

"Will that be all, then?" she asked, noticing his white shirt and black broadfall trousers, like he was going to Preaching and not off to work.

"Oh, and I'd like some hard peppermint candies, too," he said, leaning on the counter as if he might have more to say.

Here it comes, she thought, daring to raise her eyes. She spoke just as he opened his mouth. "Anything else?" She pointed at the glass display case and mentioned the freshly made peanut butter balls. But he shrugged and said maybe another time.

When she went to gather up his order, he followed her over, of all things, and stood watching. Goodness, but Eva was thankful for the steady stream of customers. Anything to keep her busy. Then again, she was afraid someone might suspect her and Alfred of being a courting couple. If not that, then certainly of being sweet on each other. Sure, they'd gone riding together a half-dozen times during the past few years, and they'd played volleyball on the same team, too. She also recalled a picnic in Central Park near downtown Lancaster, where she provided the meal, but none of that meant they were serious. Alfred was quite aware that a handful of other fellows had taken her out, as well. *All of them married now,* Eva thought grimly.

"*Denki,* Alfred, for comin' by—"

"Eva, slow down a minute," he said. "Your customers will wait."

She felt her face warm as Alfred proceeded, in front of everyone, to invite her to play Ping-Pong with him at his cousin's house.

Leaning over the work counter, she lowered her voice and replied, "You're askin' me here. . . ." She glanced behind him.

"*Jah,* 'tis all right." His eyes were smiling as he held her gaze. "So, will ya?"

She noticed their neighbor to the north pretending to study the homemade ribbon candy in the glass display case behind them. Eva felt positively mortified—what was Alfred thinking? The grapevine would have them engaged by day's end.

If I hesitate, will he stay and try to persuade me?

Pleasant and well-mannered as Alfred Dienner was, she wouldn't put that past him. *But, goodness—like a dog on a bone!*

"Um, that'll be fine," she whispered to him.

"*Des gut,* then," Alfred said with a nod.

18

She placed his order in a large sack and recited the total. "Enjoy the candy. Some very *gut* choices."

Alfred counted out the payment and dropped two quarters in the tip jar. "I hope I can make it last awhile." He gripped the bag of candy and, before turning to go, winked at her. *In front of everyone!*

CHAPTER TWO

························· ❀ ·····························

IN HOLMES COUNTY, OHIO, the maples and oaks were already flourishing against newly mown lawns and countless fields of sprouted corn. Amish farmers welcomed the season. *A time of rebirth.*

From the pinnacle of a hill, Jed Stutzman couldn't help noticing the Amish cemetery, the final resting place for his fiancée, Lydiann Coblentz. The peaceful, leafy green sanctuary of what-might've-beens was located not two miles from his work as an apprentice buggy maker. But today he urged his horse onward, not wanting to ponder what he'd so tragically lost.

Rattling past the three-acre burial ground in his elderly uncle Ervin's buckboard wagon, Jed felt the old, familiar pain, perhaps duller with the passage of a year. He'd spent hours there, contemplating his life without Lydiann, talking to his beloved as if she might hear him, and often as if she hadn't left at all.

He sped up the horse's pace. "You have to keep movin' forward," Jed told himself, drawing a breath, aware of the air's sweet fragrance. The wind had shifted in the past hour, pushing the smell of fertilizer away toward the south.

"The whiff of success," Dat says.

Jed smiled wryly and recalled Lydiann's opinion of what she'd called the *"schtinkich* scent," in spite of the fact that she'd grown up on a farm not far from his own father's. The truth was, his sweetheart had often declared how glad she was the Lord had seen fit to make her a woman, so she could keep house and cook for her future husband and keep him company by the evening fire.

"You would've been a splendid wife," Jed whispered.

Plenty of young men had thought so, too, back before Jed swooped in and began to court Lydiann. Last week at market, an *Englischer* woman who'd known Lydiann for years had declared her an angel on earth.

Lydiann trusted the Lord in a gentle yet mighty way. He considered all the times she'd prayed for God's guidance in their lives as a courting couple—they'd planned to wed this very November. Theirs had been a short-lived yet precious love story, and their mutual friends in the youth group had often remarked about the light in their eyes when they were together.

Heaven had other plans. Jed trusted in the sovereignty of their Lord. For him, as for all the People, there was no other way to approach such a profound loss.

Just ahead, he noticed his cousin Sol Troyer approaching the intersection in the black family carriage. Sol was New Order Amish, so his buggy wheels were solid rubber, which made for a quieter ride on the roads. Jed had always been interested in the difference in buggies around Berlin and surrounding towns, including carriages that were a bit fancier. Not that he'd ever desire anything but what was sanctioned by his Old Order bishop, but because he loved the craft.

"An Amish carriage must be made practically and properly," Uncle Ervin liked to say about his shop. "Built well enough to last a lifetime." This was his uncle's motto, and the man was well respected all over Holmes and Wayne counties as a result of his quality work. People came from miles around to order carriages from Ervin Stutzman.

As a lad, Jed had quickly learned that the buggy's framework was made of solid hickory, and that the steel springs and axles were the next thing to permanent if built correctly. Thanks to Uncle Ervin's patient instruction, Jed realized there weren't many ways to build a buggy right, regardless of style and whether they came from Ohio, Indiana, or Pennsylvania, where Uncle Ervin's cousin-in-law built the gray, boxlike carriages so typical of Lancaster County.

Glancing at Cousin Sol again, Jed waved, but Sol didn't see him. Jed thought of trying to get his attention, but he was mighty conscious anymore of all the ways something could go wrong on these narrow roads, especially coming into downtown Berlin with an older horse. The small town was becoming congested with eager tourists, most looking to purchase the fine souvenirs offered at Amish and Mennonite merchants.

Jed directed the horse to turn west onto Main Street. He nodded to a friend waiting for the stoplight near the flea market, where dear Lydiann had worked for a number of years. How many times had she told Jed, her expression glowing, that she could hardly wait to get to work each morning, she enjoyed it so? She'd delighted in the customers and loved attending to the children, thrilled for opportunities to spread kindness and cheer.

Jed pushed the memories aside. *She's with the Lord,* he reminded himself. It was the one and only thing that brought him solace, particularly during the first six months after her sudden death.

A few months ago, his family and closest friends had begun to encourage him to get back "into circulation," so Jed had reluctantly gone to several barn Singings and other youth-related activities, if only to test the waters.

Jed also had Uncle Ervin's retirement heavy on his mind, along with the possibility of taking over the family business. That had once seemed like a sure thing—at least until Perry Hostetler entered the picture.

My own fault, Jed thought. His uncle had always insisted the chosen successor be solidly grounded in the Amish church—a baptized member. Jed had intended to join church with Lydiann this coming September; it was all part of their plan. Now, though, he would be making his kneeling baptismal vow on his own, assuming he was ready. *I'm dragging my feet,* he thought.

Like Jed, Perry was also a buggy-building apprentice, but Uncle Ervin's cousin's son had joined church last fall. And Perry reportedly had a serious girlfriend.

Jed *had* attempted to date a few young women recently. The first, Phoebe Miller, while very nice, struck him as rather self-absorbed. Freida Burkholder, on the other hand, admittedly hadn't cracked open a book since finishing eighth grade. Eye-opening, indeed, considering Jed enjoyed reading as much as his work at the buggy shop. And pretty Mittie Raber, well, she'd chattered nonstop, gossiping like a nosy parrot, which drove Jed *narrish*—crazy.

In all truth, none of the young women had measured up to Lydiann. And he was beginning to wonder if *any* woman alive could make him forget his cherished first love.

Jed spotted the Christian bookstore on the left-hand side of the road and recalled combing through the many shelves there with Lydiann. He, looking for volumes of biblical history, and she, partial to fiction by Mennonite authors.

Continuing up the street, Jed eyed Boyd and Wurthmann Restaurant, their favorite. He and Lydiann had once snuck away to have breakfast together in the back room of the quaint eatery. Lydiann's blue eyes had brightened at her first taste of rich sausage gravy over a breakfast haystack of biscuits and eggs. Even now, Jed relished that recollection, as well as the thank-you note she'd written, starting a chain of correspondence between them, even though they'd lived within a short buggy ride of each other. From the start, she'd made up endearing closures to her letters. In Jed's opinion, Lydiann's creative sign-offs—phrases like *Love till the sea runs dry*—would take the prize for such things.

For me, she was the prize. . . .

He made the turn into the hardware store parking lot, glad for the morning sunshine. Then, tying the horse to the hitching rail, he thought of all the times he'd allowed himself to imagine the sequence of moments leading up to Lydiann's accident. He'd sometimes catch himself contemplating the foolhardy buggy race . . . with a speeding train, no less. It was no wonder the terror had managed to bombard his dreams, where he relived the devastating event. For weeks and even months afterward, Jed had privately blamed Lydiann's younger brother, known for recklessness with his fast horse and new black courting carriage. The same boy who'd lost his life as a result.

In that horrid accident, Lydiann's parents had lost two of their children, yet they had expressed acceptance of God's will. Jed had eventually learned he, too, must forgive, or he would be forever haunted by that terrible day.

Only by Gott's grace have I come this far, he thought, tying his horse to the hitching post. He willed his focus back onto the errand for Uncle Ervin.

Just today Ervin had gently prodded Jed to pray about getting baptized. "And ya might find a good Amish girl to court, too," he'd added with a wink. Jed couldn't blame Uncle Ervin for being eager to retire and wanting to leave his shop to an established Amishman. *If I don't pull it together, I'll lose this golden opportunity,* he thought, tempted to give in to defeat as he proceeded to the hardware store.

CHAPTER THREE

·············· ✿ ··············

MANY TIMES SINCE CHILDHOOD, Eva had heard the charming story of her parents' courtship, Mamma's pretty face alight with the telling.

The Plain People of Eden Valley knew well that Dottie Flaud had married Vernon Esch just one week following her eighteenth birthday. And while it wasn't required by Pennsylvania law to get parental permission at that age, Mamma did so anyway, because she felt compelled to please those in authority. Indeed, Mamma's thoughtful gesture put her fiancé on even better footing with his father-in-law-to-be, if that was possible, considering her parents had set their sights on him as a mate for their daughter back when he was but a schoolboy.

Mamma had said there was an exceptionally large turnout for the Flaud-Esch wedding day, with more than four hundred Amish guests in attendance, including Mamma's lifelong friend, Naomi Mast, like a surrogate mother to Mamma and her older sisters, since their own mother had died when Mamma was in her early teens. Naomi's daughter, Ida Mae, had wed two weeks before Mamma herself, and Ida Mae and her young husband, Joel, set up housekeeping as neighbors to Mamma and Dat on Eden Road. In fact, their dairy farm was situated at the southernmost tip of the Esch property.

But it was Naomi, twenty years older than Mamma, who was Mamma's dearest confidante and closest neighbor. Naomi enjoyed helping Mamma at the drop of a *Kapp,* and the other way around. Some thought the two friends felt duty bound to make certain the other had adequate help gardening and canning and cleaning to host Preaching. It was a remarkably sweet shared conviction.

As a result, when Mamma lost Dat to a farming accident, it was Naomi who immediately took a prominent place in the Esch kitchen, cooking and cleaning, even though Mamma's own sisters were equally sympathetic and supportive.

Then, in the days and weeks after Mamma's own unexpected passing, Naomi began to reach out to Frona, Eva, and Lily, sharing privately that before Mamma passed away, she had asked Naomi to watch over her girls, covering them with prayer and compassion. Naomi especially bonded with Eva, though Naomi was old enough to be her grandmother. It wasn't long before Eva found herself unburdening her sorrow and loss to Naomi . . . and even letting slip a few secrets about some of the fellows she'd gone with, including Alfred Dienner. This was so very out of character for Eva, who'd never shared as much with her Mamma. Yet never before had she needed such consolation, and she was grateful every day that Naomi was always there, especially when Eva felt the world caving in on her, when she needed to just sob and let it all out.

Dearest Naomi. My only motherly source of wisdom now . . .

Eva hurried to dry the supper dishes, working alongside Lily, who'd always preferred to wash. Their immediate goal was to have the kitchen spotless for Menno's arrival. Scanning the large room, Eva noticed the pantry door ajar; bags of sugar and flour inside needed straightening. And the book Lily was reading, still open, spine out, on the kitchen table.

Frona was outdoors sweeping the back porch and steps, giving them a careful once-over. It wasn't as if Menno was coming to inspect, but they'd always tidied up especially well for this rather finicky brother.

"Frona's worryin' herself into a tizzy," Lily said, letting the hot water drip off the plate before she set it in the dish rack. "Like she wants to impress Menno."

"Well, it's not like we don't try."

"He struts around like he's king, ya know."

"You might have something there," Eva replied, wondering why Lily was dawdling with the dishes.

"Yet I daresay Frona's more rattled than we've seen her since Mamma came down sick. Remember?" Lily's blue eyes were solemn. She washed the utensils last before drying her hands on her black apron. "*Nee, ab im Kopp* is what she is."

"Now, Lily. She might worry too much, but she isn't crazy."

"But just look at her." Lily nodded toward the door.

"I honestly think you're the one frettin'."

Lily laughed quietly and shook her head. "You think ya know me, sister, don't ya?"

Eva stopped drying, her dish towel in her hand. "Oh, I know you well enough, Lily. How could I not?"

Lily walked to the table and ran her hands over the back of the chair that had always been their father's. "All I'm sayin' is we oughta be ready for anything."

Eva laughed a little. "You and Frona both . . . what's got into yous?" She laid the dish towel over the rack and left the room.

Why expect the worst?

29

Naomi Mast rarely baked so late in the day, but just before supper she'd gotten word one of her English neighbors needed some cheering up. Realizing she would have no time for baking first thing tomorrow, she'd set right to work. Tomorrow, sometime after breakfast, she planned to visit daughter Ida Mae, who'd asked for help with her Lone Star quilt pattern in navy, rust, and tan.

Besides, it was good for them to keep busy, what with Dottie Esch's passing still looming in their minds. *And hearts.* Naomi wasn't one to say much about it, but she could read between the lines when Ida Mae talked about "those poor, dear Esch girls." Fatherless and now motherless, Frona, Eva, and Lily were very much on everyone's mind.

Sighing, Naomi pinched the edges of her rhubarb piecrust just so. Truth be told, she missed Dottie terribly and wanted to live up to the dear woman's faith in her to look out for her unmarried daughters.

I gave her my word.

It hadn't necessarily been easy keeping that promise, what with Lily's head-in-the-clouds attitude and Frona's anxious temperament. *Thank goodness for Eva,* thought Naomi with a twinge of guilt.

To the best of her ability, she had lovingly embraced James 1:27: *Pure religion and undefiled before God and the Father is this, To visit the fatherless and widows in their affliction. . . .*

Naomi carried the pie carefully to the counter, privately glad she wasn't the only Plain cook clinging to the old way of doing things. Of course, she'd never think of judging any of the other Amishwomen in Eden Valley who had accepted Bishop Isaac's long-ago nod to permitting gas stoves and other gas-powered kitchen appliances.

Likely the bishop's wife wanted one, thought Naomi, then chided herself.

Pulling small logs out of the kindling box, she stacked them in the belly of the old black cookstove. All the while, she thought of fair-haired Lily, whom she'd seen walking through the wild flowers in the meadow while Naomi washed windows yesterday. The dear girl was often rushing out to Eden Road to check the mailbox. It was beginning to seem that, on any given day, Dottie's youngest was in plain view. It was the oddest thing, considering all the work there was to be done with her Mamma gone.

Here lately, Lily had been wandering up to the shared phone shanty on the property of the next Amish neighbor over from Esches'. Repeatedly so, in fact. Naomi wouldn't have suspected anything amiss, except that personal calls were discouraged, so the frequency made her pause and wonder. A time or two, Naomi had actually spotted her twirling and singing, rare behavior for even Lily.

The way I must've acted when I first started courting. Naomi recalled the rapturous feeling and thought Lily might have herself a secret beau. Naturally, most serious dating relationships were kept quiet around Eden Valley.

Whatever the reason, Lily was running out to the phone shanty quite a lot, the family's snow-white Eskimo spitz, Max, chasing after her. In fact, Naomi had seen Lily with their dog earlier this morning, before Eva's candy shop opened for the day. Lily had practically skipped all the way back from the shanty to the stone wall running along one section of the road, across from Naomi's mailbox. She'd sat there preening like a bluebird beneath the sky.

Not wanting to second-guess why, Naomi placed her pies into the oven and went out to the utility room to put on a lightweight shawl. She opened the side door and stood on the porch for a time, breathing in the fragrance of dogwood and hyacinth. Why did it bother her to see Lily behaving so? Indeed, for a moment Lily had covered her mouth as if to silence laughter. Then, just that quickly, the girl's shoulders slumped and she hung her head, looking for all the world like she'd lost her dearest friend.

Naomi knew the older Esch girls had their hands full, given their household and gardening responsibilities—and that very busy candy store, too. Oh, goodness, Naomi wished her friend Dottie were still alive. If so, she would go straightaway there and talk heart-to-heart with her about Lily. But alas, that wasn't possible, and Naomi hoped and prayed Frona and Eva might be able to rein in their sister as soon as possible.

CHAPTER FOUR

EVA PICKED UP THE RED PLATE of peanut butter balls and carried it to the table, placing it smack-dab in the middle, minutes before Menno was expected to arrive. *No more than what a caring younger sister should do,* she thought. Yet she was unable to convince even herself that she was doing it for any other reason than to soften up her brother. *If Menno needs softening.* But certainly both Frona and Lily seemed to think their brother might require several of these yummy candies before they sat down to visit.

"You have a gift," Sylvia Lantz had declared outright to Eva that morning in the shop. To think Sylvia would say such a thing, and then to have Josie agree so wholeheartedly, too—it was both heartening and embarrassing. And yet Eva had been told this back when she first started concocting sweets. Especially by her father, who was always quick to compliment.

Eva loved to get up early in the morning and dream up new recipes, or sometimes she would make her confections for the next day after supper. Often she shivered with excitement as she took the very first bite, curious how her latest effort might turn out.

———————

Eva dashed to the cupboard for Mamma's best white dessert plates, conscious of Menno's horse and carriage clattering into the lane. She stacked them nearest their father's former spot at the table. *Where Menno will likely sit,* she thought, recalling his last visit.

That done, she headed for the back screen door and there spotted Frona by the rusted-out old pump, no longer in use. Lily was also outside beneath the stable overhang with their dog. "What could be wrong? She looks downright guilty," Eva whispered as she went to rest against the porch banister to await their brother.

Menno waved at Frona, and Eva could hear him suggest they set up a roadside stand once the berries started coming on. Eva wondered why he'd brought that up.

"*Wie geht's,* Eva?" Menno asked, spotting her as he came up the steps. He paused a moment to remove his straw hat.

"*Wunnerbaar-gut,* and you?"

Menno pressed his lips together. "Word's spread clear beyond Eden Valley 'bout your candy sales," he said with a smile. "Heard it again this afternoon."

"Some days I can scarcely keep up."

He nodded. "It's been a *gut* little hobby, I'll say."

Eva noticed his smile had faded, and she couldn't help wondering what he meant by *hobby.* "Frona's real pleased with the extra income. She handles all the money." It wasn't really necessary to say that when Menno was aware Frona held the purse strings. But Eva suddenly felt nervous and wondered if Frona and Lily's worries were inching into her.

Menno waved her into the house with his hat, so she led the way, and Frona followed soon after, tramping up the porch steps and inside. As for Lily, Eva hoped she might oblige and not make them have to seek her out. *Lily knows better than to be standoffish,*

Eva thought, watching Menno reach for their father's chair and sit down. She had correctly anticipated his choice. Now it would be a relief if Menno simply relaxed and enjoyed the peanut butter balls, chatting brotherly-like, with no agenda.

Proving my sisters wrong.

When Naomi was but a girl, she'd stumbled onto crocheting after watching her mother make placemats and sweaters, and was quickly hooked. Now that supper dishes were all put away, she'd gone out to the side porch, taking her crocheting with her to sit and pray while she worked on a set of white booties for one of her grandbabies. And while she prayed silently, she looked up to see if Lily Esch was still out by the stable.

Lord God in heaven, soften dear Lily's heart toward Thee, she prayed, hoping Dottie's youngest would bring honor to her family's name and parents' memory. Dottie's youngest had always seemed more bent on having a good time than on matters of faith.

Naomi watched a patch of thin clouds float past the sinking sun, veiling it for a moment. Across from the barnyard, a row of mature cottonwood trees moved gently with the breeze, their pale trunks fissured from livestock rubbing up against the bark.

Over at the Esch farm, a young Amishwoman clad in a blue dress and matching cape apron practically marched into the lane, barefoot. The girl scurried to Lily, who was leaning against the stable door, arms folded. Naomi watched as the visitor greeted Lily with a brief hug, her back to Naomi, as Max barked and wagged his long, bushy tail. Then the young woman handed Lily what looked like a white envelope, gave her a wave, and turned back toward Eden Road.

Getting a better look now, Naomi recognized Fannie Ebersol, Lily's former school friend and distant relative. "'Tis nice she has such a companion, what with her parents and grandparents all gone to Jesus," Naomi murmured.

Naomi somehow felt better as Lily opened the envelope and peered at whatever was enclosed before clasping the envelope to her heart. With a glance toward the house, Lily spotted Naomi and waved. Feeling a bit sheepish, Naomi waved back.

Lily hurried toward the house and headed inside.

All will be fine, by the looks of it, Naomi assured herself, focusing again on crocheting the booties. *"Ach,* I trust so."

⌁

"*Gut* of you to join us, Lily," said Menno when she took her place on the wooden bench next to Eva.

Lily bobbed her head but didn't speak, and Eva inched over to give her some space. "You haven't missed anything a'tall," she reassured her as Frona eyed Lily across the table.

Menno placed his straw hat on the knob of his chair and remarked cheerfully about the tasty goodies while reaching for another peanut butter ball, eyes alight.

The more he eats, thought Eva, *the better.*

A small stack of periodicals caught her eye over on the floor near the pantry, and she wished they'd spent more time redding up. Thankfully Menno hadn't seemed to notice. Not yet anyway.

Her brother drew a long sigh, sat back in the chair, and studied the ceiling. "Has there been any trouble lately with the spring rains seepin' through?" he asked no one in particular.

Frona leaned forward and folded her fleshy hands on the table. "Not once has the roof leaked since Dat had it patched."

"*Des gut.*" Menno got up suddenly and left the kitchen.

Eva and her sisters exchanged glances.

"Told ya this could get thorny," Frona whispered. "Some-thin's up."

"Wish he would just say what's on his mind." Lily slumped forward, fingering an envelope.

The day clock *tick-tock*ed the minutes away, and as was her way when she was stewing, Frona abruptly rose to make herself busy, putting some water on the stove to boil.

Eva wished Menno might return. This was no time for mystery, not the way Frona and Lily were fussing.

"Does either of yous want coffee or tea?" Frona asked over her shoulder. She yanked the utensil drawer open, rattling the teaspoons.

"*Kumme, hock dich naah!*" Lily spouted, slapping the bench with her book.

"I can't sit down just now." Frona peered toward the hallway and the front room. She squinted her eyes behind Mamma's spectacles. "Well, for pity's sake."

"What?" Lily practically leapt off the bench.

"Menno's in there measurin' the floor," Frona said.

Eva scarcely knew what to think.

"With his feet or a measuring tape?" Lily said sarcastically.

Frona wrung her hands. "He's walking and counting from one end to the other. Maybe he's planning to build an addition onto the house."

"*Wunnerbaar*," Lily said, shaking her head as she went to sit again. "Just what we need—more space for the three of us."

Eva caught Lily's eye, but she looked away, evidently as put out with Menno's strange game as Frona, who opened the cupboard and began to remove several coffee mugs.

And there they sat, waiting for Menno, who was taking his sweet time, as far as Eva could tell. Truly, she felt like a caged cat.

CHAPTER FIVE

························· ✦ ·························

EVA WAS RELIEVED when Menno finally returned to the kitchen, yet Frona looked to be holding her breath as their brother took his place at the head of the table.

"Doubtless you're wonderin' why I'm here," Menno said.

Across the table, Frona stirred uneasily.

Menno continued. "Not livin' on the premises is becoming a challenge with all the time I spend working round here, so I plan to take full possession of the farm and the house. I'll be movin' my family in as soon as I can manage it." He paused and sighed. "There might not be room here for all of yous."

Eva's mouth dropped open, but none of them spoke.

Menno cleared his throat and expounded further on his plans. When he was finished, he looked first at Frona, then at Eva. "Why are ya surprised? Surely you knew this time would come."

Eva swallowed. They *were* surprised, thinking since Menno hadn't moved in right after Mamma's passing, maybe he'd wait awhile longer. *At least till some of us marry . . .*

"It'll be a tight fit for all of us," Lily said, bless her heart—she didn't seem to grasp what Menno meant.

Frona turned toward Lily and shook her head. "That's not what Menno's sayin'."

We'll be divided up, Eva thought sadly.

"Well, yous might have to stay with Rufus or Emmanuel instead of here. But it wouldn't be the worst thing," Menno said.

Living with this brother would be! Eva thought dolefully.

"Of course, if only one of you is still single by then, you'll have a place here as a live-in mother's helper for Bena," added Menno. "At least one of you must have a beau."

Surely he'll wait to move here till wedding season, or after, Eva thought.

Lily asked, "What 'bout Eva's candy shop? Dat built it for her."

Menno bowed his head, and for a moment Eva thought he might just come up with something to soften this disappointment. But Menno was true to form. "Eva can't expect she'll spend the rest of her days making candy," he said.

Eva watched Menno closely. *The shop's my last connection to Dat.*

"I can't believe this," Frona said.

Seeing her older sister's burning expression, Eva expected her to press Menno for more information, but she merely rose to offer him some hot tea or coffee.

"Is it instant coffee?" Menno frowned.

Frona nodded. "That's all we have."

"Well then, I'll have one more peanut butter ball and be on my way," he said with a faint smile.

"We might all end up with Great-Aunt Mary Girod clear out in Berne, Indiana," Frona worried aloud. "According to her circle letters, she has plenty of room."

Menno rolled his eyes, but Eva cringed at the thought of living so far from home. *Menno's upset the fruit basket!*

"Honestly, what'd ya think of all that?" Frona asked Eva and Lily once Menno was gone.

"I'm tryin' to get used to the notion of leavin' here." Eva considered Frona's comment about Indiana. "Why'd ya bring up Aunt Mary Girod?"

"Well, she's hinted that one or more of us could go out there, is all. Says she wouldn't mind some company."

Mamma and Frona had kept in close touch with Aunt Mary through the years and learned of the differences between this Plain community and their own.

"One thing 'bout living with Aunt Mary, we'd have to learn sign language," Frona added, wrinkling her nose.

Lily looked aghast. "*Aendi* Mary's gone deaf?"

"*Jah*, happened just over the past couple of years," Frona told them.

Eva couldn't imagine being unable to communicate verbally with a woman they'd never met—another rather gloomy thought.

"Aunt Mary's also written that the average age for baptism there is seventeen. So you know what that means." Frona looked Lily's way, but she was staring out the window, seemingly unaware.

Clenching her teeth, Eva felt embarrassed by what Frona had inferred. And her heart went out to their only sibling yet to be baptized. Lily didn't need this added pressure right now. *It won't sit well with her.*

Suddenly Lily announced that she must write a quick letter and rushed upstairs.

Eva stayed put at the kitchen table, feeling numb. "Why do

ya think Menno's bringing this up now? I mean, why didn't he take over the farm after Dat died?"

Frona paced the length of the kitchen and back. "Honestly, I'd thought Menno might let us stay put for as long as need be. Guess I was wrong."

Eva found it curious Frona hadn't spoken up to him as other times in the past, particularly over farm-related issues. Not only to Menno, but also to their brother Emmanuel, who helped Menno work Dat's land each day. Frona was never unkind, but she did have a way of expressing what she thought was right and good . . . and what was best for Eva and Lily, too. She thought of herself as the head of this particular house.

Frona stopped in her tracks. "You know, it's been the longest time since I attended a Sunday Singing. I figure you've got a beau, Eva, and I wouldn't be surprised if Lily does, too, considering how secretive she's been lately."

Eva nodded but didn't correct her assumption. It was obvious Frona was thinking ahead to their future. Sadly, she was the least likely to marry, considering her age. And, too, Frona had a way about her that seemed to set some folks on edge.

Forcing a smile, Frona said, "I'm inclined to march over to Menno's place and give him an earful."

"You all right?" Eva asked quietly.

"Well, like Menno said, we weren't gonna live here forever." Trudging to the table, Frona sat in Mamma's former chair and folded her ample arms, like their mother sometimes had at that very spot. "If I didn't know better, I'd think he just wants an excuse to get us out of his hair."

Eva's head hurt. She wished Menno had stayed home with his family tonight, hadn't stirred things up. Truth be told, she felt downright glum and as miserable as Frona looked. "I think one of us should go and check on Lily."

"I have work to do," Frona murmured, then leaned her face into her hands. "Besides, you're closer to her."

Eva had always been able to get through to that sister, and the whole family knew it. She and Lily had shared a room when their brothers were still single and living at home. Yet even after the boys married and there was extra space, Lily disliked the idea of having her own bedroom. Eva didn't mind sharing if it made Lily more comfortable and at peace.

Eva excused herself and headed upstairs. She paused in the open doorway of their bedroom and looked in on Lily sitting at the corner desk, pen in hand. A white envelope was propped against the gas lantern, and Eva couldn't help but see the sad face. *Thanks to Menno.* Yet, in his defense, Menno had given them time together in their parents' house following Mamma's death, and now he'd given them fair warning. *Surely he'll wait till after harvest. . . .*

Eva stepped inside the room. "You're upset, ain't so?"

Lily turned and forced a smile. "Just thinkin'."

Eva went to sit at the foot of the bed.

"For one thing, I kinda feel sorry for Frona." Lily placed her pen on the stationery and moved the chair to face Eva. "It hasn't been easy for her, ya know . . . with fellas, I mean."

Lily's sad over that? Eva realized she evidently hadn't paid close attention to Menno's remarks. "Frona ain't *en alt Maidel* yet."

Lily rose and went to stand in front of the dresser mirror for the longest time. "She's not unattractive, but she does seem to hold a young man at arm's length."

"Frona has her nice qualities, though." Eva disliked saying negative things about anyone.

"You, on the other hand, could have Alfred Dienner," Lily said, moving to sit beside Eva. "Though I doubt you'll marry someone you don't love. Remember what Amy March says in

Little Women? 'You don't need scores of suitors. You need only one . . . if he's the right one.'"

"But no one has seriously courted me, not even Alfred, though he'd like to."

"*Jah*, well . . ." Lily paused as if lost in thought. Then her voice changed to wistful. "There are always *other* alternatives, Eva."

"Surely ya don't mean someone from the outside?" Eva was startled. "An *Englischer* . . ."

Again, Lily seemed distracted. "If you're determined to marry for the right reason, why would ya even think of settling for Alfred?" Her sister had never spoken so pointedly about a fellow.

Lily rose and went back to the dresser. She opened the lid to the box of hairpins and removed one after another from her bun till her blond hair tumbled over her shoulders and down her slender back.

"*Ach*, Lily, what're ya doin'? We haven't had evening prayers yet."

"I'm goin' to bed early." The mirror reflected Lily's pained expression.

Eva shifted, troubled. They never let their hair down before evening family worship.

Yet Lily began to brush her long tresses, making dramatic sweeps as she went to sit on the opposite side of the bed, away from the door. She hadn't ever slept on the side nearest the hallway. Eva suspected she was afraid of the dark as a child. In the spring and summer, when they kept their door and windows open for ventilation, Lily seemed quite content to sleep on the opposite side of the bed, with Eva as a buffer of sorts.

"Honestly, sister, you're too tired for Scripture reading?"

"I am," Lily admitted. "And for much of anything else round here, too."

Their eyes locked and held for a moment. Lily was the first to look away.

"What's really botherin' ya?" Eva got up and stood near the dresser.

"My heart pains me." Lily continued brushing. "Somethin' terrible."

"Missin' Mamma?"

Lily placed her brush on the dresser. "We keep losing the people we love . . . and now the house where we grew up. Where does it end, Eva?"

"You won't lose *me*," Eva reassured her.

Lily teared up.

"Is something else worrying ya?" Eva asked gently.

Lily was silent for a moment.

"Sister?"

"If only you knew." Lily was staring now at the wooden quilt hanger across the room, where their mother's prettiest quilt was on display, the most beautiful Dahlia pattern Eva had seen in all of Eden Valley, or anywhere in Lancaster County, for that matter. It was the last quilt Lily and Mamma had made together, just the two of them, before Mamma took sick.

"It's Mamma, ain't so?"

"I miss her all the time." Lily leaned her head gently on Eva's shoulder and began to cry like a child.

"I understand. I truly do." Eva slipped her arm around her. "Go ahead, sister. The Lord sees and knows your heart." Such were the very words Naomi used when Eva couldn't keep back her own tears.

"Why'd Dat and Mamma both have to die?" Lily's pitiful sobs filled the room, and Eva guessed there were many more *whys* in her sister's mind, simmering just below the surface.

"I miss them, too," Eva offered, trying to be strong yet sensitive. *Poor, dear Lily.*

"Do ya ever think 'bout what Dat would want ya to do with your future, if he was still alive?" Lily asked.

"Well, we *know*, ain't so?"

Lily pulled a face. "For me to join church and settle in with the People, *jah*?"

"Why sure." She looked at her sister, pretty as a daisy. "Why turn up your nose at that?"

Abruptly, Lily straightened and dried her wet cheeks with a hankie from her dress pocket. "That's just it. I don't know if this is the life I want. Don't you ever wonder what else is out there?"

"My life is here, Lily. But of course I have private moments when I wonder what *Gott* has planned for me, like anyone else." Eva brushed back her own tears. "Losin' our parents might be a test to see what we're made of . . . like Job of old."

Lily's shoulders drooped and she moved to the wooden wall pegs, where their long nightgowns hung on hangers. Lily's were a lovely pale pink, and Eva's plain white. "Like I said, I'm all tuckered out, sister. I'm weary of tests."

Eva returned to sit on the bed, then leaned back and stared at the ceiling. She let the air out and didn't draw another breath for a moment. Tomorrow was their baking day for the week, and while their cousin Rachel tended the candy shop, as she did each Saturday, Frona and Lily were planning to take some pies to several shut-in neighbors, as well as to the deacon's wife. If Lily really *wasn't* feeling well, maybe it was wise for her to turn in early tonight. But in the past, she'd been far sicker and still listened to the reading of the Good Book.

Rolling onto her side, Eva gave Lily some privacy as she undressed. *What would Mamma tell Lily tonight, kind and loving as she always was?*

It was Lily who broke the silence. "Will Frona be miffed if I don't go downstairs?"

"She'll think you're mad at Menno."

"Like *she* is?" Lily sighed audibly. "I'm not goin' down there." She stepped to the dresser mirror and divided her thick hair into thirds and began to braid it, her slender fingers gliding expertly through her smooth locks.

"Aw, Lily, you're not yourself tonight." Eva pushed up against the headboard.

"Well, you're one hundred percent mistaken 'bout that." Lily's firm reply hung like a thick curtain between them. There, in the room where they'd shared every imaginable sisterly secret and confided their hopes and yearnings.

All of our lives.

CHAPTER SIX

.... ❈ ....

THE MINUTE SUPPER WAS OVER, Jed Stutzman had hurried back to work a mile or so from the family farmhouse. His goal was to finish building another carriage seat by day's end.

Meanwhile, Uncle Ervin sat in the corner of the shop, leaning on his cane with wrinkled hands. Now and then, Ervin scuffed his black work shoes on the cement floor, commenting to Jed about one thing or another, his thread of a voice rising and falling in the glow of the gas lights installed in the ceiling.

A short while later, Perry also showed up and set to work with no prompting from Ervin, who had long since ceased supervising every aspect of both Perry's and Jed's excellent work.

Jed stepped back to survey his handiwork before glancing at his stooped uncle, perhaps the most respected buggy maker in all of Ohio's Amish country. *Oh, to be as shrewd as Uncle Ervin.*

"Say, Jedediah, I've been mullin' something over," Uncle Ervin said. "I thought you might wanna go to Pennsylvania for some input from Jonas Byler, my wife's cousin. He could show ya some tricks to the buggy-making trade."

"Never been there," Jed replied, glad to please his uncle. "Sounds like an interesting opportunity."

"Word has it Jonas may be callin' it quits come fall, so there's no time like the present." Ervin rose with a groan and meandered over, standing close enough for Jed to smell his pipe tobacco. "It would be an honor for you to meet him, Jed. Spend a week or so."

"I'll look forward to it."

"All right, then. I suggest ya purchase a train ticket right away." Then his uncle dropped the other shoe. "I've already arranged for you to stay with Jonas and his wife, Elsie, near Quarryville. They have a right nice granddaughter close to your age, and one a little younger. Both are mighty *perty*." Ervin winked and tapped Jed on the shoulder.

Smiling, Jed played along. He should have known his uncle had more in mind than just getting some wisdom from a master carriage maker!

***

"You feelin' all right, love?" Naomi's husband asked when she rolled over in bed for the fourth time that night, trying to find a comfortable spot.

She hadn't wanted to awaken him and felt bad she had. "Just having trouble sleeping."

Abner suggested she drink some warm milk. "Might help."

That used to work, she thought, wondering if her insomnia was the Lord's way of keeping her up to pray for someone. It wouldn't have been the first time.

She slipped from bed, donned her lightweight robe, and reached for the flashlight on the nearby table. She padded downstairs barefoot, holding on to the railing as Abner had urged her to do in recent years. Too many women her age fell and broke a hip. She smiled at her doting husband's suggestion to warm some milk. Ach, *as if for a baby.*

The plank floors felt cool to her feet as she made her way to the kitchen. Naomi shone the flashlight on the day clock above the sink and knew she hadn't slept much, if at all. "What's ailin' me?" she whispered, going to the gas fridge and reaching for the half-gallon bottle, cow-fresh just yesterday. "After midnight, for pity's sake."

She didn't bother to light the gas lamp over the table, instead letting the bright stream from the flashlight guide her movements. She carried the milk to the stove and paused, thinking she'd heard something outside. The Esches' dog barked across the way.

Walking to the side door, she peered out. The sound came again as she opened the inner door to let in some air. That certainly wasn't an animal crying, and the strange sound continued, alarming her for a reason she couldn't put her finger on.

Naomi pushed the screen door open, glad for at least a slice of a moon. Was something amiss out there? She waited, listening. Someone was crying at this hour, and in the direction of the road.

Might be one of the neighbors' teenagers.

The way the side porch was situated, Naomi could see not only the road but across to neighboring farms. Standing near the screen door, she saw someone near Esches' lane as her eyes grew more accustomed to the diminished light. *A trespasser?*

Concerned yet curious, Naomi stepped forward and reached for the porch banister. She held her breath as the slender figure dressed like an *Englischer* moved toward the road.

For a few minutes, the woman stood there as though waiting for someone. Naomi stared, and although her eyes were becoming adjusted to the dark, she was unable to determine exactly who this was. *One of the Esch girls? But if so, why dressed so fancy?*

Just then, an open buggy crept down the road and stopped in front of the neighbors' driveway. The young woman got in, and the horse headed quickly in the direction of May Post Office Road.

"What on earth?" Naomi said, her heart pounding.

※

In the wee hours, Eva stretched her hand across the mattress and realized Lily must have gone downstairs for a drink, as she sometimes did in the night. Lying in the darkness, she remembered their troubled conversation following Menno's unexpected declaration. She couldn't forget Lily's strange demeanor—the way she'd sobbed so pitifully.

O Lord in heaven, help dear Lily, she prayed silently before falling back to sleep.

She began to dream of ice-skating with Lily, holding hands and spinning over the ice together as little girls, their woolen scarves flying. They skated till they were breathless, and then Eva shared secrets about the kind of husband she wanted to marry when she grew up, whispering that she much preferred a nice man like their father—*"except not a farmer."* But Lily kept silent and shook her head when Eva asked her and pressed for an answer.

※

"Sister, you've overslept. I need your help in the kitchen." It was Frona hovering near.

Eva leaned up momentarily to look at the windup clock on the dresser. "Where's Lily?" she muttered sleepily.

Frona shook her head, her hands on her hips. "Haven't seen hide nor hair of her."

"Must be out for a walk."

"Maybe," Frona agreed, stepping back as Eva emerged from bed. "She sure wasn't herself last evening."

"None of us were." Eva reached for her bathrobe on the foot-board.

"A brisk walk might do Lily some *gut*." Frona stared at the floor.

"I'll come down as soon as I'm dressed."

"All right, then." Frona left the room.

Hazily, Eva went to the shared closet and chose a green dress and matching apron for the day. High on the shelf, she noticed the small black overnight case missing. *Did Frona lend it to someone, perhaps?* She thought little of it, but then something compelled her to move to the opposite side of the closet, to Lily's dresses. Everything was as it should be, except for one missing lavender dress and black apron.

She turned and made her way to the dresser and opened the drawer where Lily kept her undergarments. Eva's breath caught in her throat. The drawer was completely empty. "For goodness' sake," she whispered.

Going over to the desk where Lily had sat last evening, Eva looked in each of the small drawers, including the narrow one. But there was no sign of a letter there.

"I'm goin' to bed early," Lily had said. Eva clearly recalled the misery in her sister's face. *"My heart pains me. . . ."*

Eva swiftly dressed around and then also checked the petite chest of drawers across the room. There, atop the white doily, she saw an envelope addressed to her in Lily's hand. She unfolded it and began to read.

Dearest Eva,

I'm sorry if this upsets you, but I've decided to leave Eden Valley. I don't want to hurt you or Frona, or our brothers. Be assured this has nothing to do with any of you.

A friend of a friend has invited me to stay with her, so you mustn't worry over me. I've been pondering this move for

months now . . . and I've decided to go fancy. With Menno
taking over the farmhouse, the timing seems especially right.

I love you, sister, and Frona, too. I know I'll miss all of my
family, but things will be better this way.

Lily Esch

"Better . . . how?" Stunned, Eva hurried downstairs.

Frona was busy making bread. When she turned to look, she
must have caught the strained look on Eva's face. "Don't tell
me . . . it's something 'bout Lily."

"Here, read this." She handed the letter to Frona, who took
it warily, then read it, frowning.

"Did she say anything 'bout this last night?" asked Frona,
looking up.

"*Nee* . . . but it sounds like Lily's been planning this."

"Still, Menno's visit yesterday had to make things worse."

They sat together at the table, absorbing the shocking turn
of events. Any thoughts of breakfast had fled with the discovery
of the letter.

"Where would Lily go?" Frona asked.

"I have some ideas, but nothin' certain." Eva sniffed softly.
"I can't understand it. There isn't anything in her note 'bout
contacting us when she arrives at her destination."

"Lily wasn't thinkin' straight." Frona's face was solemn. "She's
been lost in her own world for months."

"Oh, sister."

"I mean it. Think back to how she was after Mamma died.
Remember?" Frona shook her head.

"I wonder if she has herself an English beau somewhere."
Considering some of Lily's comments, it certainly was plausible.

"Wouldn't she have told somebody?" Frona asked, wearing a
worried expression. "At least *you*."

Eva's heart pumped in her ears, but she rejected the urge to panic. *Lily's not familiar with the outside world.* "Surely we'll hear something from her soon."

"Let's just hope she's not taken advantage of," Frona said, her voice solemn.

The thought gave Eva goose pimples. "Lily is old enough to know her own mind, but I'm honestly concerned," she admitted. "I think I'll take the horse and buggy around the neighborhood right quick while Cousin Rachel looks after my shop. If Lily's had second thoughts and is still nearby, maybe I can help her rethink this ridiculous move."

"Our sister's never been so thoughtless, I daresay."

In that moment, Eva understood that Lily hadn't shown her true colors to Frona. No, Lily had always confided in Eva alone, at least after Mamma died. Even so, one thing was sure: Lily had never once mentioned leaving the People. *And she was writing the letter to me last evening, while I was standing there talking to her!*

Eva tried to remember everything Lily had said.

"I have an idea," Eva told Frona and rushed out the back door. Surely it wasn't too late for *some* clue as to Lily's intentions, something that might relieve their worried hearts. Perhaps Naomi Mast had seen something. . . .

The breeze shuffled the new leaves in the maples overhead as their lane straightened out near the road. Eva stopped in her path, aware of the hard, terrible lump in her throat.

Lily's left us, she realized anew, hugging herself. She took a deep breath.

"Lily's left *me.*" If Eva had been a child, she would have sobbed her heart out right there, sitting on the black iron bench her father had placed over by the tulip beds years ago. Where was Lily going? And who had influenced her to leave?

Eva stared pensively down the long road, recalling the many times she and Lily had walked to school together, meeting up with other scholars, as their teacher called them, along the way. Once she'd even used her lunch bucket to ward off a billy goat to protect young Lily.

"Is my sister in danger now?" she whispered.

CHAPTER SEVEN

DESPITE HER LACK OF SLEEP LAST NIGHT, Naomi felt the
need to get outdoors. She swept the entire back porch, then
headed toward the steps and the sidewalk, taking in the springtime morning—a time to pray about whatever came to mind.

Earlier at breakfast, Abner had readily summarized his day's
chores and mentioned he'd gotten word of an estate auction coming up next week down near the home of the well-known carriage
maker, Jonas Byler. Abner talked about that for a while, then
asked if anything more had come of their son Omar's flirtation
with the world. The last time he'd dropped by, Omar had taken
them off guard by announcing he wanted to register to vote in
the November general election.

"I haven't heard more than what you've told me." She'd paused.
"Is it all right to solicit Ida Mae's help, maybe? She and Omar
have always been close siblings."

"Well now, I hadn't thought of that." Abner folded his hands.
"I'm not getting anywhere with Omar."

"Hope he's not straddlin' the fence at his age."

"Ya wouldn't think so." Abner shook his head. "Ain't a *gut* role model for his children."

"*Nee,* that's for sure."

"But we're not to judge, remember?" Abner had gone on to compliment Naomi on her "mighty perty" pink rhododendron bushes out front. He frequently brought up such thoughtful things at mealtime.

Now, though, Naomi swept briskly, trying to erase last night's troubling image of the distraught woman waiting to be picked up in the middle of the road. She knew for certain she hadn't dreamed it, because she'd left her flashlight on the counter, along with the milk bottle, after returning indoors and going back upstairs. No, what she'd witnessed had been all too real. The flashlight batteries were kaput, and the milk warm.

Naomi inhaled the fresh air and tried to focus on spring's arrival. Sometimes she just couldn't get over the abruptness of it. One week there'd be mere soil in the barren flower beds, and the next an ocean of green sprouted up from the ground to announce a new season. "I should go over and see if the Esch sisters are all right."

But Ida Mae's expecting me, she thought as she carried the broom to the door. It was then she noticed Eva heading this way.

"*Guder Mariye,*" Naomi called.

Eva turned to wave. "*Gut* morning to you." She looked downright miserable as she crossed the road. "Oh, Naomi . . . I have the worst news ever."

Naomi braced herself.

"Lily's run away."

Startled, Naomi wasn't sure she'd heard correctly. "What'd ya say?"

"It's Lily . . . she's gone."

"*Ach,* gone to one of your cousins, maybe?"

"I hope so, but based on the letter she left, I doubt it."

A *letter?* Naomi motioned for Eva to come sit with her on the side porch, seeing how distressed the girl was.

"I saw someone walkin' outside late last night," Naomi said now, wanting to help.

"What time was that?"

"Oh . . . past midnight." She reached for Eva's hand. "And there's more, my dear." She told what she'd seen—the man in the open carriage stopping by for her.

At this, Eva looked completely *ferhoodled.* "An Amish fella?" Naomi confirmed it was.

"Tell me everything you saw," Eva pleaded. "What was she wearing . . . did ya notice?"

"Well, it was odd. But whoever it was wore fancy clothes—a white skirt and a dark sweater." Oh, she hated telling poor Eva more to compound her worries, but if this would help to locate Lily, it was worth sharing.

Eva paused as if to let this sink in. At last she said, "Sounds like my sister wouldn't be stayin' with anyone Amish, then."

"But we really don't know."

Groaning, Eva pressed her hands together. "I don't see how we missed seein' this coming." She told how stressed Lily had been last night. "And she seemed distracted when our brother Menno visited."

Naomi noticed Eva said nothing about her brother's reason for visiting.

Eva rose from the porch chair all of a sudden. "I'd planned to help Frona deliver some pies this mornin', but I really must look for Lily. If I could just talk to her, she might not . . ." Eva couldn't continue, apparently, and her eyes filled with tears.

"Would ya want me to go with ya? Help ya search?" Naomi offered, thinking Ida Mae would understand in due time.

"*Denki.* But there's no need for you to put yourself out. I don't even know where to start."

Naomi remembered something more—Fannie Ebersol's brief visit to Lily yesterday evening. Quickly, she told Eva about it and what little she'd observed. "Can't be sure it relates, but I wanted you to know."

"Fannie, ya say?" Eva bowed her head, then whispered, "Fannie's not the best influence, 'tween you and me."

"*Ach,* I'm ever so sorry."

Eva reached toward Naomi, a quiver in her lip. "We'll get through this . . . with God's help."

Naomi wasn't sure Eva was in any frame of mind to handle a road horse alone. Nevertheless, the young woman was clearly determined to find her beloved sister.

Eva rushed back to the house and told Frona what she was going to do. "I need to try an' find Lily. Or at least find someone who might know more."

"Well, is it a *gut* idea to let everyone know our business?"

"I won't sit on my hands and do nothing."

Frona shook her head sorrowfully. "You be careful, ya hear?"

"I'll be home as soon as I can." Truth be told, Eva wasn't sure that even a couple of hours would be enough time to cover all the houses up and down Eden Road and the surrounding area.

"Do ya think she's stayin' round here somewhere?" Frona rubbed her chin nervously. "I mean, considering what she wrote, an' all?"

"I pray she's gotten cold feet and stopped in at one of our relatives'. Who knows what she's thinkin'." Stiffening, Eva continued. "But if Naomi's right about what she saw last night, Lily's more than likely gone. A young man in a courting carriage stopped and picked her up."

"What?"

Eva assured her that Naomi was nearly positive it was Lily she had seen climb into the carriage. *Wearing fancy clothes, Naomi said.*

"Ach, maybe I should go with you." Frona wrung her hands.

"I'll be all right," Eva replied, preferring to go on her own. Honestly, she didn't think she could handle Frona's company just now, not when her older sister was so out of sorts. Eva hurried out to the stable and chose Prince, their best driving horse.

Eva fairly flew down Eden Road in the family carriage, uncertain which direction to take. *Where would Lily go?*

Then, remembering what Naomi had said about Fannie Ebersol, she knew where to head first.

Passing over a small bridge and the stream below, she thought of summer, fast approaching. Eva did not recall a single summertime activity that hadn't involved her closest sister.

How could Lily think of leaving?

On the way to Fannie's, Eva changed her mind. There were closer neighbors who might have seen something amiss. So she chose, instead, to work her way to Fannie's, neighbor by neighbor.

Joel and Ida Mae Yoder's pale yellow clapboard farmhouse came into view. The place had a charm all its own, with distinctive black shutters on all the upper windows. It was with some measure of trepidation that Eva tied her horse to the hitching rail near the kitchen windows and scurried around the side yard to the back door.

"Have ya seen Lily?" she blurted when Ida Mae appeared. "She left in the night."

Ida Mae looked befuddled, then outright dismayed, and Eva felt terrible for barging in like this. "Ach, I'm sorry to bother ya."

Ida Mae stared down at the thimble on her pointer finger, and the needle in her other hand, and shook her head. "*Nee*," she said. "Ain't seen her."

"In that case, I'd best be goin' on to the next house." Eva asked if she'd simply keep her eyes and ears open, then turned to leave.

"*Da Herr sei mit du*," Ida Mae called after her.

"The Lord be with you, too." Eva glanced back. "*Denki* for your prayers."

"You can count on them." Ida Mae raised her hand, not waving, just standing there straight and stiff and looking concerned.

Eva headed on toward Lester Lantz's tall farmhouse, feeling worse with each passing moment. *Why didn't Lily give me the chance to talk her out of this?*

She observed the line of lake willows set back on Lester's broad sprawl of a meadow, where as girls she and Lily had often perched themselves on the fence at summer's dusk to watch courting buggies drift by, sharing secrets about fellows at church. The grass there was tall, green, and lush, scattered with wild daisies in late spring and summer. Her heart sank as she remembered those happy days, flown away. She pulled into the Lantzes' lane and clambered out of the family buggy.

When she'd described the predicament, Sylvia Lantz encouraged her to trust in the heavenly Father's care for Lily, "wherever she is." And there in her kitchen, Sylvia promised to pray. "I surely will."

"*Denki.*"

"You mustn't lose heart," Sylvia said. "Things may look dismal, but there's always a light flickerin' at tunnel's end."

Eva thanked the thoughtful woman and headed out to the carriage. Time was short, and Frona might soon be fretting if Eva didn't hurry back.

Eva urged the horse on to the Ebersol farm, where she found

Fannie outdoors, watering her mother's flowers with a hose. When Eva told her that Lily had left, a peculiar look crossed Fannie's face. *Like she isn't surprised.*

"Do you have any idea where my sister's gone?" Deciding she had nothing to lose, Eva asked it outright before she'd even climbed out of the buggy.

Fannie twiddled with the waistband of her long black apron.

"*Ach*, Fannie, you know Lily nearly as well as I do."

"I'd best not be sayin'."

"Listen, I think you'd better tell me what ya know!"

"But I promised Lily . . ."

Eva clenched her teeth. "What if she falls into difficulties or danger? What then?"

Fannie looked away. "Lily told me very little . . . only that she was leaving."

"Goin' where?"

"She never said."

"How can that be?" Eva asked.

"I'm tellin' the truth." Fannie blinked back tears. "I warned her 'bout leaving. But she was so determined. She's kept everything so secret."

I'm getting nowhere with this girl. Then she mentioned that Naomi had reported having seen Fannie and Lily together yesterday.

"I was just sayin' good-bye, is all," Fannie explained.

"And it didn't occur to you to warn Frona and me 'bout this?"

"Lily will be fine." Fannie sighed. "She knows what she wants. Just let her be."

"What if you're wrong?"

Fannie glared at her. "Would you want *me* to stand in your way if you were bent on doin' something?"

"If it was something like this, I would. Why not? We're here to help each other." Eva kept her gaze on the accomplice, for surely Fannie was that. "Fannie, if you know anything more . . . anything at all, please tell me."

The young woman's lip trembled, but her expression hardened. "Leave me alone! It's not my fault." With that, Fannie dropped the hose, ran to turn off the spigot, and stormed inside.

Eva blew out her breath at Fannie's stubborn but misguided loyalty.

What now, O Lord?

CHAPTER EIGHT

UNABLE TO SHAKE EVA'S EARLIER LOOK of consternation, Naomi headed out on foot to Ida Mae's, having forgotten her sturdy walking stick. It wasn't that she felt old at seventy-three, but some days brought unexpected and painful twinges that were difficult to ignore. Abner encouraged her at times, saying, *"You're still my spring chicken."*

She had to smile, despite her present concerns, knowing the kind, jovial man she'd married—never a lack of laughter around the house, especially first thing in the morning. Marrying Abner Mast had been the best thing she could have ever done for herself.

Once she arrived at Ida Mae's, Naomi felt content to simply sit at the quilting frame and make tiny stitches, not bringing up what had transpired with Lily Esch.

"You're not so chatty today, Mamm." Her daughter's big hazel eyes were intent. "Somethin's bothering ya."

The grapevine would have its way soon enough, but for their time together, Naomi preferred to skirt the tension.

"Are ya worried 'bout Lily?"

Naomi's breath caught in her throat. "You've heard?"

"Eva dropped by just a bit ago, askin' if I knew anything of her sister's whereabouts."

"'Tis a pity. The Esch girls have had more than their share of challenges."

Ida Mae reached inside her gray dress sleeve for a handkerchief and patted her eyes. "I wondered recently if Lily wasn't itchin' to get out and see the world. 'Specially after Dottie passed away— Lily seemed restless to me." She shook her head, sighing. "Guess she finally did it."

"Are ya sayin' she wanted to travel to other places—just to see new sights?" Naomi wondered if Lily wasn't actually interested in *living* in the outside world; maybe she just wanted to experience it during her *Rumschpringe*—the running-around time before joining church. *But where'd she get the money?*

Her daughter rose to make some hot tea. "I s'pose it must be enticing for a curious young woman, wanting to understand fancy ways," Ida Mae said, reaching for two teacups. "All the perty pictures of other states in those geography books, ya know. I remember how it stirred up ideas in me, too, back when."

Sightseeing? thought Naomi. *Is that what Lily is up to?*

"I wouldn't be surprised if her brother Menno didn't play a part in this," Ida Mae was saying as she carried some honey to the table. "Bena told me the other day that her Menno's ready to take over the Esch farm, which might leave the girls scrambling for another place to live."

"Well, now." No wonder Eva mentioned Menno's visit. But she hadn't revealed any of this. *Why not?* Naomi's heart sank. Still, she might've known this would eventually happen, given his parents were both gone now. Naomi supposed Menno was the designated heir to the old homestead.

When the water came to a boil, Ida Mae poured it into the floral cups and offered her mother a variety of teas to choose

66

from. They sat awhile, stirring and sipping, and Naomi's heart went out to all three Esch girls.

Later, when Naomi had drunk her tea and completed a row of stitches, she put down her needle and thimble. "I wanted to mention somethin' else, Ida Mae. Your father and I were talkin' earlier about your brother Omar. Has he said anything about wanting to vote in the presidential election come November?"

Ida Mae's head bobbed up. "*Ach*, why would he want to?"

"Honestly, he's so intrigued by Ronald Reagan and politics in general, makes your father and me a bit concerned."

"Omar's prob'ly itchin' for lower taxes for farmers."

Naomi shook her head. "Who's to say?"

"Well, voting ain't something Joel and I would ever consider doin'. Might be only a handful of Amish who would. Maybe Joel knows more 'bout what Omar's thinkin'."

"*Jah*, talk to your husband and see." Naomi poured a second cup of tea. "Still, I hope Omar's changed his mind. The bishop's not so keen on getting involved with national politics. We're sojourners here, just a-passin' through."

Ida Mae agreed. "There's plenty to do just to keep our churches runnin' smoothly. I say, let the world run the government!"

❧

Some time later, Alan Yoder, Ida Mae's nephew-in-law, arrived with a baker's dozen of fresh biscuits from his mother. Right away he started talking about Lily. "I heard this morning from Fannie Ebersol's brother Thomas that Lily's left for good."

Word's traveling fast, Naomi thought.

Once people heard the news, likely it would be weeks before some sense of calm returned to Eden Valley. She couldn't help wondering if young Alan had used this delivery as a way to spread gossip.

"Lily asked me to take her to town just last week," Alan said, eyes wide. "She never said what she was doin', but it seemed mighty important."

Ida Mae glanced at Naomi. "What do you mean?"

Alan pushed his fists into his trouser pockets. "Well, she made me wait for her, and when she came out of the mall, she was clutching a small, flat paper sack." He looked up now, singling out Ida Mae. "Didn't think nothin' of it at the time."

Ida Mae stared at him. "What're ya sayin', Alan?"

"*Puh!* My big mouth." He had the good sense to look sheepish.

Naomi's interest was piqued. And because she didn't wish to *renkle*, she bit her lip. Disgusted, she said nicely yet firmly, "It's kind of you to drop by, Alan. Now, don't ya have some other deliveries to make?"

With that, the lad turned and headed outdoors.

Feeling all in, Naomi returned to the front room and sat down at the quilting frame. *Without a doubt, there's more to all of this than poor Eva may ever know,* she realized. *Once young folks leave to become* Englischers, *they're rarely heard from again. . . .*

⁂

Fannie's attitude this morning continued to disturb Eva, and she did not understand why Lily, who'd written of wanting a life away from the People, would arrange for an Amishman to pick her up last night.

Surely, Lily will become disillusioned with the modern world and come back, Eva thought. This hope squeezed her heart, and she tried to take comfort from Sylvia Lantz's wisdom that God's hand was on her dear sister.

Eva slowed the horse and headed back toward home, discouraged. The sun was inching ever higher; Frona was likely cooking the noon meal.

A mere quarter mile from home, she noticed Alfred Dienner pulling out of his father's dirt lane in his buggy. Alfred spotted her, too, and waved politely, his smile enveloping his tan face. She felt a twinge of guilt for having accepted his invitation to play Ping-Pong.

"Alfred's heart turns to sauce when you're around," Lily had once teased, insisting there was nothing wrong with marrying a farmer. *"If you love him enough,"* she'd added.

If anyone took hard work seriously, it was Alfred. He was well respected in the community, too. *"Your love would grow,"* Eva could imagine Mamma saying.

It might, if the Lord wills, Eva thought, putting on a smile for Alfred as she slowed Prince to less than a trot.

She felt a twinge of sadness. A farmer's wife had no time to keep up with a thriving candy store. *Maybe someday in the future, once the children are grown.*

Alfred pulled up beside her, but his smile had faded. In fact, he looked downright somber. "I was just headin' over your way, Eva. Funny runnin' into you."

"Have ya already eaten your stash of candy?"

He gripped the reins and turned slightly in his seat, his manner unusually tentative. "I received an unexpected letter this mornin'," he said. "I'm afraid it changes everything for us, Eva."

She waited for him to continue as his strange phrasing echoed in her head: *"Changes everything for us." He's stretching things,* she thought.

"I'm leaving for Kingston, Wisconsin, at first light tomorrow," he said in a quick flow of words. "I wanted you to know."

"You're goin' away?" This was the last thing she'd expected.

"Till sometime this fall."

A long time!

"I need to lend a hand to my father's cousin. He's laid up with a bad back."

"Your family will surely miss ya."

"I didn't want you to think I quit goin' to youth gatherings and whatnot." Alfred seemed to struggle with what to say. "My father thinks it'll be a *gut* change for me." He nodded as though affirming this to himself. "Doing something besides farming, ya know."

She was baffled. "What will you be doin'?" She embarrassed herself with her sudden curiosity.

"Woodworking," he said, but she noticed his expression, like his heart wasn't much in it.

"You might enjoy yourself, *jah?*"

"Hard to imagine," Alfred admitted. "But that's not all I wanted to discuss with you." He leaned across his buggy seat, smiling again. "I know we haven't spent much time together, but I'd like to write to you while I'm away . . . if you're agreeable. Maybe court ya by mail."

She gasped inwardly. It struck Eva as ironic that, after her hesitations about becoming a farmer's wife, Alfred was seemingly being transferred to Wisconsin to learn a trade. And while he hadn't hidden his interest in her, he'd never seemed quite so serious as now.

"Alfred, this is all so sudden."

His countenance dropped. "I'll write more 'bout what I'm thinking, if that suits ya." He paused. "A *gut* way to keep in touch, *jah?*"

She opened her mouth to answer but stopped. Alfred was staring at the floor of his buggy, and she felt just terrible. *What should I say?*

"Eva?" he asked, clearly anxious for her answer.

"Sure, if you'd like to, Alfred," she heard herself reply.

"*Wunnerbaar!*" He clicked his tongue to the horse and waved as it pulled him forward.

During the ride home, Eva felt as if she were at the bottom of a lake, struggling to reach the surface for a gasp of air. By the time she directed Prince into their driveway, she was so flustered she didn't know which she was more worried about: her sister's worldly future or her own.

Chapter Nine

·························· ✿ ··························

Jed awakened in the wee hours the following Monday, anxious to catch the early train to Lancaster, Pennsylvania. He'd jumped at the chance to please Uncle Ervin by going on this trip but was also concerned the shop might fall behind on orders, even though Perry would continue working in Jed's absence. Uncle Ervin had reassured him all would be well. He'd even suggested Jed make sure he took time for socializing while there. *The better for matchmaking?*

As he put on his Sunday best—black broadfall trousers and vest, and a crisp white shirt—his thoughts drifted easily to Lydiann. Bits and pieces of conversation when they were out riding or walking came to his remembrance, and images of her smiling knowingly, reading him the way she did so well. And oh, her wonderful sense of humor!

"Once we're married, I'll have to know how you like your eggs," she'd said once.

"Over easy." He'd played along.

"No omelets, then?"

73

"I'll eat whatever slides off your skillet."

"Careful now, Jed. You might live to regret that."

They'd shared the heartiest laugh.

Jed pushed the memory from his mind, wondering if his youngest sister would remember to wake up early enough to make breakfast. He hadn't wanted to trouble his mother to do so.

Opening his bedroom door, he immediately smelled the familiar aroma of eggs and sausage and walked to the kitchen, where seventeen-year-old Bettina was already dressed for the day. She looked wide-awake as she carried his plate over from the stove and set it down in front of him before taking a seat herself.

It was still dark outside, and Jed could hear the ticking of insects from the slightly open window behind him. The wide plank floors showed the marks of the years in the soft yellow light of the gas lamp over the oak table.

"How long will ya be gone, *Bruder?*" Bettina asked, thoughtful as always. It was no wonder this tenderhearted, soft-spoken sister already had a serious beau at such a young age. She sat across from him, eyes alert and hair parted straight down the middle. Her face was already sprinkled with freckles from hours spent in the sun planting the family garden with Mamm.

"Only a week." He explained why Uncle Ervin was sending him, leaving off the possibility of meeting Jonas Byler's granddaughters. Bettina would have had too much fun with that little tidbit.

"Might be *gut* to get away for a while." She looked kindly at him.

He nodded. "It's been a while, ain't?"

"Maybe ya won't be so *ferhoodled* when ya come back."

"Somebody's gotta keep you on your toes," he said.

"With brothers like you, I'm gonna need more toes." She left the table and brought back a cup of coffee, setting it down near his plate. "Seriously, I'll be prayin' for ya, Jed. You could use some happiness."

"*Denki.*"

She laughed a little, her spirits high this morning. "I might have something to confide in ya when you're back," she whispered, leaning forward.

"Surely it's not—"

Bettina put her finger to her lips. "Shh, 'tis a secret."

He had a sinking feeling but ignored it. There was plenty of time to deal with whatever it was. Besides, he knew her well enough not to probe further. "Ain't goin' New Order on me, are ya?"

She chuckled and shook her head. "Can you imagine *me* drivin' a car?"

"Well, I've seen ya drive a buggy. . . ."

She frowned with mock annoyance. "Are you pickin' on the sister who woke up early to make breakfast?"

"And it was mighty tasty, let me say."

Sighing, she regarded him with a wistful look, and a long moment passed between them. "*Ach*, Jed. It's so *gut* to see ya smile again. I've missed that."

He took a hesitant sip of coffee and glanced over the top at her. "I know ya wouldn't have gotten up before dawn for just any brother."

"*Jah*, you're the fortunate one."

When he finished, she removed his plate and took it to the sink, and he headed upstairs to close his suitcase. *Go before me today, Lord God, I pray. And make Thy will known to me.*

⌒﹏⌒

When Seth Keim, the hired van driver, arrived, Jed was surprised to see other passengers in the second and third seats. He slipped into the passenger side up front with Seth, a slight man in his early forties who had been driving the Amish for at least a decade. They exchanged brief greetings and Jed settled in for the ride, not wanting to add to the talk.

One woman was chattering excitedly about her "little loom room," where she wove different yarns into "the pertiest rugs you ever did see!" Jed didn't glance back, but by the sound of it, she was trying to encourage, even recruit, another woman to do the same. "A room like that's the best place in the house to retreat from *die Kinnerzucht*. A separate place to call your own, for sewing or weaving and whatnot, is a must sometimes."

Jed couldn't imagine his own mother admitting that her children were too noisy or underfoot. In all truth, he doubted his mother would have even wanted a hideaway workroom like the woman behind him. None of Jed's aunts or grandmothers had ever clamored for a separate sewing room, either, that he knew of. *Somehow, they managed. And I think we're better off for the time they took with us.*

He recalled his youngest sister's sweet-spirited temperament. Bettina, being the baby of the family, had been somewhat doted upon—much as his Lydiann had been. Yet neither of them had turned out the least bit spoiled.

Another woman in the van spoke up behind him now. "S'pose I *could* use a quiet place set apart . . . but for my ailin' mother," she said, her voice lowering as she continued. "Mamm's been planning her funeral here lately—every detail, right down to the kind of food she wants served."

"She needs privacy for that?" The first woman sounded shocked.

"Well, she's jittery a lot and needs her rest. Plus, she doesn't want anyone to see what she's writing in her journal. There are days she talks of setting fire to it . . . must be she doesn't want us to see who she's blowing off steam about."

Jed smiled to himself, and if he wasn't mistaken, Seth was over there chuckling behind the wheel. Jed had never heard of someone planning a funeral in advance, but then, it took all types of personalities.

He decided to ignore the frivolous conversation. Alliance was just one hour away. There, he would catch his train to Lancaster.

It was still too dark to read the old classic *The Pilgrim's Progress.* He'd read the book once before but liked to carry reading material wherever he went, even in the buggy. *"You never know when a good book might come in handy,"* his father liked to say, particularly when Mamm or Bettina needed a ride somewhere to shop. *Daed* was of a mind that a book was his "insurance" against waiting idly for his womenfolk in town.

Something else his father had urged Jed and his seven siblings to do was trust in God's provision for the direction of their lives. *"This means believing the Lord will stand strong when you cannot . . . that He will hold you up,"* Daed had said.

This wisdom had been essential for Jed this past year—each time he was tempted to doubt, thinking he couldn't continue on without Lydiann.

"Real *gut* to see ya headin' to Pennsylvania," Seth said, glancing his way. "A change of place is sometimes helpful."

"Just doin' my boss's bidding."

"Well, have yourself a nice time."

"*Denki,*" Jed said. And for the first time since Lydiann's death, he realized he was looking forward to something new, if only for a few days.

⟢⟡⟣

While waiting in the crowd of passengers to board the eastbound train, Jed overheard an older man telling a young boy about the various train cars they could explore on their trip. "There are dining cars, lounge cars, sleeping cars, and even a dome car where you can look at the sky and all around. You'll see."

"Is there ice cream in the dining car?" the boy asked, his face hopeful.

"We'll find out, won't we?" the older man replied as he ruffled the boy's hair.

Everywhere Jed turned, people were paired up—young couples holding hands, elderly couples assisting each other, families with children. *People in love.*

Once he was on board the train, Jed chose a window seat on the right side of the aisle. As of the first jerk forward, the seat next to him was still vacant. *Like usual.* He turned to gaze out the window and embraced the new day with another silent prayer.

⟨❦⟩

Unknowingly, Jed had drifted off to sleep and was awakened, startled, when someone sneezed. In his groggy state, he bumped something hard wedged between the seat and the coach wall. A brief investigation revealed it was a hardback copy of *Little Women*. He'd seen Bettina reading the classic novel last summer.

Opening the book, Jed saw no name or identification on the front pages. With his own treasured library—accumulated over more than a decade—he'd always printed his full name and address in plain view on the front page.

Thumbing through, he discovered a wrinkled photograph tucked between pages forty-four and forty-five—a pretty Amish girl, possibly in her late teens. He studied the picture more closely, finding it curious that the young woman looked so boldly into the camera while wearing a white prayer *Kapp* shaped like a heart—the characteristic head covering for the Lancaster County Old Order Amish. Though the picture was black and white, it was clear she wore a cape dress and matching apron, as well. The

BEVERLY LEWIS

photo looked as though it had been torn from a strip of others, with the bottom of the next picture showing a young woman's folded hands.

Why would a devout girl have her picture taken?

He turned the photograph over and saw penned on the back: *The best and worst day of my life.*

Still more curious, Jed returned the picture to its place between the pages and scanned through the book, quickly noting that the story was focused on four young sisters growing up in New England during the time of the Civil War.

Definitely not my choice of reading material!

Yet, while paging through the book, he came across many notes penciled in the margin—the note writer's own thoughts about family and grief and death, as well as a few tender words about romance and love.

There were also underlined passages, such as *"You are like a chestnut burr, prickly outside, but silky-soft within, and a sweet kernel, if one can only get at it. Love will make you show your heart some day, and then the rough burr will fall off."*

Jed smiled and wondered if the book's owner had been thinking of someone in particular. Certainly he had known a few people who could fit that description!

***

Two hours later, when the train slowed and then came to a stop in Pittsburgh, a number of passengers got off. By now, Jed had already breezed through a good portion of the book's margin notes and underlined passages, glancing now and then at the photograph to put the words and the note writer together in his mind.

The new passengers boarded and rustled about, taking their places and making conversation with seatmates. Once again no one occupied the seat next to him, leaving him alone for the duration of the journey, but this time the prospect pleased Jed.

He returned to the pages, captivated by the girl's thoughts, sensing a growing connection to her, at times moved by her delicate honesty.

He closed the book, recalling how quickly he and Lydiann had bonded, how rapidly he had known she was the girl for him. *Almost immediately.* That sort of connection came once in a lifetime, or so he presumed. He leaned back in his seat, allowing a gentle sadness to wash over him.

Whatever he'd had with Lydiann was gone forever. There was no point in wishing for it again.

CHAPTER TEN

••••••••••••••••••••••••••••••• ❀ •••••••••••••••••••••••••••••••

TWO DAYS HAD PASSED since the unthinkable had happened. In the meantime, Eva and Frona, and their brothers, too, tried to make the best of it. Menno and Rufus had taken it upon themselves to cover nearly all of Eden Valley, the areas beyond Eva's Saturday search, but to no avail. It seemed no one had heard from Lily.

This morning Eva had written in her diary, hoping Lily might simply walk in the door at any moment, having changed her mind. *"I'm sorry I worried you,"* she might say, and whatever agony they'd all felt would be drowned out by sheer relief.

Presently, Eva and Frona were having a dinner of baked chicken and rice, taking their time to plan the week, since they'd gotten the Monday washing hung out much earlier.

Eva suggested, "We might take your tasty jams and my specialty candies down to the Quarryville market come Thursday. What do ya say?" Eva was certain going to market might distract them for a while, at least, from their mutual woes. And, too, perhaps someone might know something about Lily farther south of them.

Frona nodded. "Fine with me." She looked up from her meal. "Word has it a lot of people are comin' into the area for an auction."

"Farm or cattle sale?"

"It's an estate auction takin' place two farms down from the Byler carriage shop," Frona informed her.

"Is that right?"

"Should be quite the all-day event, what with not only the house and everything in it being auctioned off, but the barn equipment and the animals, too."

Eva listened and hoped they might have time to attend.

"I also heard that Jonas Byler may retire come this fall," Frona said. "Might leave a hole in the buggy-making business round here."

Eva wondered how that would be for the highly sought after buggy maker, respected all over Lancaster County. Was Jonas Byler looking forward to the change? "It's hard to hear of older folks having to give up what they've loved doing so long."

"We don't know if it's for his health's sake." Frona reached for the butter dish, a homemade biscuit in her other hand.

"Might just be," Eva said, realizing how much less laundry there had been today. Goodness, but it seemed Lily had nearly as many dresses and aprons as both Eva and Frona combined. *There's something about the sharp smell of our homemade soap that Lily loves,* Eva thought sadly.

In spite of what they did to keep themselves occupied, Lily was in the background of Eva's every thought.

They finished the meal without saying much more to each other, and when dessert was served, Eva made over Frona's chocolate macaroons, still deliciously soft.

"Lily's favorite," Frona remarked. "I'd be willin' to make them every day if she'd just return," she added.

"Maybe she's missing us and already thinkin' of starting home." Frona nodded slowly, like she wasn't so sure.

Eva reached for another cookie. Not that it helped anything, but the sweet taste couldn't hurt.

Later, while she and Frona were redding up the kitchen, Eva mentioned an upcoming work frolic. The deacon had invited all the young men and women in the church district to help clean up the schoolhouse. "Would ya like to go with me?" she asked. "There'll likely be some nice young men there."

"What on earth. Who are ya thinkin' of—me or you?"

"It's been a while."

"*Puh!*" Frona muttered, the dishes clattering. Another moment passed. "When is it?"

"About two weeks away."

Frona's eyes instantly looked more gray than blue. She stopped washing the dish in her hand and frowned. "You must still be thinking 'bout Menno's announcement."

"His *what?*"

"Well, what would you call it?" Frona said.

Eva shrugged. *She's so dramatic. . . .*

"Well, you were here when he laid it all out." Frona resumed washing the dishes. "I'm thinkin' of going to see him after the clothes are brought in and folded."

"To try an' change his mind?"

"Give him a piece of mine, maybe."

"Oh dear."

"It can't hurt, can it?"

Sure might, Eva thought. She wished Frona would forget about arguing with Menno. What she really wanted was for Frona to commit to going to the work frolic at the schoolhouse. It would get their mind off things. She brought it up again.

"I'll have to think on it." The evasive answer gave Eva little hope of Frona's agreeing.

She knew better than to push too hard with this sister.

⁕

Jed was met at the Lancaster train depot that afternoon by Jonas's grandnephew Wallie Byler, who introduced Jed to the short, dark-haired driver, Neil Zimmerman. "It's *gut* of you to come," Jed told them as Neil turned the key in the ignition and backed out of the parking space. A small orange cat with a cheesy grin swung from the rearview mirror—a character Jed had seen once or twice in a cartoon strip.

"Wouldn't have it any other way," Wallie said right next to Jed in the second row.

They made small talk about the weather and tomorrow's auction near Quarryville. During a lull in conversation, Neil switched on the radio and Jed was shocked to hear the news from faraway South Korea—an uprising was following what a reporter called "a massacre" in Gwangju. "These protests against martial law are the necessary crucible of a grassroots movement to overturn a repressive regime," the reporter said. "More than two hundred students died for freedom."

Wallie glanced at Jed and shook his head. "If folks could just get along, what a better world this would be."

So tragic. Hearing of such mayhem made Jed all the more grateful he had not had to take part in any wars, even to serve overseas as a noncombatant like some of his male relatives had during the war in Vietnam.

Neil turned down the volume and asked if Jed and Wallie wanted to get a quick bite to eat. They were definitely in agreement, and Neil made the turn into a fast-food place.

"It's nearly suppertime round here," Wallie said with a tug on his black suspenders. His light hair showed a distinct dent from his straw hat, which he must have worn earlier. "Did ya have anything to eat on the trip?"

Jed nodded. "My youngest sister sent along ham sandwiches, but I sure could go for a cheeseburger now."

Right quick, Wallie pulled out his wallet while they waited in line at the drive-through. "Uncle Jonas insisted on treating."

"*Ach*, can't let him do that." Jed reached into his pocket.

"*Nee*, better let him have the last word on this, or I'll be in hot water." Wallie laughed. "If you don't know what I mean, you will shortly."

Jed looked forward to meeting Jonas Byler. "Will either of yous be goin' to the neighbors' estate auction, then?" he asked.

"Bright an' early. But I'm just goin' for the food."

Jed chuckled.

Wallie went on to talk about his big dairy operation near Gap. "But I'm happy to help Uncle Jonas out . . . and glad to meet you, too."

When they picked up their burgers and fries and the chocolate milkshakes Wallie had ordered, they headed south on Route 272 toward Quarryville.

They stopped for additional Amish passengers near an area known as Willow Street, including one younger couple who seemed taken with each other. *Plainly in love.* Jed thought again of the book he'd found on the train, and it crossed his mind: What if he could meet the note writer, the pretty girl in the photograph?

It was a crazy idea. *Besides,* he realized, *whoever wrote in the book might be mortified to know someone else is privy to her thoughts.*

Away from curious and judgmental eyes, he would look again at the forbidden photo later. Maybe he'd missed something about the young woman. *Maybe someone around Quarryville might recognize her . . . if she's from that area.*

He shook his head at the fanciful notion. He couldn't bear to put such a thoughtful soul at risk by showing the picture around, even if it meant he might find her.

CHAPTER ELEVEN

························ ✿ ························

JONAS BYLER'S HANDSHAKE was unexpectedly vigorous for as spindly as he looked—a tall, tanned man in his late seventies. Jonas graciously greeted Jed, then motioned for his wife to come over. "This here's Jedediah from Berlin, Ohio—Ervin Stutzman's nephew, ya know." Jonas introduced him to Elsie before pointing the way into the light and airy kitchen.

Austere in its simplicity, the kitchen reminded Jed of his paternal grandmother's with its low windows along the south side of the room and a considerable freestanding pine hutch, yellowed with age.

"*Willkumm*," Elsie said, her black apron a menu of baking projects—splotches of flour and something sticky, like jam.

"I appreciate your hospitality."

"We hope you'll feel free to stay as long as you'd like." Elsie grinned at Jed and gestured for Jonas to take him upstairs to the spare room. "There's a washroom just down the hallway up there," she added. "We're tryin' to keep up with the times, I guess you could say." She laughed a nervous little laugh.

Jed was surprised she felt it necessary to excuse the indoor plumbing. His parents' home had been updated that way back in the mid-fifties. *Before I was born.*

"We'll have a later supper than usual," Elsie called again up the stairs. "Chust take your time getting settled."

Jed didn't have the heart to say he'd wolfed down a hamburger and fries on the way there.

Leading the way, Jonas opened the door to Jed's room. "My son and family are comin' for the meal tonight—Mose and Bekah and their two youngest daughters . . . both courtin' age." Jonas winked slyly.

Keeping his smile in check, Jed assumed Uncle Ervin must have put a bug in Jonas's ear. *Could be interesting,* he thought and quickly unpacked, then went to freshen up. Strubblich *hair will never do for this meal!*

⌒⌒⌒

When Sylvia Lantz stepped into The Sweet Tooth around closing time at four o'clock, Eva smiled. "Happy to see ya," she said, going around the counter to greet her neighbor.

"Came to bring some cheer." Sylvia was all dressed up in a pretty black cape dress and matching apron and wearing her crisp white *Kapp.*

"You couldn't have arrived at a better time." Eva went to the display case and removed the last two bonbons, setting them in a bowl. "Let's go over and sit in the kitchen and have ourselves a little taste of chocolate."

Sylvia was quick to agree, and as they walked through the hall and into the main house, she mentioned receiving a letter from her daughter Tilly Barrows, who lived in Rockport, Massachusetts, with her family. As a youth, Tilly had decided against joining church and had eventually married an outsider after moving to the English world. She and her husband, Kris, had three children—nearly seven-year-old identical twin daughters, Jenya and Tavani, and eighteen-month-old Mel, named for Tilly's brother, Melvin Lantz.

"Will they be comin' for another visit?" Eva hoped so for Sylvia's sake.

"As soon as the twins are out of school for the summer." Sylvia opened the letter once they'd seated themselves at the kitchen table. "Just thought I'd read a little bit of it to you. All right?"

Eva was glad Frona was upstairs—she could hear the footsteps overhead. For her own part, she was all for listening to Tilly's letter, as she'd always liked Sylvia, possibly because Mamma had thought so highly of her.

"I won't tire you with everything Tilly wrote," Sylvia said as she scanned through the lines. "Ah, here we are."

She began to read aloud.

"Our twins have learned to make beautiful little quilting stitches, Mamma—isn't that such happy news? And they can say simple words and phrases in *Deitsch*, even though they haven't grown up with the People, as I did. Seems that Ruth and I let that slip into our conversation more than we know! I thought it might be an encouragement to you and Dat, hearing that some of the Plain culture has found its way to your English grandchildren."

Sylvia looked up from the letter, tears threatening. "Oh, Eva, isn't this the dearest thing? Like a melody to my heart."

Eva hardly knew what to say. Was Sylvia trying to offer her some hope about Lily? But it wasn't hope really; it seemed more like giving Lily up to the world and being satisfied with a letter or two.

"I never dreamed I'd get such letters from our Tilly, tellin' the truth."

Eva knew that Tilly and her younger sister, Ruth, had nearly broken Sylvia's and Lester's hearts. But seeing Sylvia's response to this letter, Eva sensed Sylvia had made peace with losing her dear children to the outside world. Perhaps the years had washed away the worst of the pain.

"Sometimes I wish they'd all relocate to Eden Valley so I could get my fill of seein' them and my grandchildren."

"Ain't likely they'd become Amish, is it?" Eva asked, knowing her own mother had posed the same question to Sylvia after Tilly and Ruth left the People. Against her husband's advice, Sylvia had clung to that hope, even though she'd confided in Eva's mother that she knew in her heart that Tilly and her family would never think of such a move.

"*Nee*, not likely, though I'd like nothing more." Sylvia dried her eyes with a hankie from her pocket. "A mother's heart is never far from her children."

When Frona came downstairs, Eva offered some of her chocolate macaroons to Sylvia, which brought smiles all around. "I do believe I've had my fill of sweets for the week," Sylvia said, thanking them.

Later, Eva walked with her to the end of the lane, aware of the pungent smell of manure in the air. "I'm glad you stopped in." She paused.

"If I know you, you're prayin' for Lily." Sylvia gave her a kiss on the cheek. "Dottie raised you well."

Standing in the road, Eva watched her mother's friend head back down the road, Sylvia's black dress swirling around her bare ankles.

She wondered what had motivated Tilly to leave her family behind and strike out into unfamiliar territory. *Was it frightening for her at first? Or an adventure?*

Thinking again of Lily, she trembled. *Oh, write to me, sister, please write soon!*

❧

Jed was seated to the left of Mose Byler at the long table that evening, with Mose's wife, Bekah, and their daughters Lovina and Orpha across from Jed. *To encourage conversation, no doubt,* he thought.

Elsie sat to the right of Jonas, who presided at the head of the table. She passed the food first to her husband, and then the platters went to the men—pork chops with mashed potatoes and gravy, baked beans, and corn pudding.

Jonas and his son Mose talked for a while, but it wasn't long before Jed, too, was drawn into the conversation. He was mindful of the bashful though pretty blond girls across the table. Orpha, who said she was nineteen, and Lovina, twenty-one, glanced up from their plates every so often. Mose helped things along, mentioning that both young women would be at the auction tomorrow.

"They're helping with the food," Jonas interjected, leaning forward to catch Jed's eye. "*Wunnerbaar-gut* cooking."

"Home cooking's best," Jed replied, smiling back at Orpha, who seemed the more outgoing of the two. "What type of food?"

Orpha replied, "Oh, nearly whatever you have a hankerin' for. Delicious soups: ham and bean, ya know, and chicken corn soup, too. There'll be ham and cheese sandwiches, hot dogs, barbecue, whoopie pies, cream-filled doughnuts, homemade ice cream, and all kinds of pies, including banana cream."

"My mouth's watering already."

"*Des gut,*" Orpha replied, glancing curiously at Lovina.

"Ever been to an auction round here?" Mose Byler asked, eyes intent.

91

"This is my first visit to the area."

"And you're enjoying working in Ohio with my mother's cousin Ervin Stutzman?" Mose said.

"So far, I'm just an apprentice."

Orpha glanced at Elsie, then at her mother. "That's the best way to start, ain't so?" she said at last.

Jed nodded, smiling back at her. *She's coming out of her shell.*

When it was time for dessert, Elsie's strawberry pie got calls for seconds from Jonas and Mose, but considering Jed's full stomach, he respectfully declined.

Later, Jed found himself alone with Orpha and sitting on the back porch. They weren't by themselves for long. Lovina and her mother wandered outside a few minutes later, heading around the walkway to visit Elsie's older sister living in the *Dawdi Haus.* Then, not so long after, Mose and Jonas appeared and pretended not to see Jed and Orpha there as they made their way over to the carriage shop, full of talk.

When it was just the two of them again, Jed commented on the peacefulness of the hilly countryside around his native Berlin farmland, and Orpha was quick to say how nice it was right there in rural Quarryville. They talked about hobbies and favorite activities—he surmised volleyball was the one commonality between them. The longer they visited, the more he missed the easy style of conversation he'd enjoyed with Lydiann. He wanted to be companionable to Orpha, but everything he said came out awkward and stilted.

Am I trying too hard?

Later, when Mose and Bekah and their daughters left for home, he was invited to join Jonas and Elsie for their Bible reading in the front room. Thankful for this quiet and reflective time, Jed asked again for the Lord's guidance, as he did every night during the prayer time.

When he'd said good-night, Jed headed upstairs, where he spotted *Little Women* on the table near the bed. He hesitated for a moment, feeling more than a little silly as he finally gave in to his whim and turned to the page where he'd left off, marked by the photograph.

Another neatly printed note ran down the side of the page: *How will I know when I find true love?*

Jed closed the book. If he hadn't met Lydiann, he might have wondered this himself. Lydiann hadn't just been his "true love." She herself had been *true*, a young woman of the highest character and noble intention, earnest to do God's will.

That's true love, he thought.

Looking at the photo once more, Jed knew the owner was obviously living too close to the world. It wasn't uncommon for restless Amish girls in *Rumschpringe* to follow their boyfriends right out of the community.

He studied the woman's eyes in the picture. They were kind and bright, but something was amiss.

Again he deliberated the notion of searching for this young woman, who despite her struggles with the ordinance, had written such poignant thoughts about life. By the looks of the delicate *Kapp*, surely the girl lived somewhere in Lancaster County.

But where?

The grandfather clock downstairs chimed ten times, and Jed prepared to retire for the night. Morning would come on cat's paws, sneaking up on him.

CHAPTER TWELVE

·· ❋ ··

EARLY THE NEXT MORNING after breakfast, Jed left Jonas's house to peruse the barn equipment up the road, already displayed for the auction. Other men were trickling onto the property, a smattering of Amish and Mennonites and even a handful of English farmers—many of them milling about and surveying the tools and other offerings.

A number of men had gravitated to the stable, talking rapidly in *Deitsch*, a few puffing on pipes, a habit Jed hadn't noticed much in public places back home. *Except for some of the older Amishmen who smoke on their own property, like Uncle Ervin.*

It was certain there would be plenty of competition in the bidding for the barn's and house's contents, all of which were to be sold in separate lots.

Jed observed Mose and his wife riding into the lane, Lovina and Orpha squeezed into the second bench seat with two other younger girls. Right now, though, Jed needed to go over to sign up for his bidding number, in case he saw something that caught his interest.

Several older men were chewing the fat as Jed made his way into the line for the bidding numbers. "Word has it a clinic in Philly has health screening tests for seniors, free of charge," one of the long-bearded men was saying.

"Hadn't heard that," said another.

"How old do ya have to be?" asked a third.

"A senior."

"Well, I've got a few years yet till I hit eighty," the second man said.

"Seems to me that's a super-senior," the first man said with a chuckle.

Jed grinned, and when he'd acquired his number, he moseyed out to the barn to have a look at the animals, eager for the day when he might own more than one road horse and perhaps some goats or chickens.

Later, on his way back toward the yard, he noticed Mose tie his mare to the hitching post, the girls standing in a cluster nearby. The thought of having to talk exclusively with Orpha Byler again felt uncomfortable in light of last evening's porch encounter.

⁜

As they lingered at the breakfast table, Naomi Mast pressed Abner about the estate auction down near Quarryville. "Wouldn't it be nice to go for just a little while?"

Paging through *The Budget*, Abner appeared to have other things on his mind. "There's nothin' I'm looking to buy."

"Are ya so sure we wouldn't enjoy ourselves?" she pleaded.

"Fairly sure."

Naomi set her teacup down and added, "We could have some delicious food while we walk around a bit."

Abner inclined his head toward her. "This must mean a lot to ya."

"Well, I've been a-turnin' the idea round and round this morning, is all. We meet such interesting people at these sales, and some of our grandchildren might be there, too. Our son Elam will be, for sure."

Abner set his paper down and came over to the sink to plant a kiss on her lips. "I remember that perty smile of yours, Naomi, and I haven't seen it yet this mornin'. S'pose that means we best be ridin' down to that auction you're so keen on."

"Oh, Abner, ya mean it?" She couldn't keep from smiling as she leaned happily into his strong arms.

"I do indeed."

∽✦∽

Their rhubarb was coming on fast now, and from the kitchen window, Eva observed Frona basking in the sunlight like a child. She'd gone out to pick right after breakfast while Eva laid out her candies and other goodies for tomorrow's customers.

Frona was happiest, Eva decided, when she was putting up jam, something she did for the tourists who came to The Sweet Tooth and discovered the preserves for sale alongside Eva's confections. *Sweets upon sweets!*

To keep from going *narrish* over Lily's departure, Eva poured her heart into her own work. And whenever she thought of Lily, she breathed a prayer and ached for whatever pain had propelled her sister away.

A little while later, Ida Mae dropped by with some fresh bread to share. "You two oughta be down at the Quarryville estate auction, selling your jams and homemade candies," she suggested to Eva when Frona came inside. "Might lift your spirits some."

"Oh, there'll be plenty of goodies, I'm sure," Eva replied.

"Your Dat and Mamm are goin'," Frona said, turning from the

sink, where she was washing rhubarb. "Naomi said so when I was out mailin' some letters this morning."

Eva brightened. "I'm *sure* Abner's excited."

Ida Mae laughed. "No doubt she had to twist his arm."

"Your Mamm likes to mingle with new folks," Eva told Ida Mae. "She's a social butterfly, my mother always said."

"Well, Dottie would've known," Ida Mae said.

When Ida Mae was gone, Frona returned to the rhubarb. "Are ya lookin' forward to going to market Thursday?" she asked Eva as she took out the cutting board and began to slice the stalks for jam.

"*Jah*, and for the same reason Naomi's goin' to the auction."

"You're itchin' to see some new faces, I 'spect." Frona squinted at her. "Ain't still hoping to meet someone who might know where Lily's gone, are ya?"

"It *would* be helpful to know if she's safe somewhere, ain't so?"

"I 'spect we'll hear something when she runs out of money," Frona spouted.

And the sooner, the better, Eva thought sadly.

❧

"I got thirty dollars . . . now give me forty," the Amish auctioneer rattled off from where he stood high on a flatbed wagon. "Thirty, thirty . . . give me forty?"

Jed raised his head to the younger man reciting bids while keeping track of indications from the throng of bidders as various items were presented.

"Got a forty-dollar bid—will ya give me fifty?" called the auctioneer.

This was the third item that had caught Jed's eye, but he'd dropped out of the bidding when the price went higher than he felt the particular tool was worth. *I can't see paying these prices.*

By ten-thirty, his stomach was rumbling, and he'd struck out further with each item he'd tried to secure. He wandered over to the buggy shed to have a look at the food selection. The place was crowded with church benches and tables set up on one side. Orpha and two other girls he didn't recognize were helping with the food, and he stepped up to order a barbecue sandwich.

Orpha spotted him and smiled, the roses in her cheeks growing brighter. *I have to admit,* he thought, *she's very friendly. And pretty, too.*

"Anything else you'd like?" Orpha asked, pointing out the soda options.

"There's also plenty of pie and ice cream," another of the girls piped up.

"I'll be back for dessert later," he said, paying for his sandwich and going to sit at one of the only spots available.

While he ate, he wondered if he might have been too quick to judge Orpha. *Should I give it another go?*

After all, he was interested in marrying a level-headed, responsible young woman, and Orpha seemed to be that. She didn't, however, come across as a book reader, though she was smart. His uncle would be pleased if he came home with good news to report.

Still, she's nothing like Lydiann, he thought. And that was the heart of the issue, the answer behind every dating-related question.

The day was mild and sunshine plentiful. The occasional scent of lilacs wafted on the breeze as Naomi walked along with Abner at the auction late that morning. They greeted two other Plain couples, one with young children in tow, and Naomi savored this chance to mingle.

On the other side of the corncrib, Naomi spotted their youngest son, Elam, with his little boy, two-and-a-half-year-old Sammy. The very instant the child laid eyes on his *Mammi* Naomi, he began pulling on his father's sleeve, asking in *Deitsch* if he could walk around with her and *Dawdi* Abner. Elam agreed and told Naomi he'd catch up with them in a little while.

Sammy's blue eyes sparkled as he looked up at Naomi, who delighted in feeling his small hand tucked into hers. "Such a nice surprise," she said. "Maybe you'd like some ice cream."

Abner tapped their grandson's miniature straw hat, which leaned jauntily toward the back of his little head. "I'm going to amble over to look at the farming equipment," he told Naomi.

Naomi nodded and happily led Sammy to the concessions area, where dozens of folks were lining up. While in the crush of the crowd, Sammy managed to slip away from her.

She turned quickly, calling his name. *How'd he get loose?* she wondered, scurrying about.

Leaving the area, she went in search of the dear child, thinking now that he must have spotted his father and changed his mind, wanting to be with Elam instead. *Like* Kinner *are known to do.*

But she couldn't locate him—it was hard to spot such a tiny boy amidst the throng.

Naomi's heart raced as she headed toward the wagons where the larger tools were laid out. Nearby, she saw one of Abner's cousins talking to another man, but there was no sign of little Sammy. *Help me, Lord!* she prayed, hoping she might find the lad before he became frightened, small as he was.

Jed was pleased to finally have taken the bid on an apparently coveted set of hammers and pliers. He reasoned it was sensible to pay a little more when they were so well made.

He'd brought his prize back to Jonas's house and was eager to return to the jovial atmosphere. When he was on the grounds again, he felt a sudden tug on his pant leg. Looking down, his gaze was met by a small boy staring up at him.

As if embarrassed, the little fellow stepped away and put his hands behind his back.

He thought he recognized me. Jed crouched down. "Hey, there, aren't you the smallest bidder ever?"

The boy swallowed, and a wee smile crept back onto his features.

"Are you lost, young man?"

The boy nodded.

"Well, I think it's time to find out who you belong to," Jed replied. "But first, do ya know what might help our search?"

The boy shook his head.

"Some ice cream, maybe with whipped cream and sprinkles."

The boy giggled and all was well. The towheaded child began babbling in *Deitsch*, talking about his Mammi Naomi. A moment later, however, and his smile disappeared again; he rubbed his eyes, his lower lip stuck out.

Jed summed up the situation. "Here, let's get you a better view so you can find your family." Reaching down, he hoisted the boy onto his shoulders. The small straw hat fell off, and Jed caught it, then passed it up to the child. "*Was is dei Naame?*" he asked.

"Sammy," the boy said and clapped his hands with glee perched up there so high.

His Mammi will spot him now. Jed left the bidding area and headed across the field toward the concession table. "Do ya like whoopie pies better than ice cream, maybe?"

More clapping came from above and a pocket-sized "*Jah.*"

"All right, then, let's go."

Jed purchased a whoopie pie, and Sammy's smile returned.

101

Pulling the wrapping off as quickly as he could, Jed handed the treat to the boy. "We need to find your Mammi, young fella. She's gonna worry."

Sammy shook his head, pointing to his treat.

Jed laughed. "Don't worry. You can finish that first."

CHAPTER THIRTEEN

"WHAT DO YA SAY we go to the auction now?" Eva suggested to Frona as her sister wiped down the jar rims. "I'll even hitch up for ya."

Frona shrugged casually. "I guess it'd be nice to have the noon meal there. I've been hungry for a nice bowl of ham and bean soup."

"All right, then. I'll hurry." Eva rushed off to the stable, ever so ready for a change of scenery.

When they arrived at the auction, neither was shocked at the size of the crowd—word of mouth never failed to spread such news. Eva recommended they get right in line for something to eat. Frona agreed, and after the ham and bean soup Frona was hankering for, she went for some vanilla ice cream and a large peanut butter cookie.

They weren't poky at the table, since so many families were present. When they'd finished eating, Frona spotted some friends. "I'll catch up with ya later, sister."

103

"Sure, take your time." The sun felt so good on her back and shoulders. Eva lingered near a cluster of tall oak trees, enjoying the gaiety and observing all the goings-on. At one point, she raised her face to the sky, wishing she might have more opportunities to work outdoors—her little shop kept her inside several days a week.

She remembered the first time she and Lily had gone to a mud sale—an Amish auction to raise money for local fire departments. They were only young girls, and the mud from spring rains had been so deep that Lily had gotten stuck, her little rubber boots nearly buried in the mushy mess. As Eva called to their Dat for help, she had managed to pull her out partway. She'd never forgotten how their dear father had run over and scooped little Lily into his arms, not caring how terribly soiled his black coat and trousers might get. Dat took Eva by the hand as he carried Lily all the way across the mucky field to their carriage. There, he wiped Lily's tears with his clean white handkerchief.

Eva sighed and turned her attention again to the pleasant drone of the large gathering. Not far away was a tall man with a darling little boy perched on his squared shoulders. Watching them, she noticed the boy's smile; his tiny arm raised high overhead. *He's playing horsey*, she thought, smiling at this from her vantage point.

Then, looking closer, she realized the child was Naomi Mast's grandson. But then, who was the fellow with the strawberry blond hair hauling him around? Eva made note of the young man's hat brim, certainly narrower than those she was accustomed to seeing. Her curiosity got the best of her and she called to Sammy, waving to him.

The man turned toward her, and the youngster grinned, saying her name, "Eva . . . Eva!"

They moved in her direction, the cordial-looking man picking up his pace. But as they approached, his contagious smile suddenly disappeared, and he frowned slightly, his eyes narrowed, almost as if startled by her appearance.

Does he know me? She measured his peculiar expression, but considering his attire, he was certainly not local, and she was quite sure they'd never met.

"I'm Eva Esch," she introduced herself before pointing to Sammy. "And I know this little friend of yours." She reached up to touch the boy's hand, and he laughed.

"He's lost . . . unless you're his Mammi." The handsome fellow's steady gaze was unsettling, but she could see a trace of humor there.

"Well, I do know both of Sammy's grandmothers," Eva said, her neck and face warm in the sunlight. "One is my neighbor, in fact . . . my friend Naomi." Eva astonished herself, talking so freely to a stranger, of all things.

The man continued to study her, his head tilted, his expression serious.

"I'll help ya find Naomi Mast," she said, feeling awkward because the young man still hadn't offered his name. "Do I know you, maybe?"

"*Nee,*" he replied softly. "Just never expected to meet you here. . . ."

She felt her forehead crinkle to a frown at the odd response. "Sorry?"

"I . . . I meant," he began, blinking all of a sudden, as though snapping out of a dream or a momentary memory snag. "Forgive me, it's just that—"

"Mammi Naomi!" young Sammy called, jostling up and down, clearly wanting to keep going.

"Jed Stutzman's my name." He gave Eva an engaging smile. "From Berlin, Ohio. I'm in town for the week," he added.

"Lookin' for treasures today like everyone else?"

105

"Unfortunately, I haven't ended up with many."

Sammy was still bouncing around, trying to get Jed moving again and calling for Naomi.

Jed glanced over his shoulder. "Do you happen to see Sammy's grandmother anywhere?"

Eva scanned the nearest group of people and shook her head. The bidders were clustered around another wagon, and from where she stood, she could see the flat crowns of a sea of straw hats. "Walk with me," she said. "I have an idea where she might be."

"*Wunnerbaar-gut*," Jed said, clasping Sammy's feet, which dangled near his chest.

They walked so slowly at first, she wondered if Jed might be reluctant to head back into the crowd. It sure seemed that way, considering he kept glancing at her.

"By the way, I'm interested in going to a local market while I'm here," he said unexpectedly. "Do you know of one nearby?"

"Just thataway on Thursdays." She pointed in the direction of Quarryville. "You could prob'ly go on foot; it's quite close." Without thinking, she added, "My sister and I will be tending a table there, actually."

He nodded, eyes brightening all the more. "*Gut*, then, I'll keep an eye out for ya."

"*Denki*." His winning way made her heart flutter, yet she hardly knew what to think.

They walked farther, Jed telling about his uncle in Ohio arranging for his stay with Jonas Byler and his wife, just two farms over. "They're mighty nice, I'll say. The salt of the earth." He went on to say his uncle was also a carriage maker, and that he and Jonas intended for Jed to spend the whole week learning about Jonas's techniques and perspective on the trade.

"I wonder what the buggy-man, as we call him, will do with

his time once he's retired in a few months," she said, falling into step with Jed.

"I, for one, can't imagine not workin'."

She mentioned her little candy shop, just for fun. "It's my pride and joy, but in a *gut* way, if ya know what I mean."

"More womenfolk are opening small shops like this in their homes," Jed replied. "At least out in my area of Ohio."

"Is that right?" She found this interesting. "My father got me all set up back when I was young."

"Hey, maybe *you* blazed the trail." He chuckled.

Just then they heard a woman's voice. "Sammy Mast!"

When they turned, Eva saw Orpha Byler waving, along with two other young women. "Ah, there's one of Jonas's granddaughters with some of her cousins," Eva told him.

Orpha was all a-chatter. "Well, lookee who's got ya, sweetie," she said, reaching to playfully poke Sammy's arm. Then she proceeded to introduce Jed Stutzman to her cousins, Linda and Rebecca, who blushed simultaneously. "That was one delicious supper Mammi Elsie fixed last evening, ain't so?" Orpha declared.

Orpha seemed intent on singling out Jed and making it clear they'd spent time together.

Jed turned respectfully to Eva. "Orpha, have ya met Eva Esch?"

"Oh *jah*. Seen her at market over the years," Orpha said, eyeing her. "But we attend different church districts."

Still more families were arriving now that the house furnishings were going up for bid. Eva looked around for Frona, wondering if she'd decided to spend all of her time with friends.

"It's nice to see you again, Orpha," Eva said, then looked up at little Sammy, who was beginning to pout. "You know what? I'm going to run over and see if Naomi's where I think she is. She's surely worried by now."

Jed nodded agreeably.

"I'll bring her right over, once I find her," Eva assured him.

"I guess we'll be seein' ya later, Jed," Orpha said before leaning closer to whisper in Jed's ear—something about "homemade ice cream, up at the house."

She's carrying a torch for him! thought Eva and wondered if he liked pushy girls.

Orpha and her followers waved at Jed and wandered off.

"Sorry 'bout that," Jed said just as Eva was about to take her own leave.

She shrugged and wondered why he'd apologized.

Just then, from behind them, Naomi came hurrying over, her face as bright as a red beet egg. Then, seeing Eva, too, the dear woman slowed her pace. She looked bewildered as she walked right up to Jed and reached for her grandson. Sammy leaned down and tumbled into her arms. "Where, oh where have ya been, *mei Buwli?*" Naomi kissed his chubby cheeks, hugging the daylights out of him.

"Naomi, this is Jed Stutzman. He's the one who found your Sammy-boy," Eva told her.

"*Denki* for findin' my *Kinskind.*" She smiled and nodded at Jed, then hugged Sammy again.

"He actually found *me.*" Jed explained how the boy had walked up to him and indicated he was lost.

Naomi surveyed Sammy's chubby cheeks again, wiping at them with her fingers. "Looks like someone's been eating sweets, ain't?"

Comically, Sammy pointed an accusing finger at Jed and grinned.

"Mighty glad to help," Jed said, offering a handshake. "Sammy, nice to meet ya!"

The little tyke reached over and shook his hand like a grown-up.

Naomi's eyes widened. "Well, I never."

Eva had to smother her laughter. She was even more aware of the bond between Jed and the boy whom he'd just met.

She and Jed waved good-bye to Sammy; then Naomi took his hand, a look of relief on her face. At Jed's request, Eva lingered, enjoying his company.

After the auction, and following a light supper of homemade bread and jam, cold cuts, and Jell-O, similar to the shared meal after a Preaching service, Jed and his hosts indulged in some homemade ice cream. Orpha and her parents seemed eager to spend more time with Jed, as well, and Jonas talked about his work-related plans with Jed for the week.

Later, Jonas brought out the cards for Dutch Blitz, and the suppertime gathering was extended. Orpha Byler positioned herself in his group of players, and as the game progressed, she smiled at him frequently, clearly sending a message of interest. For her sake—and for the sake of his wonderful host—Jed did his best to keep an open mind.

Even so, despite all the distraction, it was Eva Esch who lingered on his mind. *The girl in the photograph . . .*

CHAPTER FOURTEEN

.... ✿ ....

EVA AND FRONA HAD BEEN TEMPTED to take the long way home after the auction, and they soaked up the lovely evening— mild enough for light shawls in the carriage. The ride brought with it a sense of quiet, ideal for relaxing as the horse pulled them steadily toward Eden Valley. Along the way, they encountered other Amish buggies, everyone waving and calling greetings in *Deitsch* to one another.

"You had yourself a fine time," Frona said, her hands on the driving lines.

"*Jah*, helpin' Sammy Mast find Naomi," Eva said. "He got himself lost somehow."

"That's not what I meant."

"Oh," Eva replied, suddenly feeling a little shy.

"But you certainly did seem to enjoy the search for Naomi. Or, at least, the prospect of it." Frona let out a rare smile. "And you seemed to stick together for a *gut* long time after Sammy went off with Naomi."

Her sister was having fun with this, no question. "Well,

Orpha Byler didn't bother hiding her opinion of Jed, now, did she?" Eva volunteered, wondering how long Frona had been observing her.

"Oh, it's just Jed already . . . is it?" Frona's eyes narrowed with mischievous delight.

"*Jah*, Jed Stutzman from Ohio. His boss is related to Jonas Byler by marriage."

"Well, 'just Jed' looks 'bout our age," Frona noted.

Eva didn't know how much more she wanted to divulge. Now, if it were Lily asking, she wouldn't have had any problem with telling all.

"It wonders me how Orpha got so chummy with him, at liberty to march over there with her cousins." Frona was inching into the prying side of things.

Eva began to hum "What a Friend We Have in Jesus" and let the comment be, grateful when Frona didn't weasel for more information. Besides, it was only a single encounter. Who knew if Jed would actually appear at market on Thursday.

You just never know about out-of-towners, she decided, leaning near the window, glad they were nearing the turnoff toward home.

❦

"You ain't listenin', love," Naomi told Abner, who'd admitted he was feeling almost too droopy to drive the carriage after all the pie and ice cream he'd enjoyed at the auction. "I daresay the fella from Ohio seemed awful nice, and a progressive Amishman at that. Did ya notice that right fancy hat brim?"

"You just wanna see Eva happily married, like you?" Abner winked at her. "Is that what you're going to say next?"

"Oh, you!"

He reached for her hand, and she pulled away playfully.

"Come on over here, woman," Abner teased.

"It's still daylight, dear," Naomi cautioned him. "We ain't youngsters no more."

"Well, the fire ain't out yet."

Submitting to her husband's flirtation, she leaned her hand on the seat between them so no one could see as they passed other buggies.

Abner linked his big fingers around hers. "Aw, that's my girl."

"So, what do ya *really* think 'bout the Ohio fella?" she asked.

"No need to think; I've heard all I need to know from Jonas Byler himself."

She held her breath.

"Seems one of Jonas's granddaughters might be interested in him." Abner smiled. "Some competition's always *gut*, of course."

"If I know Eva Esch, she's not one to put herself forward."

"She's one sweet girl, I'll say. But Jed'll only be around till Monday sometime, so it may be a moot point."

Naomi sighed. *Poor Eva.*

They didn't talk much more about it. And eventually, when Naomi felt her husband's hand go limp around hers, she looked over and saw him catching more than just flies while their reliable horse kept trotting, heading homeward.

Much later that evening, once the house was quiet and after the second night of Bible reading with Jonas and Elsie, Jed settled into his room. He'd placed the peculiar photograph next to the bed and glanced over at it occasionally, still puzzled. He was reasonably certain, if not convinced, that Eva Esch and the girl in the photo were one and the same. In which case, Eva, kind and thoughtful as she seemed, must have had a defiant side earlier in her life, defiant enough to flout the Old Order's ban on personal photos. If so, she'd hidden it very well today.

Before meeting Eva, he'd considered privately showing Elsie Byler to see if she recognized the young woman. But he was glad now he hadn't been so foolish. *I might have jeopardized my chance to get to know Eva better. After all, Elsie would surely favor Orpha over Eva.*

After a few minutes of rereading some of the notes in the margins, Jed closed the book and went to outen the gas lamp. He wondered when Eva had taken the train west. Perhaps Thursday at market, if the opportunity presented itself, he would ask her. Nothing pointed or prying, just a simple, casual question.

⌒﹏⌒

Lily's done more than leave us; she's made it clear we don't count for much, Eva decided as she wandered out to the stable with the lantern. Max bounded over and sat near her, panting, keeping her company. The air was still, and the katydids and crickets were making a ruckus.

She took down the grooming brush and went to Prince's stall. Poor fellow, he'd trotted ever so hard coming up the incline from the auction hours ago. She would put her angst over Lily to good work on their favorite horse. *Like a pet.*

"You miss Lily, too, don't ya?" she whispered, leaning against Prince's velvety nose.

There were times when Lily's absence felt like a stab in her heart, though not as painful as when Dat had died so suddenly.

"Lily sure changed things by goin' away," Eva muttered as she worked on the thick black mane.

How different this moment would be if Lily were still living at home. They might have come to water the horses together, like many other nights. Eva dearly missed the whispering and laughing. How many times had Lily waited up for Eva after a date, and the other way around?

One night, though, when Lily had stayed out longer than usual, Eva had sat up for hours, wondering if she shouldn't just go to bed. It was the evening Lily had finally agreed to go riding with a fellow outside their church district. The nighttime breezes had helped cool the rooms upstairs, and Eva had gone to the open window and leaned on the sill, peering out at the stars.

She'd never planned to eavesdrop or observe Lily with Manny, but there they were walking toward the house in the moonlight. At first, Eva looked away. Then, realizing something seemed amiss, she hurried downstairs and out to the screened-in porch, listening and watching. Manny was telling Lily that he wanted to see her again, and very soon—even before next weekend—in a demanding tone.

Lily backed away, saying she was getting home awful late.

"It'll be even later next time," Manny had said as he reached for Lily, but she brushed him away.

Concerned, Eva opened the screen door and hurried out. "Everything all right over there?" she'd called gently, mindful of their sleeping mother.

Relieved, Lily had come running toward her as Manny turned back down the driveway toward his buggy, his footsteps quick on the gravel.

Upstairs, Lily had been terribly quiet as she dressed for bed. Eva prayed for wisdom all the while. And after they'd turned out the gas lamp and settled into bed, Lily confided that Manny definitely wasn't for her. "No matter how nice he was at the Singing last week." Even though Lily had assured Eva that nothing appalling had taken place, she refused to put herself at risk with such a fellow.

Lily was so careful then. Why was she now so willing to take a risk like running away? Eva wondered.

She finished brushing Prince, then gave him additional water and headed for the house, Max alongside her as the night sounds filled up the darkness.

_____

Inside, Eva said good-night to Frona and took time to wash up, getting ready for bed. Then, sitting at the desk where she'd last seen Lily, Eva took out her journal and began to write.

Tuesday, May 20
  With everything in me, I wish Lily would let us know where she is. It would help so much to know she's safe. Frona would rest easier and so would I. Our brothers seem worried, enough so that all of them have spent time questioning various neighbors and relatives. So Lily's whereabouts are a mystery to us all.
  It wonders me if someday Lily might recognize that she belongs here and not out in the world. Oh, I do hope she will, before she marries outside the church and it's too late.
  At some point, I'm going to have to stop holding my breath. I can't cry for her the rest of my life, even though I would if I thought it might somehow help.
  O, dear Lord above, please watch over our befuddled sister. I do pray this in Thy holy name. Amen.

Then, because Eva hadn't taken time after the auction to make any more candies for tomorrow's customers, she set her windup alarm clock for five. Anxious for some good rest, she blew out the lamp and slipped into the soft bedcovers, reaching for the lightweight quilt Mamma had made. Her mind wandered to the fair-haired young man she'd met today.

Ah, Mamma, what would you think of Jed Stutzman?

Eva couldn't settle down, wondering about the strange but

116

sweet way she and Jed had simply stumbled upon each other. *Thanks to little Sammy.*

But more than that, she couldn't get over the surprisingly tender way she felt about him, even now as she tucked the covers under her chin and watched the moonlight's dance on the wall. She let her mind flit back to all that Jed had said to her, and she to him, and then felt a little ridiculous. *I just met him, for goodness' sake!*

Truth be known, she cherished this day. After the trauma of Lily's departure, such unexpected companionship was the salve her soul craved.

Then, thinking of Naomi and how frantic she had been to find Sammy—*like we are to find Lily*—Eva reconsidered Lily's unreasonable behavior, running off to no one knew where. And while Eva wanted to hold the day's memories close to heart, she began to question the wisdom of entertaining romantic notions about someone from so far away, no matter how kindhearted Jed Stutzman seemed.

CHAPTER FIFTEEN

WEDNESDAY MORNING BEFORE BREAKFAST, but after a stiff cup of black coffee, Jed walked with Jonas Byler out to the carriage shop on Jonas's property. "Your shop looks bigger than Uncle Ervin's," Jed remarked, eager to finally get a good look around.

"I'd say it's pretty typical for a workshop round here—two hundred feet by one hundred—but it's divided into four sections."

"Are ya lookin' forward to retiring soon?" Jed slowed his pace to be respectful to the older man.

"Oh *jah*, I s'pose, but I'll always be workin' somewhere till the Lord calls me home . . . helping one farmer or another, no doubt. Just not the day-to-day business of the carriage shop." Jonas's chest rose and fell. "It's a shame none of my boys wanted to learn the trade. 'Tis mighty important to pass it down through the generations."

Jed agreed.

"That's why I'm seriously thinkin' of selling."

His sons must already be established in their chosen work, Jed assumed.

119

At Jonas's shop, Jed stepped inside and felt right at home, thanks to a layout similar to Uncle Ervin's. "Real nice and tidy," he said.

"It's fairly well organized today," Jonas said, wiping his beard. "Shoulda seen it last week." He let out a chuckle. "Then again, it's a *gut* thing ya didn't!"

"There are just some days, *jah?*"

Jonas led the way to the impressively orderly back area, where workbenches were set up for building a buggy's wooden base. All across the wall hung hand tools like those Jed was accustomed to using.

Another large room was set aside for storing materials for manufacturing the buggy, including the bench seat in surreys and parts for the hacks or buckboards. The latter were similar to an *Englischer's* pickup truck, the area behind the seat providing a flat bed for hauling.

"Now, here's something. Ever see a dashboard like this?" Jonas pointed to a panel of inlaid wood with holes drilled for switches for inside and outside buggy lights, as well as turn signals.

Jed ran his hand over its smoothness. "Real fancy compared to some."

Jonas shook his head, amused. "Makes me wonder what the owner's thinkin'—some of the nonsense we put in. *Ach*, the carpet colors, several years back, were downright loud. Just depends on what's allowed in a particular church district . . . how strict the bishop is." Jonas motioned toward the next area. "Say, do your Swartzentruber neighbors still use kerosene lanterns for their buggy lights?"

"They do." Jed was surprised Jonas knew this.

The older man went on to say that the brakes, wheels, and spokes were all made less than ten miles from his shop. "I 'spect it's similar out there, ain't?"

"Probably closer to fifteen miles."

"That far?"

Nodding, Jed found the shoptalk stimulating and was glad Uncle Ervin had suggested the visit with the great buggy maker. *And matchmaker, too.*

❧

Blackbirds pecked at one another in the field near the roadside as Eva and Frona set out for market Thursday morning. The skies were overcast and rain was predicted for later that afternoon.

"Hope we get home before a downpour," Frona said, her attention on the road.

"I guess I don't care one way or the other," Eva said.

"Well, ain't you somethin'?"

"Just glad for any chance of moisture. My garden could really use it."

"*Your* garden?" Frona gave her a look.

Eva wasn't going to remind her that *she* had done the tilling and planting during her days in between working at The Sweet Tooth. *How could Frona forget?* Of course, Frona had single-handedly done all the weeding here lately, so doubtless that's what she meant.

Striving to think pleasant thoughts, Eva peered out at the silvery windmill just ahead as the carriage rumbled along.

"*Just because a fella promises something, doesn't mean it'll happen,*" she remembered Mamma saying, and she wondered if Jed would show up today.

"You sure are deep in thought," Frona said, interrupting her daydream. "Thinking 'bout your young man, maybe?"

Eva sighed. "He's not mine, *Schweschder.*"

"Oh, well, it's just a matter of time." Frona didn't wait for a response. "I saw how he looked at you at the auction—'tis a *gut* thing, too, what with Menno's plans. There's really only room for one of us when they move in, remember."

Eva squelched a smile. Not only did Frona have Eva nearly hitched up with Jed, but poor Frona was still fretting about Menno's move.

The good Lord will see to the future. And that's that, she thought.

<hr>

The warmth of the morning sun and the strong scent of mown grass heightened Jed's anticipation for the day. He'd slept restlessly, caught up in the hope of seeing Eva Esch again. Truthfully, he hadn't felt such anticipation since Lydiann.

He caught a ride with Mose Byler, who was on his way to the east side of Quarryville to make a delivery for his father—ideal for Jed to get to market around opening time.

"You'll return on foot, then?" Mose asked, sitting tall in the driver's seat.

Jed nodded. "Mighty grateful for the lift."

"Be sure an' take the umbrella," offered Mose, pointing to the back of the buggy. "S'posed to pour cats and dogs later."

Jed went around and opened the back. "*Denki!*"

"*Gem gschehne!*" Mose lifted the reins and clicked his tongue before heading out of the parking lot.

Inside the market, the place was already busy with folding tables being moved about and set up amidst vendors greeting each other. Jed didn't want to be in the way if he showed up too soon to Eva's table, so he wandered about, heading up the first long aisle. A large glass display case featuring homemade fudge caught his attention, and perusing the options, he considered a purchase. He thought of buying something for Eva but didn't want her to feel awkward.

Even so, he continued searching the fudge counter for a gift, recalling Lydiann's cravings for chocolate.

"Ach, *you spoil me, Jed.*" Lydiann had smiled sweetly that day. "*But, of course, if you really want to buy that chunk of chocolate, I won't refuse.*"

He'd whipped out his wallet before she could change her mind. "*It's yours, then.*"

And she'd laughed so merrily the sound lingered in his mind for the rest of the week, till he saw her again that Saturday evening.

What if Eva doesn't care much for chocolate? he thought, although he had a hard time imagining it. He recalled what she'd said about her confectionary shop. Was it possible to create sweets and not enjoy them?

"What's your fancy?" asked the large woman behind the counter. Her shoulders slouched as she leaned heavily on the display case.

Jed pointed to the smallest package, covered in a pretty red wrapping. He didn't want to seem stingy, yet a token might actually be better than something too big for a first gift.

"It's buy one, get the second one half off," the smiling clerk told him. "How can ya pass it up?"

He took his time, looking at several other options.

"If ya pick something bigger, well, same deal for that, too," she said.

In the end he stuck with his original order, glad to have the treat for Eva in the little sack the clerk handed to him.

⌘

"I think changing the arrangement sometimes *is* wise," Eva was telling Mary Riehl, another market vendor.

Mary had taken it upon herself to stride across the aisle and rearrange Frona's and Eva's wares without their say-so. The middle-aged woman had a mind of her own, but prior to this she'd never demonstrated it in such a radical manner. "Just thought I'd offer a bit of help, is all." Mary gave a flamboyant wave and headed back to her own table.

Frona had cause to frown for sure. And later, when Mary was out of earshot, she told Eva she felt like changing it all back to the way it was. "What do ya say to that?"

"Just let it be. Sometimes it's *gut* to vary things."

Frona stared at their goodies, including her jams and preserves. "Well, if it's already workin' one way, why bother?"

"Honestly, customers don't care 'bout the arrangement, do they?"

"If they're repeat customers, maybe not. But I still like things the way we had them."

Eva could sense there was no compromising with Frona today. "If you put it all back, you can be the one to explain to Mary . . . if she comes marchin' back over here."

"*Puh!*" Frona shook her head. "The woman's got some nerve!"

The whole thing seemed petty to Eva. *Why's Frona so tetchy?*

A half hour or more later, while she was making change and answering questions, Eva noticed Jed standing back near the periphery of a dozen or more customers. *He's here*, she thought, trying not to smile too broadly. But he'd seen her spot him. *Oh, goodness!* And to think there was no way to greet him the way she wanted to, with so many folks there for her candies and Frona's jars of jam and whatnot.

Will he wait around?

Eva disliked feeling so unnerved and torn.

To her great surprise, Jed came around to the side and over to her. "Hullo, Eva. Looks like you're mighty busy."

"It's been this way ever since we opened."

"Ya know what? I'll walk around a bit and come back later." His smile warmed her heart. Once again there was a glint of recognition in his eyes, like he knew her from somewhere.

"All right" was all she could manage, uncomfortable at being observed so, particularly by Frona, who was glancing their way.

Jed left as quickly as he'd come into view.

In a few minutes, Naomi Mast and her daughter Ida Mae arrived carrying shopping baskets. "*Wie bischt?*" Eva asked.

"Just fine . . . you?" Naomi replied.

"Oh, trying to keep the customers smilin'," Eva said.

"Hullo," said Ida Mae, shifting her empty basket. "Looks like you've got your hands full."

"Are ya lookin' to buy some of Frona's delicious rhubarb jam?"

"Ida Mae is," Naomi volunteered and beamed at her daughter. "Ain't ya, dear?"

Ida Mae motioned that she was going to slip into the back of the line.

Meanwhile, Naomi stood with Eva, asking when she'd like to come over again for some dessert. "Just to talk."

Eva was pleased by the thoughtful invitation, especially on the heels of seeing Jed again. "I could come over after supper tonight."

"Suits me fine." Naomi smiled encouragingly. "I'll bake some cookies for us."

"Is Abner along today?"

"One of the cows came down with milk fever, so he's at home getting an IV started."

"Abner's always been conscientious thataway." *Dat was, too.*

"Well, I'd better let you get back to work," Naomi said, giving her shoulder a pat now.

"Glad ya dropped by." Eva watched her go and looked forward to opening her heart to the woman who'd come to understand

125

her so well. *Surely she'll have some advice for me about an out-of-town fella. . . .*

———

At only twenty-eight, Menno already had a rather arrogant swagger. Eva witnessed this very trait as he moved through the aisle toward them, not making eye contact with a soul.

She was thankful the earlier crowd had thinned out as Menno approached their table. Without even greeting them, he reached down and picked up one of Frona's jars of jam, deliberately turning it in his hand.

"How many have ya sold this mornin'?" he asked.

"More than four dozen," Frona said.

Eva wondered why he'd come. "You needin' some jam?" *Bena's surely got plenty for him at home.*

He waved vaguely. "I've been weighing something and wanted to ask what ya thought." He wandered behind the table, making himself at home, then motioned them into a huddle like the menfolk made before Preaching services. "Bishop Isaac came to see me the other day. He thinks we oughta try and follow Lily's path, so to speak. He wants her back in the fold right away."

Frona nearly gasped. "The bishop, ya say?"

"No need to worry," Menno cautioned. "He's adamant that someone should go lookin' for her. Who knows where she'll end up? Ain't safe for such a girl."

"I tried to get some leads," Eva admitted, "but there was really only one."

It was Menno's turn to be flabbergasted. "Well, let's hear it."

Eva recounted Fannie Ebersol's evasive behavior the morning after Lily had fled. "I've wondered if Fannie knows something she isn't tellin' . . . maybe even where Lily headed." She sighed as she recalled her suspicion and frustration that first day.

"Why have ya kept this to yourself?"

Eva hoped Menno wouldn't cause a scene. "Fannie refused to say. She was convinced that Lily wanted to leave Eden Valley, and there was no stopping her."

Menno looked stricken. "Tell that to the bishop!" He scoffed. "The man of God believes Lily is too young to know what's good for her—and I happen to think he's right."

"Of course ya do," Frona said.

Eva glanced at her sister, who'd turned rather agreeable, as though trying to get on Menno's good side.

Menno nodded emphatically. "I'd hate to think she'd do something to bring more disgrace to the family."

More than just leaving the People, thought Eva. "I'm prayin' for her."

Frona nodded. "In all truth, both of us are."

"What do our other brothers and the bishop think is the best way to handle this?" Eva had to know.

"No one's sayin', really. But Bishop Isaac has urged us to go after her—'get her home!'"

"Against Lily's will?" Eva asked. "If it comes to that?"

"*Jah,* if she's not thinkin' straight—which she ain't. That's mighty clear." Menno nodded, then abruptly turned and left Eva standing there with Frona.

Eva was shocked he had sought them out at market, of all places. And just that quick, she knew it had been a mistake for Menno to approach them about such a private matter there. Mary Riehl and another woman were eyeing them, wagging their heads, and a short line of customers had formed at their table.

Eva's heart sank with shame. For a fleeting moment, she wished Jed might forget to stop by again. *Not the way I feel right now . . .*

CHAPTER SIXTEEN

· ✿ ·

ON THE RIDE BACK FROM MARKET, Naomi Mast was thankful her daughter insisted on taking the driving lines in hand. Naomi guessed Ida Mae hadn't liked the way she'd handled the horse on the way there. It didn't really matter the excuse; she was glad to relax during the uphill journey home.

"Not sure if you noticed it or not," Ida Mae mentioned when they were about a third of the way. "But Fannie Ebersol was cryin' like her heart might break."

"When was this?"

"Before we left . . . while you were occupied with Mary Riehl." Ida Mae frowned. "What's odd was that Menno Esch was standing nearby, his arms folded and his expression severe. It sure looked like he'd given Fannie a talkin' to."

Naomi groaned. "Anyone else witness this?"

"Only me that I could tell."

"Where was Fannie's sister? Doesn't she usually help tend the market table?"

"That's just it. Fannie was by herself."

129

"Maybe the rest of the family ain't feelin' well." The spring flu was making its rounds, Naomi thought.

"You know what I think?" Ida Mae said, turning to face her. "I heard Menno say something 'bout Lily Esch. And it sure sounded like he was accusing Fannie of knowin' more than she was telling."

Naomi had known Menno to be a rather bigheaded man when it came to what he thought and how he wanted things done. Nearly proud, especially since his father passed away. "Things must be worrisome if Menno's pressuring Lily's friend for more information."

"All I know is he headed straight for Fannie, talked to her, then waited for her to say something—'*Spit it out, ya hear?*' is what he honestly said. Then, after waiting a while and getting nowhere with her, Menno spun on his heels and left."

Naomi didn't like the sound of this. As dogmatic as Menno Esch had become, she'd never known him to behave so rudely. "I'll admit to feelin' sorry for Fannie," she said softly.

"But what if she is stonewalling and knows something 'bout Lily, Mamm? It might help the family find her."

"'Tis true." Naomi wished she had a cat to put on her lap right this minute. A purring pet could perhaps ease her nerves. Oh, she prayed Lily's disappearance wouldn't disrupt the whole community of the People.

⌘

A steady hum filled the marketplace—vendors selling their wares, people stopping by to see what items were new or just to visit and catch up on the previous week. Popcorn was popping one aisle over, behind Eva and Frona's table.

It must have been the Lord's good timing when Jed returned quite a while later. A half-dozen people were milling about near their long table, listening attentively to Frona's method for making her strawberry-rhubarb jam—all *Englischers*.

Eva rose and went to stand near the aisle.

"Here, I bought something for ya." Jed gave her a pretty red package.

She couldn't help but smile.

"Hope ya like fudge."

"I surely do!" She was pleased he'd think to do this. "But I won't eat it in front of you, unless you'd like a piece."

He shook his head, blue eyes fixed on her. "It's all for you."

"*Denki.*" She wondered what people were thinking, seeing them like this.

"Would it be wrong to ask if you have time to take a quick walk through the aisles?" He glanced about, undoubtedly surveying the number of customers.

Now that Jed was here and the embarrassment she'd felt over Menno had faded, Eva wished she *could* slip out with Jed. "I shouldn't leave my sister to handle all the customers," she said, smiling up at him. "Hope you understand."

He nodded, respecting her wishes. "How about a buggy ride Saturday afternoon or evening—would that suit ya?"

"Sounds nice," she said in a near whisper. "Evening's better."

Jed's face broke into a satisfied smile. "I'm hopin' we might get better acquainted."

Before he leaves. The realization made her sad. "I'll meet you halfway between my house and our neighbors to the east, all right?" She told him the address of her father's farmhouse on Eden Road.

"Around dusk, then?"

Nodding, she smiled again, suddenly wishing this moment might freeze in time. She was drawn to him, yet she hardly knew him. But what Eva did know, she liked very much.

Jed made his way along the road early that afternoon, pummeled by rain in spite of the borrowed umbrella. Walking in the direction of Jonas Byler's big spread, he was offered numerous rides by Amish farmers. But he wanted to be alone with his thoughts while he could still hear Eva's sweet voice in his mind, so he politely refused the offers.

He pulled the photo from his pocket, hunched over to protect it from the rain, and studied it. The picture was creased in places and soiled a bit, probably taken a few years ago, when Eva was younger. *It's gotta be her,* he thought. *I'm certain of it.*

Perhaps by now Eva was sorry she'd had it taken. If she was a baptized church member, she might even have confessed it to the ministerial brethren.

Replacing the picture, he began to whistle. He was getting drenched but didn't mind. Just having the photo in his wallet gave him an exhilarating feeling, though it was surely against the church *Ordnung.*

Since Jed planned to be in town till Monday afternoon, it crossed his mind to find out where Eva would be attending Preaching. On the other hand, being Jonas and Elsie's guest, he ought to go with them, if it wasn't their off-Sunday. Otherwise, he should accompany them wherever they'd like to go. He just hoped the day might not include their granddaughter Orpha again.

Thankfully, Eva finished up her chores before scaring up something to eat with Frona that afternoon. She felt like she was walking on a cloud as she recalled Jed's handsome face and blue eyes. And oh, that grin!

Frona had looked at her askance more than once as they made

small talk while Frona washed dishes and Eva dried. "Eva, are ya even listenin'?"

Eva apologized, her mind whirling with the day's events—Jed's seeking her out at market, his confident smile, that look in his eyes, as if he'd known her for years.

"You're daydreamin' again," Frona said.

"Prob'ly so."

Eva dried faster, wondering if Frona had ever had special feelings for a young man. "Naomi's expectin' me over there soon."

Frona made a small groan. "Don't mind me. I'll be workin' on the pile of mending."

Eva instantly felt sorry. "S'pose I could go another day. We *did* miss out on a few tasks, bein' at market and all."

"What? And miss the chance to share your heart with Naomi? You mustn't keep her waiting."

She's upset. Eva wished she'd done a better job of keeping her giddiness to herself. "Frona, I—"

Her sister waved as if to silence any further discussion, then continued with the dishes, her head bowed.

Pursing her lips, Eva continued drying. Sometimes it was easy to forget that Frona, for all her anxious prickliness, was sensitive, too.

I need to be more forgiving, Eva thought. *And more aware.*

They finished redding up, working silently for a time. Then, out of the blue, Frona mentioned Menno's surprising visit at market and his determination to confront Fannie.

"I can't help wondering how that'll go," Eva said. "Menno can be . . . a little harsh."

"Well, I don't feel sorry for Fannie. I mean, what's she thinkin'?"

"*Jah,*" Eva replied sadly. How had everything gotten so *verkehrt*—topsy-turvy?

When the table and counters were wiped clean, Frona leaned

against the sink and gazed out the window, her eyes misty and expression grim.

"I'll be back right quick," Eva said as she hung up the tea towel. "In time for evening prayers."

Seemingly lost in her own worries again, Frona shook her head, working her lips. "Everything's a-changin', Eva." Frona shifted her weight, and the floor creaked.

She's afraid, Eva thought. "Remember, we can count on our Lord . . . for today and for tomorrow."

"Now you sound like Mamma."

Eva gave her a smile. "Besides, no matter what happens, you're still stuck with me."

"Don't make promises you can't keep, Eva. You'll end up leavin' like Lily. You'll be marryin' Alfred—that is, if the fella from Ohio who was makin' googly eyes at ya doesn't win your heart."

Eva's mouth dropped open. "What kind of eyes?"

"Oh dear," Frona muttered, setting her chin.

The kitchen was hushed, tension evident between them, until Eva could hold it in no longer. One giggle was followed by another, and then they were both laughing.

"You'd better get goin'," Frona finally said. "I can't handle all this fun."

Ain't that the truth, Eva thought, grinning as she headed out the door. "See ya later, sister!"

⚜

Eva waited on this side of the road while Abner Mast pulled his open wagon out of his driveway. She had checked for mail this late, thinking surely Lily would realize she must get in touch with her family. But there was nothing from Lily or anyone.

Eva thought again of how she'd left Frona with the unfinished mending. *I'll sew a new dress and apron for her,* she decided, wanting to do something nice for her.

Once Abner was out on the road and ready to head on, he waved his hand over his head. "Naomi just took the cookies fresh out of the oven for ya," he called in his deep voice, a grin on his pleasant ruddy face.

"*Denki!*" She crossed narrow Eden Road after the horse pulled forward.

Inside Naomi's sparkling kitchen, the place smelled of cinnamon and vanilla. "Let me guess. You made snickerdoodles, *jah?*"

"That's a right *gut* smeller." Naomi motioned for her. "*Kumme,* sit at the table with me."

Eva hugged her friend and got settled at the table. She began to share her private hope that her brothers might not be so caught up with their own families and focus more on finding Lily.

"Well, they love Lily just as you and Frona do," Naomi said. "Just 'cause you don't see them all too often doesn't mean they don't care. You know what's in their hearts."

"*Jah,* s'pose."

"No s'posin' about it." Naomi folded her plump arms. "Listen, my dear. I bumped into Bena at market, and she said Menno's been worried sick over Lily. It keeps him up at night."

"Menno himself stopped by to see Frona and me today about her." Eva felt she should own up to that much.

"So, see there?" Naomi smiled, her round face rosy.

Eva took a second warm cookie from the pretty plate. "These are so delicious," she said, changing the subject.

Thankfully, Naomi seemed to understand and let it drop. She had that way about her.

Then they got to talking about ways Eva could help direct her worries to praying whenever Lily came to mind. "Prayin' while you make your delicious candies, too," Naomi suggested.

Sighing, Eva thought of her wonderful little shop. "I guess my whole world can't just be making sweets and selling them."

"'Tis true, and I, for one, know it ain't."

Eva wondered what, if anything, to say about Jed Stutzman. Unsure of herself, she ate more cookies than necessary and let Naomi talk gently about how the best exercise for one's heart was to practice reaching out to pick someone up—"and carryin' them, if need be."

"I certainly would reach out to Lily if I knew where she was."

"I know ya would." Naomi's eyes shone with sympathy.

Eva held her breath, refusing tears.

Naomi got up and poured some homemade meadow tea and set it down in front of Eva. "Now, I've been doin' my share of talking. Is there anything you'd like to bring up that we haven't already discussed?"

"Well . . . you remember meeting Jed Stutzman, the fella who took care of little Sammy at the auction?" She paused. "He invited me to go riding come Saturday."

Naomi's eyes sparkled. "*Ach*, isn't that nice?"

No words of caution?

"It'll be fun," Eva agreed.

"And something to look forward to during this sad time." Naomi tilted her head toward her. "Jed's his name?"

"*Jah*. And not a very common name round here."

Naomi looked away, her chest rising and falling. "I daresay if you two fall in love, he'll take you away from us."

Just like Frona said, Eva thought.

"And I'd have to say selfishly that I'd miss you something awful."

"It's just a carriage ride," Eva said, but it sounded empty even to her. Buggy rides could lead to courtship, even marriage, and she recognized that the interest she was feeling from Jed was unlike anything she'd experienced before.

At that precise moment, someone knocked at the back door, and Eva was relieved at the interruption. But then she saw who it was—Fannie Ebersol, who looked sheepish when she noticed Eva sitting there.

"Goodness, Eva, never expected to see *you* here."

What on earth? Eva thought.

Fannie's firm jaw—the way she cast her gaze at first Eva, then Naomi—gave Eva a twinge of misgiving.

CHAPTER SEVENTEEN

* * *

"WHAT DO YA MEAN you pledged on your honor?" Eva asked Fannie when she was seated at Naomi's table.

"Your sister was determined," Fannie answered. "She didn't want anyone to keep her from leavin', or even to go lookin' for her. That's why I didn't tell you where she went."

Naomi's face fell. "You've known all along?"

Fannie nodded her head, eyes lowered. "I wanted to keep my word to Lily, since she . . . well, kept all *my* secrets."

"Oh dear," Naomi whispered.

Eva felt she might burst. "So where's Lily now?"

"Do ya promise you'll never say where ya heard this?" Fannie looked pale.

Eva glanced at Naomi. "If it saves Lily from ruin, what's it matter?"

There was a long and painful silence. At last Fannie said, "I'll only tell you what Lily told me 'cause she hasn't written like she said she would . . . and I'm worried."

Eva held her breath.

Fannie began to share more. "Lily's staying somewhere in Ohio."

"Where in Ohio?" Eva asked.

"I'm not sure, really," Fannie said. "Lily talked 'bout different places over several weeks' time, but I don't remember now."

How could she forget? Eva wondered. "Please try," she urged. "If you could just remember the city or town . . . that would help us ever so much." She felt frantic.

"Well, if it helps any, Lily was supposedly gonna stay with her boyfriend's married sister and family for a while."

Eva's mouth dropped open. "A boyfriend? That's why she left?"

Fannie bit her lip. "I hate bein' the one to say. . . ."

Hearing it helped in some ways but also raised so many questions that both Eva and Naomi started talking at the same time. "Go ahead," Eva said, motioning for Naomi to continue.

"*Nee* . . . you first, she's your sister." Naomi eased back into her chair.

"Since Lily's gone fancy," Eva said, scarcely able to get it all out, "then her beau must surely be English."

"*Jah.*" Fannie continued, seemingly eager now to reveal that the young man in Lily's life was twenty-one and a mighty *gut* horse trainer. "He's from somewhere over near Canton, if I remember correctly. Lily met him a year ago when she went with my family and me to Kidron to visit relatives. She hit it off with this *Englischer* fella and said that he hardly noticed she was Amish, which kinda had me surprised."

She ran off to be with a worldly beau. Eva tried to let this sink in.

"He must've been writing to her all this time to influence her so," Naomi said, looking thoughtfully at Eva.

"That's where I came in—the go-between," Fannie confessed, sounding somewhat embarrassed. "Lily gave her boyfriend my

140

address, which meant the envelope was always addressed to me, but with no return address. My mother actually thought *I* had a beau in Ohio."

Eva struggled to remain calm. "How'd Lily get out there?"

"My brother Thomas picked her up that night and took her to Strasburg, where she met a van driver. She wouldn't tell me much else. And Lily kept other things secret, too," Fannie admitted. "It was the oddest thing—she was open 'bout certain things but not others."

"And you haven't heard from her to know if she got there in one piece?" Naomi asked, looking concerned.

Fannie shook her head. "I can't understand it for the life of me. She promised to keep in close touch."

A tremor ran down Eva's back. "Is it possible Lily changed her mind about where she wanted to end up? Maybe she didn't go to Ohio, after all."

Fannie sighed loudly and leaned her face into her hands. Then, after a time, she looked out the window. "Makes no sense why she hasn't written to me . . . or to *you*, Eva."

Fannie's emotions and her obvious concern for Lily seemed to point to the fact that she was finally telling the truth. Or so Eva believed.

<hr/>

Jed's pulse raced as he drove toward Eden Valley that evening in Jonas's buggy, thinking it wise to chart his course to the spot where Eva had suggested meeting on Saturday. He'd made a mistake, having failed to ask her out for tonight, since he planned to leave for home next Monday afternoon.

Even now, he could not erase Eva's guileless expression when he'd first seen her at the auction and her surprise when she'd spotted Sammy riding on his shoulders. And her pretty face—

the delightful yet unexpected connection to the photograph in his pocket.

Providential, he thought. *And yet . . .*

The fly in the ointment was the forbidden photo itself, lingering proof of Eva's disobedience. On the other hand, if she *hadn't* had her photo taken, Jed might never have sought her out.

Can anything good come of something so wrong?

Hidden beneath his struggle was the biggest question of all. Why had Eva had her picture taken? *Do I dare ask?*

The prospect was both exciting and alarming.

On Eden Road, he got stuck behind a slow-moving buggy—*probably an older horse*—and decided not to attempt to pass, but slowed up and sat back in his seat. Passing by a large farmhouse, he saw three little Amish girls jumping rope while their older brothers hung back near the stable, heads together. *They're up to something, guaranteed.* He smiled and remembered when he was their age, always looking for a way to make mischief with his brothers after chores were done or on lazy Sunday afternoons. And some evenings, too, when the older youth were busy at Singings and other gatherings.

Finally the pokey horse and carriage turned off, and Jed urged the horse onward, noticing a young woman walking this way, her head down. He slowed again, staying well inside the right lane.

It was still light enough that as he came closer to the woman, he saw that it was Eva, deep in thought. Goodness, if he didn't keep running into her, although it was less surprising when he was traipsing around her neck of the woods.

Pulling over, he waved to her, leaning out the right side of the enclosed carriage. "Eva . . . it's Jed. Would ya like a ride somewhere?"

She looked startled, so he quickly reassured her. "I was just out here double-checking where we're going to meet Saturday evening."

She smiled at his explanation. "'Tis a welcome surprise."

Jed got out and stood near the horse, holding the driving lines. "We could ride a little while now, if you'd like."

She didn't say at first if she would or not but glanced over her shoulder, presumably toward her house. "My sister's expecting me home."

"Of course. I didn't mean to interrupt. Need some time alone, maybe?"

She shook her head and crossed the road, then got right into the buggy. "I don't mean to be standoffish. It's just a nice evening for a walk," she added.

Something's bothering her, he thought as he returned to the carriage. He could sense it, and not because she was reluctant to talk. Eva was completely different than she'd been today at market. Her exuberance had vanished.

She folded her arms and turned to look out the window on her side. For a good minute or longer she was silent.

"Everything okay?" he asked.

Eva took a breath and let it out slowly. Another moment passed before she turned to him. "My younger sister's run off. It's that simple, really, and it's ever so hard on my family . . . and embarrassing, too. But most everyone here knows, so I guess you might as well hear it, too."

Jed was at a loss for words.

"I think I've shocked ya," Eva added.

"You're obviously worried for her."

"Putting it mildly, *jah*." Eva hung her head again. Then, sighing, she sat up straighter and said, "I just learned Lily's gone to live in Ohio."

"A long way off," he said, then added feebly, "Stayin' with relatives?"

Eva shook her head, visibly upset. "You don't understand, Jed.

She left without tellin' us where she was going—not a word, not a clue."

He wondered if this sister was sowing her wild oats as some did before joining church. Eva shared more of her concerns, admitting she didn't think Lily was capable of handling herself among strangers. "We've all been through a sad time with my mother's recent passing," she added. "My candy shop has made the biggest difference for me, keeping me busy. Lily didn't have anything like that." She stopped talking and peered at him. "Listen to me, rambling on."

He felt so drawn to her, pulled into her heart and her life, and deeply touched by her compassion for her missing sister.

"I really need to get home," she said abruptly. "I don't want Frona to worry that I've jumped the fence, too."

He didn't know how to respond.

Eva sat without speaking as Jed drove to the spot where she'd said they should meet Saturday evening. On the way, they passed a makeshift sign, *Homemade Soaps for Sale*, and Eva explained that when these neighbors had first started selling soaps, Lily had insisted her mother and sisters go over and buy several as an encouragement.

"Sounds like Lily's a very caring person."

"*Jah*, she is." Eva bit her lip. "She's just mixed up right now."

A curtain of silence fell between them once more; then Jed decided to speak up. "I really want to get to know *you*, Eva." By this, he hoped to assure her that Lily's issues would not interfere with that.

Yet Eva remained quiet until she got out of the buggy. "I'll see ya Saturday, Jed."

He watched her hurry up the road and wondered if she might have preferred to cancel their upcoming date. *I'm glad she didn't*, he thought and hoped he wasn't being selfish. As it was, he had little time to win her heart.

Jed slapped the reins and considered Eva's rebellious sister, who'd apparently escaped to his home state, of all places. Indeed, he felt sorry for Eva and her family. *Surely Eva has moved past the mistake of having her photo taken—a youthful indiscretion.* He presumed she'd be mortified if he brought it up, particularly now, with Lily's disappearance on her mind. He preferred not to risk doing anything to break the connection he felt with the sensitive young woman. *Eva's been through a lot.*

On her way back to the house, Eva's eyes caught sight of the large bushes alongside the house, where the back sidewalk met the driveway. She and Lily had often tossed their scooters into the shade of those bushes when they were little. Oh, she wished Lily were around so she could share her thoughts of Jed. Talking with Frona about such things just wasn't the same.

"Frona!" she called as she rounded the house and stepped into the empty kitchen. "I have to talk to you!" She darted from room to room, looking for her sister. "Fro-na!"

Just about the time she was beginning to think her sister had gone somewhere, Eva found her out in the stable pouring grain into a feeding trough. "I've been lookin' all over for ya," she said breathlessly.

"I thought you were over at Naomi's."

"I was." Oh, she felt so *ferhoodled.*

"What's the matter, Eva? Your face looks all red." Frona came forward. "*Ach,* you've been cryin'."

"Fannie Ebersol finally talked about Lily. She thinks Lily's somewhere in Ohio."

"It's 'bout time Fannie coughed up what she's been keepin' to herself."

"And there's more. Lily's got herself a worldly boyfriend." Telling Frona this made Eva feel all the worse.

"Well now. We should've expected as much."

"I guess Fannie felt persuaded to tell because she's worried 'bout Lily, too, since she hasn't heard from her. This time I'm sure she wasn't makin' it all up."

Frona's face softened. "Slow down now. Start at the beginning."

Eva recounted what Fannie had said about Lily's *Englischer* boyfriend and where she'd met him.

Frona shook her head, dismayed but also determined. "I know just what to do. I'll send out word to our Ohio relatives. If Lily has shown up in a small town, maybe, how could she keep this sort of thing quiet?"

"You wouldn't think it's possible."

"Someone will surely know and make the connection, the Lord willing," Frona continued, stooping to pet Max. "Well, Lily went to that there town—Kidron—last summer with Ebersols!"

"Why didn't we go with her?" Eva shook her head. "We should've!"

"You and I didn't accept the Ebersols' invitation because Mamma needed help with gardening, and you couldn't leave the candy shop untended during tourist season." Frona hung the feed scoop on the designated nail and wiped her brow. "Remember?"

"After Lily returned from that trip, I found some fashion magazines and dress catalogues under our bed—a few love stories, too, especially contemporary novels like Mamma's always discouraged," Eva said. Lily had always loved to read and had once declared to Eva and all of their girl cousins that she was going to read a book every single day for the rest of her life. But up till last summer, her interest had only been in the classics.

Lily's words when confronted came back now. "*Books can't be the only way to experience the rest of the world,*" her sister had said. "*As much as I love to read, I don't want to just imagine what's out there!*"

At the time, Eva had hoped this wasn't going to turn into a phase, like the curiosity of a handful of other youth in the community. *Lily must have given in to her inquisitiveness,* she thought as Frona headed to the house.

"Would she still be here if I'd said something?" Eva wondered aloud, giving their Eskimo spitz a gentle pat. She recalled the look of surprise on Jed's face when she'd told him about Lily. *He must think little of our family now. He's probably glad to return home soon.*

But that wasn't her biggest concern. Right now Eva couldn't understand why Lily hadn't kept her word to Fannie. *Why didn't Lily contact her? Or us?*

CHAPTER EIGHTEEN

THAT EVENING, AFTER A LATE DESSERT of lemon sponge pie, Naomi Mast lingered at the table with Abner. She listened as he talked of his long day spreading fertilizer on their alfalfa field and of having some troubles with one of the mules, causing the whole team difficulties.

When Abner paused for more coffee, she mentioned her unexpected visitor that afternoon. "Evidently, someone thinks she knows where Lily Esch ran off to."

"Really now?" Abner blew on his coffee.

"*Jah*, Fannie Ebersol says she didn't feel at liberty to tell till now, wanting to keep her promise to Lily."

"What's different now?"

"She has some concerns about Lily, too . . . and it didn't hurt that Menno confronted Fannie at market, putting pressure on her to tell what she knows." Naomi paused. "I'm not sure how certain Fannie is 'bout any of it, honestly."

"Well, I ran into Menno just this morning. He's been appointed by the bishop to find Lily and bring her home."

"Who better than her brother?" Naomi revealed that Lily was supposedly living in Ohio with her English boyfriend's sister.

Abner muttered under his breath.

"What're ya sayin', dear?"

"*Puh!* I'm gonna say it right out, right now." Abner shook his head. "I partly blame those battery-operated boom boxes and whatnot for so much of the *Druwwel* with our youth. There's a general fascination with the world, and those just feed into it. "

Naomi scratched her head. "The radios young people are listening to in their courting carriages are causin' them to run away?"

"Trust me on this: It's just one more temptation tuggin' on them," Abner said, picking up his coffee cup and holding it in front of his beard. "Worldly music is a trick of the devil . . . and it's infiltrating the Plain community faster than you can say *Sis en Sin un e Schand.*"

"A sin and a shame," Naomi whispered. "So do the other menfolk also blame radios for our youth's troubles?"

"Oh *jah.* You should hear what they're sayin'."

Since the arrival of warmer weather, Naomi had been awakened by some of those boom boxes in the dead of Saturday nights. "Well, I know one thing: Spring is in the air . . . and with it, notions of romance."

He rose with a smile on his face. "That, my dear, ain't no foolin'." And he leaned over and kissed her soundly.

❦

"'The best and worst day of my life.'" Jed recited the words on the back of the photograph as he drove toward Eden Valley for his date with Eva Saturday evening. He'd spent a beneficial day with Jonas Byler, even though by late afternoon Jed was anxious to get cleaned up and out the door. Yesterday had been equally interesting, meeting a number of Jonas's loyal customers and suppliers, as well as learning a few new techniques for buggy making that Jed was eager to pass along to Uncle Ervin.

One of the leisure stops this morning, however, had been to Mose Byler's place, where Orpha had been sitting out on the porch, as though expecting him, wearing her ever-present smile. While the others remained in the kitchen to eat their three-berry pie, Jed had taken the opportunity to thank her for being so welcoming. Along with casual talk, she had shared her concern over one of their ailing ministers.

Jed was touched by her empathy for the man of God, and knowing it wasn't fair or right to encourage Orpha to believe that they might further their friendship, he had tried to gently let her down. Surprisingly, Orpha took it well, although her unchanged demeanor made him uncertain she'd accepted the message. At least he had been forthright with her, difficult as it was.

Presently, Jed slowed the horse as he topped the hill before the turnoff from the highway. If he was a good judge of how things were developing with Eva, the potential for a relationship seemed good. Consequently, showing her the photograph tonight could prove disastrous. Besides, he wouldn't think of putting her on the spot.

"But I *can* test the waters." He began to formulate a plan while directing Jonas's black gelding onto Eden Road.

Jed saw Eva waiting near some underbrush and slowed the horse with a "Whoa." He pulled back on the reins as the carriage rolled to a stop. "Hope ya don't mind ridin' in Jonas's old family buggy again," he said as he got out to meet her, waiting till she was settled in on the left side of the seat.

"That's fine," she said. "*Denki*."

Then, hurrying around to climb back in, he jokingly added, "Of course, we can be sure this carriage is well built, *jah*?"

She smiled in the fading light.

He picked up the reins and signaled the horse to move forward, relieved Eva was in better spirits this evening. "Jonas gave me *gut* directions to a place for dessert later."

She nodded, her hands in her lap.

"I like chocolate cake. Do you?" he asked.

She said she did, and he was pleased Eva wasn't as bashful as one of the girls he'd taken out riding in recent months. He was relieved, too, that she didn't seem nervous about being alone with him. Had that been part of the reason for her reticence Thursday evening?

Jed was conscious of her nearness, aware of the lightly scented perfume she must have dabbed behind her ears, like his youngest sister did before going out with her beau. The scent reminded him of lilacs or honeysuckle, and he wished he might transport Eva to Berlin for the summer, so they could take their time getting to know each other.

"My younger sister, Bettina, likes to wear a similar fragrance," he said. "She's just seventeen and is very active in her buddy group." Jed brought up the rest of his siblings and then mentioned Eva's older sister, reminding her that he'd seen Frona at market. But he purposely didn't refer to Lily.

Eva was quiet now, and akin to last time, they rode in a haze of silence.

Suddenly she faced him. "You might like to know more about my family."

"I would indeed."

"Well, my mother isn't the only one who's deceased," she told him softly. "My father is, too."

The words jarred him, and he carefully weighed his response. "I'm very sorry."

"My parents were much too young," she added. "Dat died in

a farming accident, and Mamma got sick and just couldn't get well. She passed away last winter."

Not so long ago . . .

"Do you and Frona live with a married brother and his family, perhaps?" he asked, diverting the topic.

"It's the preferred way round here, but because Frona's older and able to run the house—and likes doin' so—our brother Menno has been letting us live there alone since Mamma's death. He and Bena will be moving in soon enough, though."

"Ah, so he must be the youngest of the sons?"

"*Jah,* that too."

He looked at her, unsure what she meant. "Sorry?"

"Menno can be severe at times."

Jed didn't press for an explanation. He let Eva talk about whatever was on her mind. And there was plenty, beginning with her seeming interest in his hometown of Berlin—what sort of carriages he built, his daily life, and if the Plain community there catered much to the tourist trade, like in Lancaster County.

Is she curious because Lily's gone there? he wondered.

The more Eva talked, the more he found himself comparing the way she spoke to the words she'd written in the margins of *Little Women,* down to the similar phrases she used to describe her feelings.

I know her better than she thinks, he thought, feeling a little guilty. After all, her notes had given him a window into how she expressed herself, an idea of what things were important to her. *Would she forgive me if she knew?*

In spite of his distraction, he attempted to answer her questions, still uncertain if she was making polite small talk or if she was actually curious about his life and work. And Jed considered when he should slip in the question that weighed on his mind.

Could he do that without interrupting the easy flow of their conversation?

"How do you like Lancaster County?" she asked.

"I'm very glad my uncle Ervin suggested I glean some knowledge from Jonas Byler. Jonas is a cousin to Ervin's wife," he added.

"Oh, so that's why you stayed with them."

He waited for her to mention Orpha, perhaps, but Eva was already on to another subject.

"What sorts of quilt patterns do your sisters make out in Ohio?"

"You'd have to ask them." Jed chuckled.

Now she, too, was laughing. "I guess men don't pay much attention to such things."

"Well, we have our own ideas about what's important."

"Like what's for supper?"

He smiled, enjoying her all the more for her spunkiness.

"You don't have open surreys out there, do ya?" she asked.

"Only the courting carriages are open. Why do you ask?"

She mentioned an elderly aunt who lived in Berne, Indiana, where all the carriages, even the family ones, were open, no matter the season. "It's surprising, the differences between church districts, 'specially between states."

Jed agreed.

"Yet some things don't change. The cloistered life can be stifling for some young folks."

"You must be thinkin' of Lily," he said.

"S'pose I am."

Quickly, Eva moved from Lily and their Indiana aunt to how nice the weather was for the ride.

"The sky's clear," he agreed. "And in a little while, we should be able to see Venus, the evening star." He pointed toward the west, and she leaned forward to look.

"I wonder if Lily can see it where she is," Eva whispered.

"She can if she's searchin' for it." He sensed Eva's great affection for her sister—and apprehension. Curious, Jed dared another glance at her, pleased they had this time together.

Eva watched for the golden glow of gas lamps in each Amish home as they rode, speculating how far toward May Post Office Road Jed would take the horse and carriage. She enjoyed that he was more talkative than most fellows she'd dated, even Alfred, especially when the topic of conversation surrounded family, either Jed's or hers. It wasn't odd for Jed to bring up Lily, considering all Eva had told him. Still, she felt *naerfich*—nervous—and protective of her strong-willed sister. *Or am I simply overreacting?* This respectable young man certainly wasn't nosey.

"How 'bout if we ride up to White Oak Road?" Jed asked, breaking the silence. "Jonas Byler suggested it."

"Sure." She was glad she didn't have to propose their route.

Jed smiled at her, though she could scarcely see his features now that the sun was down and the shooting rays of light had vanished from the sky.

"Are ya lookin' forward to getting back to work?" She was anxious to start the conversation again.

"We do have a backlog of orders. Besides that, Bettina might have some news for me when I return."

"What sort of news?"

"She loves a *gut* mystery, so she's makin' me wait . . . and wonder. But I do have an inkling. Best not to say more till she confirms it, though." Jed also mentioned their recent celebration of Ascension Day, which he said most Ohio Amish communities observed. "I do know of Amish in Indiana who treat it like any other day, however."

"*Ach*, our bishop wouldn't hear of that."

Jed nodded. "The businesses in Berlin close, and *die Youngie*

155

team up to play softball or volleyball. What 'bout here—what did you do?"

"Mostly just played games and went visiting, like a no-Preaching Sunday. Frona encouraged us to spend time thinking 'bout how the day commemorates the Lord's physical ascension into heaven." She paused a moment. "Some districts have church; it just depends on the bishop, I guess . . . and the standard custom."

Jed shifted on the seat beside her. "Would ya say your bishop is traditionally strict, then? 'Specially with the youth?"

"Oh, prob'ly as strict as most older bishops. He's in his mid-seventies, same as Abner Mast across the road. Abner is my friend Naomi's husband."

"It sounds like Jonas's bishop is also firm on the *Ordnung*," Jed said.

"Well, that's because his bishop and ours happen to be one and the same."

"I would've guessed the two church districts might be closer in proximity, then."

"Actually, it's been that way since I was little."

He glanced at her. "May I be so bold as to ask why Naomi is such a close friend?"

"Honestly, Lily was when we were growin' up. She was my best sounding board, too, but that changed after Mamma died. Naomi became more of a confidante then. She was so close to my mother . . . really wanted me to know I wasn't alone." Eva had stuck her neck out and hoped to goodness he wouldn't probe further. She wasn't sure she was up to talking more about either Lily or Mamma tonight.

Jed's voice grew softer. "Life throws us curve balls sometimes."

"Still, I like to remember that the heart of love is always kindness, even with a difficult family member."

Jed was mum.

"*Ach*, sorry. I didn't mean to talk out of turn," she said.

"Sometimes the ones closest to us are the real test." Jed seemed to understand. "In fact, my Dawdi Stutzman has often said that 'familiarity breeds contempt.'"

"He must've read Aesop's fables, then."

"As a matter of fact, he has. What about your family—are they big readers?"

"We all are. It's a *gut* way to experience new things without ever leavin' home." She also told him she liked to read the Bible to start the day.

"Then you must know Psalm 50? Maybe from memory: 'And call upon me in the day of trouble: I will deliver thee, and thou shalt glorify me,'" he recited, smiling when Eva joined him for the last phrase.

"That's such a comfort," she said, considering it. "We're taught to regularly read *die Biewel* in both *Deitsch* and King James English, but we don't purposely memorize Scripture. I s'pose after reading passages often enough, though, they become part of our thoughts. And that's certainly one of them."

"Our bishop actually encourages us to study and memorize passages from Scripture."

She found this interesting but didn't care to debate the differences between their church districts. Not on their first and possibly only date.

After some time, a half-moon rose, and Eva was able to see Jed better as they made their way along the two-lane road toward the small junction at Nickel Mines. She looked forward to being able to see his expressions as they talked across the table during dessert.

Jed directed the horse into a small café parking lot, where newly painted white lines marked individual spots. "Are you hungry yet?"

"Mostly thirsty . . . maybe for a root beer float."

Jed grinned, looking quite dapper in his straw hat with its narrow brim. "Whatever you'd like."

She waited for him to tie the horse to the hitching post, then come around and open her side of the carriage. When he offered his hand, she took it and felt her heart skip a beat.

CHAPTER NINETEEN

THE NICKEL MINES CAFÉ'S DINING ROOM was a narrow space with windows on both sides. The soda fountain sat at the far north end, where, from Eva's vantage point, its counter shone with a glossy finish. A lone yellow rose adorned each of a handful of tables, the one in the middle of their particular table having lost its vitality. Eva reached out to touch its pretty petals and tried to prop up the blossom with the stem's leaves. "Looks like we might be the last customers today," she whispered.

Jed glanced around. "Are you all right here, or would ya like to move to a different spot?"

"One with a perkier flower, maybe?" she joked, surprising herself. Now that she could see his face better, she felt more comfortable. The waning light of the ride over had felt a bit distancing.

He grinned. "So, are ya sure it's just a root beer float for you?"

The waitress was heading their way, a pencil pushed into her hair above one ear.

"Sounds *gut*." Eva leaned back in her chair, letting him order. Once the waitress retreated to put in their requests, Eva brought up his apprenticeship, and they settled into another interesting conversation. And later, she enjoyed seeing him become even more talkative after a few bites of carrot cake. *Must be the sugar,* she thought.

"I'd like to see you again before I leave Monday afternoon," Jed said, appealing to her with his engaging eyes. The way he looked at her, so inquisitively at times, made her wonder what he was thinking. "Is there a place we could go walkin' tomorrow afternoon following your Preaching service?" he asked.

"I know a spot." She felt pleased. "Naomi and her husband have a large property with a big pond—I'll bring some bread crusts to feed the ducks."

Jed nodded. "I haven't done that in years. Are ya sure your neighbors won't mind?"

"Not in the least," she said most assuredly, her heart already beating more quickly at the prospect of seeing him again.

Why don't I feel like this with Alfred?

⬥

Jed did his best to keep the horse trotting steadily as they headed back toward Eden Valley. He wished the night would slow down. Eva was not only fun to be with; she seemed to be warming up to him.

"What if I wrote you a letter when I get home to Ohio?" He didn't think it was too soon to ask.

"Well, I'd read it, of course."

He laughed. "And if you read it, would you write back?"

"Depends on what you write."

He delighted in her bantering. "I'll be careful what I say," he promised.

"*Gut,* then."

And they left it right there as their time together drew to a close.

He glanced at her, and she was smiling. Her eyes caught his, and her pretty face brightened all the more. The moment passed between them, and within it was an understanding that neither wanted to let it go.

When they pulled up to the end of her driveway, Jed tied the horse to the nearby fence post and went to help Eva down from the buggy, happy to offer his hand again, wishing he could keep hers in his. *Too soon for such affection,* he reminded himself as he walked with her to the back door and said good-night.

He returned to the carriage and untied the horse, and it was all he could do to keep from leaping into the driver's side. Not delaying, he urged the horse back out to the highway, and up and down the hills toward the Bylers'.

A glance at his watch with the help of a flashlight showed that it was much later than he'd planned, and he hoped Eva's older sister hadn't waited up. And what might Jonas and Elsie Byler think of his borrowing their buggy and returning it so late? *Especially since I'm not out with their granddaughter Orpha!*

He remembered something Eva had said earlier tonight, when they were talking. *"The heart of love is always kindness."*

He'd read that before, but where? *In her book, perhaps?*

Pulling into the Bylers' long lane, Jed wondered what Lydiann might have thought of Eva. Would she have liked her, too? What a peculiar thought, yet considering how much he'd loved his fiancée, he realized it wasn't strange after all.

Jah, thought Jed, *she would definitely approve.*

CHAPTER TWENTY

By THE TIME THEY ARRIVED at Bishop Isaac's farm a little before eight o'clock Sunday morning, Eva felt somewhat settled, enough to attend worship. But as soon as she and Frona stepped into line with the other womenfolk, one after another began to whisper concerns about Lily. Some even had questions.

Everyone knows, Eva thought, stiffening.

"Have ya heard from your dear sister?" Sylvia Lantz's grand-mother Suzanne asked, blinking her milky blue eyes, her cane dangling off her arm.

"*Ach*, you mustn't worry," Frona said. "Not at your age!" and then added something Eva could not hear in a reassuring tone.

Others, just as well meaning, asked how she and Frona were getting along. Although Eva knew it was all in a spirit of compassion, it nevertheless was beginning to wear thin.

When Menno's wife, Bena, arrived, Eva observed her walk across the backyard with little Katie Ann in tow. Their match-ing blue mother-daughter dresses moved gracefully around their calves, and they had on new black shoes.

"We'll sit with ya," Bena said with a sweet smile when she approached. This sister-in-law had always been one to exhibit the utmost reverence for the Lord's Day. It was one of the reasons Eva's mother had liked her so well for Menno when they were first dating. Mamma had shared this with Eva when she also reached courting age, wanting to note a good example.

"*Denki,*" Eva whispered and lowered her head, hoping not to attract any more attention to Frona and herself.

During Preaching, Eva fought to keep her mind on the ministers' sermons—the first one an hour long—and also during the second, lengthier sermon. Their pointed words were a clear warning to young people not to entertain foolish notions. *Like Lily's,* thought Eva.

When it was time for the final silent prayer, they all turned to kneel at their wooden benches, and Eva beseeched almighty God to lead Lily home according to His loving and sovereign will. *I trust Thy wisdom, heavenly Father. Be our compassionate guide, and strength and comfort. May Thy protecting hand cover my wayward sister, Lily, and grant all of us divine peace.*

After the announcements, Eva made her way outside with the other young women her age while the benches were converted into tables for the shared meal. She noticed Alfred Dienner's mother, Miriam, talking with Naomi Mast on the back porch. Miriam and her sister had been assisting the bishop's wife with serving cold cuts and pie, but Miriam made a real show of smiling and waving at Eva.

For goodness' sake, thought Eva. *What has Alfred told her?*

With a bag of bread crusts in hand, Eva waited for Jed beneath two sheltering oaks that balmy Lord's Day afternoon. Since her first unexpected meeting with him, Eva believed she'd crossed an imaginary line in her mind, and perhaps in her heart. *My sister leaves . . . and Jed arrives*, she thought, torn between sadness and exuberance.

She recalled Naomi's endearing smile after the common meal, when Eva asked if it was all right to go walking with Jed around the Masts' pond. Not only had Naomi said repeatedly that it was fine, but she offered to leave some treats and cold lemonade in the backyard gazebo, *"if you won't think I'm interfering."*

Now, spotting the Bylers' gray carriage coming into view, Eva's heart thrilled to see Jed wave out the window. His enthusiasm delighted her, and she waved back.

The sun dazzled everything in sight—suddenly the meadow looked greener and Naomi's climbing roses a brighter pink, as if Eva's surroundings were tinged by her own happiness.

"I'm glad to see you again, Eva." Jed's voice was warm as he offered her a hand up, then went around the buggy to get into the driver's side.

"It's all right if you want to pull into Abner's lane," she suggested with a smile. "He won't mind."

"What if we just ride for a while first? All right with you?"

Eva was perfectly content to sit there next to him and asked about his morning, knowing the Bylers' church district had an off-Sunday, since their shared bishop had held the Preaching service for Eden Valley at his own house. Jed mentioned a quiet breakfast with Jonas and his wife, then family worship, followed by a long walk around their property.

"How was your Preaching service today?" he inquired.

"The house was packed," she said softly. "I don't think anyone was missing, come to think of it." She caught herself. "Except for Lily. And I almost wonder if that wasn't the reason for the larger than usual attendance." She mentioned a good number of people had offered to pray for Lily.

"Reminds me of our church." Jed tilted his head thoughtfully. "It's God's way—the People lookin' after each other."

She nodded in full agreement. "It does help, but it doesn't always ease the pain."

"I understand," he said quietly, taking his time. At last he met her gaze. "You see, I lost my fiancée to an accident a year ago."

"Oh, Jed." Her heart broke for him.

He inhaled deeply. "Lydiann died instantly, I was told . . . a blessing for her, but . . ." He paused, clearly uncomfortable with the recollection. "Not for the rest of us. At the time, I didn't think I could bear it."

"I'm so sorry." Eva didn't ask about the accident. *Some things are just too painful.*

"It was shocking, sure, but no more than your father's death was for you and your family."

"There's no time to say good-bye with a sudden loss, but it's quick and over with for the person," she said. "A lingering illness gives time for the family to accept the death, but the patient suffers more—like Mamma did."

Jed glanced at her, his expression caring. "Afterward, I remember feeling exhausted all the time. I couldn't seem to get enough sleep."

"Oh, and ya feel so alone," she admitted, swallowing the lump in her throat. "At Mamma's burial service, I kept wonderin' if anyone could see how forlorn I felt . . . ever so lost." She glanced at Jed. "Like the orphan I am."

Jed was nodding his head. "For me, it seemed like my hopes and plans dried up. It took days, even weeks, for the truth to sink in. I kept wakin' up and thinking it was a horrible dream."

"I felt that way for months, too, but not so much about my future hopes as for the giant hole in our family."

"Did you find yourself wishing you'd done something different the day of your father's death?" he asked.

"For sure. To this day, I wish I had cut one more piece of my birthday cake for him."

Jed's eyebrows rose. "Your father died on your birthday?"

She bowed her head. "My sixteenth—four years ago. It was terrible."

They talked further, more slowly now. Then Eva asked, "What about you? Did ya wish you could change anything 'bout the day Lydiann died?"

"Over and over, I wish I'd offered to take her to visit her aunt, instead of letting her go with her younger brother—as if *I* had the power to change God's will."

He turned to face her again, and in his eyes she saw the pain he carried, the enormous loss.

"I'm learning a lot about faith through grieving—trusting that our sovereign Lord knows what is best for each of us . . . about everything," Eva whispered, blinking away tears. "To be honest, it's a difficult journey."

"*Jah*, for certain." Jed reached for her hand, and despite her sadness at what she had lost, Eva felt an irrepressible joy.

After the ride, Jed pulled into the Masts' lane and tied up the horse under a shade tree. They set off walking toward the pond, where there was a grove of willows along one side, nourished by the water. Jed set an easy pace as they enjoyed soothing breezes beneath the graceful branches. The place was peaceful, hidden by dozens of green tendrils.

"My father cautioned me against bitterness in the early days after the accident," Jed admitted. "I was sorely tempted to fall into that pit. *Ach*, there were days . . ."

She purposely didn't look at him, lest he was struggling. "I can't imagine your loss, Jed."

167

"And I can't know *yours*. I have a feeling that each loss is different . . . and unique, too, in how a person grieves."

"With my father's death, I mostly fought the disbelief—the shock of it—and with Mamma's illness, I felt so helpless. Oh, the sorrow, the ache in my heart for them both once they were gone."

Jed glanced at the sky, then back at her. He mentioned someone had indicated he'd taken Lydiann's loss too hard, that he should have gotten over his sadness sooner, since they hadn't married yet. "But no one can really say how another person should grieve, or for how long."

Eva fully understood. *Oh, do I ever!*

A cloud concealed the sun from their view as they emerged from the willow grove. Eva spotted several ducks gliding through the water toward them. "I think they must know somethin'," she whispered, opening the bag and breaking off a long piece of crust for Jed. "Lookee there."

She pinched off a small piece and tossed it, and then another, and Jed did the same. He looked so handsome in his Sunday clothes—black trousers, white shirt, and black suspenders, and his narrow-brimmed straw hat, too. She had to remind herself to feed the ducks instead of watching Jed squat to toss the crumbs into the pond.

Soon, two larger ducks waddled out of the water and came right up to Jed, quacking for more. He held his hand flat, and the first duck ate off of his palm.

"They're not afraid of you." Eva was intrigued. "Lily can do that, too. The ducks and Canada geese come right up to her."

Jed looked at her. "You've suffered a third loss," he said so tenderly she thought she might cry. "Lily's leaving an' all."

"A frustrating kind of loss, *jah*." *Because no one knows how it'll end.*

He rose and brushed off his hands, but the two ducks stood there quacking for more.

"Here, why don't you take the rest." She was amused by his interaction with the more persistent birds.

Jed pinched off a few more pieces and moved closer to the water. Now many more ducks were swimming this way, some flapping their dark wings and splashing as they came.

Once the crumbs were gone, Jed and Eva walked twice around the pond's perimeter, and each time, when they wandered beneath the willows, Jed took her hand.

"I'd like to see your candy shop before I leave town," he said. "Might I drop by tomorrow?"

"Well, I open later on Mondays to help with the washing. If ya stop in after the noon meal, that'd be best."

"Fewer customers then?"

"Possibly." She couldn't help but smile.

"Do you have a Closed sign?" He winked at her.

She blushed. "I do, actually."

"So maybe we could slip away for another walk."

She liked the idea. Then, second-guessing it, she said, "Honestly, it might be better to stay put in the shop to visit.'"

He seemed to acquiesce. "I don't want to leave without sayin' so long, ya know?"

She encouraged him to come by The Sweet Tooth around twelve-thirty, after dishes were done.

"Will it be all right with Frona?" he asked.

"I don't plan to tell her," Eva replied with a little laugh. "Hopefully, if anyone spots you, they'll assume you're there to purchase sweets."

One last visit with Jed . . .

CHAPTER TWENTY-ONE

················ ✿ ················

THE WONDERFUL SMELL OF BREAD DOUGH filled the
kitchen as Eva made her way down the cellar steps on washday
morning. Frona was fretting about coming that close to getting her fingers stuck in the wringer. "*Ach,* I'm glad ya didn't!"
Eva said, hurrying to help lift the heavy, wet clothes out of the
washer and carefully feeding them through the wringer with
her sister's assistance.

Later, once the first load was out on the line and they'd loaded
the second batch, they stopped to have a cup of tea. And after
the breakfast dishes were washed and put away, Eva rushed to
the mailbox and found a letter from Alfred Dienner. Truth be
known, she wasn't very excited to hear from him, especially since
meeting Jed.

Nevertheless, she slipped away to her room to read Alfred's
letter.

Dear Eva,
  *How are you? Are you keeping busy with your candy making
and your customers?*

I've been doing quite a lot in the woodworking shop here, more than I realized would be necessary. That's why I haven't written sooner, even though I do think of you every day.

Have you given any thought to our last conversation? Ach, I sometimes wish I could hear your voice. Maybe I'll call you at the phone shanty sometime, even though it might be frowned on if we talk too often that way.

There are some fine places to eat here in Wisconsin, but I haven't found a shoofly pie like my Mamm's. I will say, though, that the cheese is very tasty!

As for learning the woodworking trade, I enjoy the creativity involved more than I ever expected.

Alfred's letter continued by describing some of the folks he'd met since first arriving there, and even though he seemed happy enough, sharing his activities with her, Eva could tell he must be homesick. It was odd, because she didn't know how she should think about Alfred, uncertain how her new friendship with Jed Stutzman would play out once he returned to Ohio.

It's unusual to have the attention of two young men at the same time, and for both to be out of state, she thought as she pushed Alfred's letter into her dresser drawer.

Two buggies rolled into the driveway, and she figured they were candy customers. Happily, she hurried downstairs and into The Sweet Tooth just as they pulled into the parking spaces.

⚜

As planned, Naomi stopped at Ida Mae's after the washing was on the line. She'd noticed Frona and Eva outdoors exceptionally early getting theirs up, too. Not that she was in competition, but her neighbor to the west certainly made a valiant attempt to be first on *Weschdaag* mornings. After years of this nonsense,

Naomi just let her win. What was the point? She'd once told this to Abner, who'd chortled.

"Your father went to see Bishop Isaac first thing today," Naomi informed Ida Mae on their ride to the General Store for sewing notions. "I know you'll keep it to yourself, but it was 'bout Lily Esch's possible whereabouts in Ohio. He's mighty worried, as are the Esch boys."

Ida Mae gasped. "Lily's made it all the way there?"

"Evidently, there's a young fella involved . . . an *Englischer.*"

"Lily's always been such a *gut* girl. What's gotten into her?"

Naomi nodded. "Poor thing, losing her mother threw her, I gather. We all know Dottie raised her girls right."

"*Ach,* Dottie would weep if she knew."

Naomi tried to relax her grip on the reins. "Have ya thought any more 'bout traveling to Paradise with me the end of this week to help with some sewin' for your second cousin?"

"Poor Connie must be really bad off if she can't even hold a needle."

"She can't thread one either, her wrist's so painful," Naomi added.

"Honestly, I don't see why she doesn't have it put in a cast."

"Well, you and I both know why."

Ida Mae looked away, pulling on her shawl. "It wonders me why some people are timid 'bout getting medical help and others ain't. It's just odd."

"The community's split down the middle on that." Naomi waited for Ida Mae to say whether she would go or not.

"I s'pose I could take one of my impatiens plants to Cousin Connie. Cheer her up, maybe."

"I think she'd like that, I surely do." Naomi was relieved, since she hadn't wanted to travel alone all the way south, though she'd made the trip by herself before.

Naomi tapped on the carriage brake when they reached a steep decline. There was something else she thought Ida Mae should know. "Your brother Omar also went to speak with Bishop Isaac today. Sounds like your father bumped into him on the way in. Anyway, Omar asked outright what Bishop thought of him going ahead and registering to vote in the election."

Ida Mae's eyes popped. "*Ach*, really?"

"Know what the bishop said? He told Omar that if he fasted and prayed 'bout it for three days, the Lord God would show him what to do."

Ida Mae clapped her hands. "Well, ain't that the best answer ya ever did hear?"

"Your Dat completely agreed."

"And what did Omar say?"

"Knowin' Omar's penchant for food, I would've thought he would say he'd keel over with starvation in three days." Naomi shook her head. "But he's considerin' it." She went on to say that when she'd tried to talk sense to him, he was as closed as a book. "The bishop was mighty prudent, if ya think about it, putting the decision right back in Omar's hands."

"I do hope my brother is willing to fast and pray like the man of God asked."

"If he refuses, the voting issue will be the least of our fears."

They talked about other things for a while. Then, as they neared the store, Naomi asked, "By the way, how early did ya get your washing hung out today?"

"Before breakfast. Why?"

Naomi grinned at her. "Just curious."

⁓

At 12:42 that afternoon, Eva saw Jed pull into the parking area in front of The Sweet Tooth. She knew the exact time because she'd been watching the clock since the last few customers left, hoping Frona was busy writing to a couple of Ohio relatives about Lily's whereabouts, as she'd volunteered to do.

Eva put the last few triple chocolate–nut clusters onto wax paper to cool, so delighted at seeing him again, she did spontaneous little steps in place. Not a dance but nearly. "What if we *did* slip away for another walk?" she murmured, recalling yesterday and how they'd shared their hearts. She'd felt sad for his loss of his first love.

Eva could hear Jed whistling as he tied the horse to the hitching rail out back. Shaking out the lower part of her black apron, she wanted to look as neat and presentable as she could once Jed came up the walkway and opened the shop door. Watching him from afar, she felt almost dazed at her good fortune—this especially handsome and kind young man seemed so eager to see her again.

He wants to write to me, she reminded herself, aware of her own widening smile.

Jed's stride was long and even, and his hair shone in the sunlight as he approached the shop. His black suspenders were stark against his long-sleeved white shirt, its sleeves rolled up.

"Hullo again." He came inside and turned to quietly close the door.

"You're nearly on time," she teased. It occurred to her how very comfortable she already felt with him.

"I might've been earlier if there hadn't been an accident out yonder."

"Oh dear. Hope no one was hurt."

"It looked like just a fender bender. Might've been a tourist who'd lost his way—the driver gawking about and not paying attention."

She'd seen plenty of automobiles racing around buggies, but

she had never run across two cars in such a mishap. "Well, I'm glad *you're* in one piece, Jed."

He brightened as he met her gaze, then looked around the place. "So this is where you spend much of your time?"

"The shop is only open four days a week—Monday, Wednesday, Friday, and Saturday—and never for more than a few hours. I do spend a fair amount of time makin' goodies, though! Would ya like a tour of this small corner of my world?" She showed him the little kitchen, where she pointed out the chocolate-nut clusters cooling on the counter. Then she brought him back to the display case to show him other favorite offerings, including the Butterfinger truffles made with semisweet chocolate, fresh cream, and Butterfinger candy bars.

"Choose a sample or two, if you'd like."

"They all look *wunnerbaar-gut*," Jed said with a grin.

She even led him behind the counter so he could see all the cubbyholes for storing paper bags and boxes, string, tape, and the like.

"You're very organized." He moved closer to the display case, eyeing the truffles. "I'll purchase a few of these," he said, his nose practically touching the glass.

"They were flyin' off the shelf earlier."

Jed reached for his wallet and set it on the counter.

She shook her head. "*Ach*, you treated me at the café . . . won't ya let me treat you?"

"That was our *date*, Eva. And if I lived round here, this would be just the first of many purchases."

She smiled and felt her face flush, surely as pink as the geraniums on Naomi's porch. "I'd like to send some sweets along for your trip, all right?"

Jed reluctantly gave in, and it took no time for her to gather up a half-dozen truffles and wrap them. "I've hired a van driver, since there are a few tools and other items to take back," he explained. "Couldn't see storin' any of that in the luggage hold of a train, not when there's a driver already going that direction."

"Sounds like you've got everything planned." Oh, she wished he didn't have to leave.

He walked around the counter while she pulled out a small sack. A glance out the window reassured Eva that no other customers had arrived, and they still had a moment or two to themselves.

"I meant what I said the other night 'bout writing, Eva," Jed said as she handed him the truffles.

"It'll be real nice to hear from ya."

"That you will." He picked up his wallet and a small picture fell out, landing facedown on the counter.

She leaned forward to retrieve it, but just as quickly, Jed reached for it. The photo slipped from his grasp and fluttered away. "*Nee!*" he muttered, trying to seize it.

His obvious nervousness startled her.

"I've got it," he said, finally getting a grasp on it, but not before she'd caught a glimpse.

Her heart stopped, then sank. *What on earth?*

"Jed . . . who *is* that?" Eva asked, though she was certain she knew.

He reddened. "I found this photo on the train," he said, looking at the picture before reluctantly offering it to her.

Tears sprang to Eva's eyes as she gazed upon the face of the last person she would have expected to see. *Lily.* "It's my dear missing sister."

After a moment, she raised her gaze to his own befuddled expression.

"Did *you* take this picture?" she asked at last.

"Of course not," he stammered. "Like I said . . . I found it on the train." He frowned. "But wait . . . did you say *Lily?*"

"*Jah*, this is a photo of my sister." She stared at him, still wondering why this photo was in his possession but now equally perplexed by his present confusion.

He must not have known it was Lily. . . .

And then it came to her: Jed had thought *she* was the girl in the picture.

"Go ahead and keep it," Jed said, attempting a smile.

"Lily and I do look quite a bit alike," she said, taking a deep breath. "Or at least people say we do."

Jed removed his straw hat and stared down at it. "I don't know what to say. . . . I honestly thought . . ."

That I was the girl, Eva thought again, stunned. "I don't know anything 'bout this photo or where it was taken. What could have prompted Lily to do this?" She slid it into one of the cubbyholes beneath her cash register, wishing it might vanish just as her sister had.

It was evident now why Jed had looked so inquisitively at her when they'd first met at the auction. *Like he'd seen me before.*

The awkwardness was strewn before them like broken glass, and every bit as painful to step on. *Was he looking to meet Lily?* she wondered. *Is that why we met?*

"I hope I haven't offended you, Eva." Jed stepped toward her, then, as if out of bounds, he inched back.

Her head was spinning.

"Listen, I don't care about the photograph," he began again before hesitating, but the way he said it wasn't very convincing.

I feel like crying. How on earth had everything gone so wrong so suddenly?

"Eva . . . I thought about telling you, but then I wasn't sure what you'd think."

They heard the sound of the doorknob turning and the door whisking open. Eva spotted Bishop Isaac smiling at them beneath his formidable-looking black hat. Except for his long-sleeved white shirt, he was dressed all in black.

"I'd best be goin'," Jed said abruptly. "You have another customer."

"Ain't necessary to go," she heard herself say. But it was apparently pointless for him to remain to pursue the young woman he'd assumed Eva to be. She managed to nod her head. "*Jah*, maybe 'tis best." She sighed. "So long, Jed."

He turned slowly and then glanced back at her, as if still trying to reconcile her face with the photograph. He reached for the door as the bishop stepped up to the counter. Once again, Jed looked back at her and nodded politely.

The worst timing! she thought.

"*Willkumm*, Bishop," she said. "What sweets might ya be interested in?"

Her heart sank anew as through the window she saw Jed hurrying to his buggy.

"Nothing today." The bishop kept on his black felt hat. "But I'd like you to follow me into the main house, where Frona's waiting."

What else can go wrong?

"Let me just hang up my Closed sign," she said, thankful now that she and Jed hadn't set out for a walk. But then Lily's forbidden photo might still be safely tucked away in Jed's wallet.

All this time, Jed thought I was the girl in the photograph.

CHAPTER TWENTY-TWO

✿

EVA SAT RESPECTFULLY AT THE TABLE while Frona informed the bishop that Menno had stopped by earlier. It was surprising to hear that Menno had contacted their cousin Jeptha King in Apple Creek, Ohio. "Jeptha's agreed to nose around some of the surrounding towns . . . see what he can find out about Lily," Frona said with a glance at Eva.

After what had just transpired in the candy shop, it was hard to keep her mind on what the bishop was saying in response. Eva was still so baffled Lily had dared to have a picture made of herself . . . and that Jed had found it on the very train he'd taken here. The whole thing was mind-boggling.

"Menno's a conscientious farmer," Bishop Isaac was telling Frona. "I understand why he can't just up and leave, 'specially with cultivating filling his hours."

"I'm doin' my part to help," Frona chimed in, explaining she'd written to some Ohio relatives. "It shouldn't take long to find out something, I wouldn't think."

"But what will happen if Lily refuses to come home?" Eva asked softly.

Bishop Isaac folded his big, callused hands on the table where their father had always sat. "*Gott* has a sovereign plan for your sister, and I believe it's right here with the People. No doubt in my mind."

Eva hoped with all of her heart he was right. After all, he was the man chosen by God to shepherd the flock here.

"In the long run, though, it'll be up to Lily to surrender her prideful independence," Bishop Isaac said.

All the same, Eva fought against the idea of someone forcing Lily to return against her will. *If she's even still single*, she thought. That was the only way it could possibly work, because if Lily had already eloped . . . Oh, she didn't want to think about that. They must find her, and soon!

"We'll put our complete trust in our heavenly Father." The bishop rose and made his way toward the door. "I'll leave you sisters to your work now."

"*Denki* for comin', bishop," Frona said right quick.

But Eva said nothing.

❦

Jed tortured himself on the ride to Quarryville, where he was scheduled to meet the van driver for the trip home. "How could I have made such a fool of myself?" He could not escape the memory of Eva's utter disappointment. And the way she'd wanted him to stay, then changed her mind and agreed he should take his leave. *What a time for the bishop to appear. . . .*

Lily certainly resembled Eva. But now Jed's disappointment was less over the girl in the photo than the realization that Eva wasn't the author of the notes in the book's margins. To think he didn't know her as well as he'd imagined! That was the most disappointing fact of all.

"Just when I was beginning to think God had brought us together in the most unlikely way," he muttered miserably.

Eva waited until the bishop backed out of the driveway before she dashed over to the candy shop. There, she found Lily's picture and brought it into the kitchen to show Frona, who was busy slicing the fresh bread.

"Where do ya think Lily had this taken?" She pushed it in front of Frona, who leaned forward for a better look.

"Where'd ya get this?" she demanded.

Eva hesitated, unwilling to say. "I just came across it . . . and want to know what you think."

"I think you'd better burn it, that's what."

Eva nodded and studied it again. "*Ach*, I wonder if Fannie has an opinion 'bout it. She seems to know more than I would've guessed 'bout our sister."

"True. You could ask her." Frona glanced out the window. "Right now, though, it looks like you're getting a customer."

Eva could see the carriage pulling in. "Come to think of it, maybe this photo might help Cousin Jeptha locate Lily."

"Well now, ain't that a thought?"

"It would help a lot if they could narrow things down—Ohio's an awful big state," Eva said, picking up the photograph. "Cousin Jeptha can't just run around all over, ya know."

"*Nee*, that's for certain." Frona bobbed her head toward the shop. "Hurry up, now."

"I'm goin'," Eva exclaimed, leaving Lily's photo there on the counter.

Jed loaded his tools into the back of the van to make room for five other paying passengers. The driver, Arnie Strout, informed him it wasn't necessary to skimp on space since none of the other passengers had much luggage.

Sitting in the front passenger seat, Jed was plagued by Eva's disillusionment. *What a mess*, he thought. *It was ridiculous of me to carry that photo around in the first place!*

And he had made a terrible mistake in assuming Eva was the girl in the picture. *I should have known she wouldn't do such a thing.*

Jed recalled everything Eva had said about her younger sister. She had been pretty tight-lipped, perhaps to protect Lily. He didn't know and wasn't sure he was supposed to know.

Now he felt convinced that finding the book on the train had been purely coincidental. *Anyone could've picked it up. . . .*

"Was there a crowd at the auction?" Arnie asked, interrupting Jed's thoughts.

"It was well attended."

"I wonder if the sellers will spend winters in Florida like other Amish retirees are starting to do."

"Is that so?" Jed hadn't heard this.

"Oh yes, and Pinecraft's the place for Plain snowbirds. At least that's what I'm told."

"I don't know of any Amish who go there." Jed was truly interested. "Is it a set-apart community?"

"I guess it's somewhat isolated from the more modern surrounding neighborhoods. Some of the cottages have electricity, though, but since these are mostly rentals and most folks are only there for a few months out of the year, the bishops are looking the other way." Arnie added, "Once a person experiences the warmer temperatures, it's doubly hard to endure another Pennsylvania winter."

The conversation lulled, and Jed found himself contemplating the way he'd left things with Orpha Byler. Had she finally accepted the fact that Jed was only interested in a casual friendship and nothing more? Indeed, yesterday he'd almost thought Orpha and her family might come again for dessert after supper, but he was relieved when the meal rolled around and it was just him and his hosts seated at the table.

He hoped his uncle wouldn't be frustrated to learn that things had gone nowhere with Jonas's granddaughters. Jed simply hadn't been able to think of anyone but Eva once he'd encountered her at the auction.

And now I've ruined that.

CHAPTER TWENTY-THREE

JED'S YOUNGEST SISTER met him in the kitchen that night, sporting a big smile.

"I want you to hear this from me first," Bettina said, eyes dancing as she told him of her wedding plans come November.

He knew she was hoping for his brotherly blessing. "I'd be happier if you were a little older. What's the big hurry, sis?"

"Aw, Jed . . ."

"Well now, think about it. You've only been goin' to Singings a year."

"Levi and I *love* each other," she said, wringing her hands. "Why should we wait?"

She was far from ready to be a wife, young as she was. "Have ya thought of talkin' to Dat and Mamm?"

She ignored his question. "I forgot to tell you—Levi wants you to be one of his side sitters at our wedding."

"Shouldn't *he* be askin'? That's traditionally the way it's done."

"Oh, Jed, I'm just so thrilled! I can hardly think straight."

Thinking straight should come first. . . .

"Remember, Lord willing, you'll be married to Levi for a long time—might be sixty years or more," he offered kindly. "Besides, isn't Levi the only fella you've ever gone with?"

She nodded. "And he's the one for me, so there's no point in arguing that." Bettina sighed. "*Ach*, you're too tired to be happy for me, I daresay."

He *was* tired. Evidently undaunted, Bettina left the kitchen to go upstairs.

Jed recalled Eva's interest in Bettina's possible news, but he pushed the thought away. What did it matter now?

He headed back to his bedroom, adjacent to the front room, and noticed Lily's book lying on the dresser. There hadn't been time to give it another look during the trip from Lancaster County, what with all the conversation in the van. Jed had wanted to be considerate of his driver and fellow passengers.

I could mail it to Lily, he thought. *If I knew where she was.*

He heard voices drifting down the stairs now and assumed Bettina had taken his suggestion to heart, although Jed supposed their parents might have guessed something was up. *The way she's prancing about like a young filly.*

Their father might also caution about Bettina's young age, although Daed had married Mamm the year they each turned eighteen.

Flipping through the book's pages, Jed zeroed in on a note: *Love gladly sacrifices itself for the beloved.*

He closed the book, still aware of the muffled conversation. *Bettina's arguing for her own beloved,* he thought as he leaned back onto the bed, his hands behind his head.

I have no right to discourage her.

❦

The next morning, Jed rose an hour before the alarm clock went off, anxious to turn up at work before Uncle Ervin arrived.

Considering the raucous birds outside his window, he'd needed no further incentive.

O Lord, pave the way for me today with Uncle Ervin, he prayed, on edge about whether his absence might have proved a boon to Perry.

Bettina met him in the kitchen, looking like she hadn't slept much. "Well, I did your bidding," she said conspiratorially.

He nodded. "How'd it go?"

"Not the way I expected. And Mamma's not feelin' so well this morning because of it." She groaned and went to the fridge and reached for some orange juice and milk. "I hate causin' her worry," she said as she opened the cupboard and brought over two choices of cold cereal.

Jed picked up the cereal box. "This is all I get?" He rose to get a clean bowl from the shelf and returned to help himself to a large amount of Wheaties without saying more. He was dismayed by his sister's apparent mind-set. It wasn't *his* doing she'd gotten herself engaged too young.

"Mamma was cryin' by the end of our talk," Bettina volunteered.

He kept his mouth shut, except to eat, believing anything he might say could make things worse.

"So now you're not talkin' to me?" Bettina poured orange juice into a tall glass and set it down in front of him.

He thanked her with a nod, but she ignored him and left with a sad face.

A dramatic start to the day, Jed thought.

❧

Ervin Stutzman wasn't the easiest boss to please, despite the fact that Jed was related to him. He was known to expect perfection, or close to it, and he wanted his employees to work long hours when necessary. Now that he'd had two apprentices for some time, Uncle Ervin's exceedingly high standards were even higher than before, although here lately he was nearly too frail to bark orders.

These thoughts were running through Jed's mind as he walked up the familiar lane to the shop and pushed the door open.

Surprisingly, there sat Ervin, smoking his pipe, surrounded by stacked plywood for seats and the main box of the buggy, as well as lumber for the canopy frames. He sputtered when he spotted Jed. "Didn't expect ya this early."

"Mornin', *Onkel*. Just thought I'd get a head start since I've been gone."

His uncle gave him a nod and returned to puffing away. "*Willkumm* back."

Jed proceeded to tell him about Jonas Byler's carriage shop—the equipment, the setup, and the various techniques he'd learned there. "Found it takes Jonas and his employees about a hundred and fifty hours to make a buggy, same as here."

Ervin smiled and slowly nodded his head. "It's never right to cut corners, *niemols*."

"Jonas has quite the big operation," Jed said, catching his uncle up on all that he'd seen and heard.

"And how was your visit with Lovina and Orpha Byler?" Ervin asked with a quirk of his eyebrow.

Jed might have guessed this would be next. "The Byler sisters were pleasant enough," he replied. *But that's where it stops.* His uncle didn't need to know the rest of the story.

Uncle Ervin got up and leaned heavily on his cane. "They were pleasant, ya say? Just pleasant?"

Jed smiled. "Orpha seems like a real *schmaert* and helpful young woman, too," he added.

"Helpful is *gut*, but ya don't sound like a would-be beau. She *chust* ain't for you?"

190

"'Fraid not."

Quickly, Jed changed the subject. "I'm wondering if Perry finished makin' the seat for the surrey he's been building."

"*Jah,* and one of the curtained doors and the hinged door in back, too. Perry's a fine welder and painter and mechanic, but he needs to work on his upholstering and painting. Ain't nearly as *sarchsam*—painstaking—as you in all areas of work."

Rare affirmation.

Jed set to measuring the vinyl-covered black cloth for the new buggy tops, sides, and back and decided the day was turning out better than it started.

CHAPTER TWENTY-FOUR

································· ❖ ·································

EVA HEARD ONE OF ABNER MAST'S HEIFERS bellowing across the road as she emptied the trash early Tuesday afternoon. Frona was finishing up the ironing, and Eva had felt restless, going from room to room to gather up the wastepaper baskets. She felt she needed to get away from her sister, who had nothing good to say today. *She's out of sorts, stewing over Lily.*

Returning from behind the barn, Eva saw Sylvia Lantz pull into the driveway in her family carriage, waving. Eva hurried her step, then set the empty trash can down near the old hand pump. "Nice to see ya," she called to their neighbor.

Sylvia got out and went around to the opposite side of the buggy, where she removed a large casserole dish nestled in her handmade quilted carryall. "I decided to bring some supper over as a surprise," she said. "Since it's your day off from the candy shop, I thought I'd catch ya before you start cookin'."

"Perfect timing." Eva was especially pleased because it was her day to cook. She walked with Sylvia into the house. "Heard from Naomi that you're expectin' company this weekend."

Sylvia nodded. "*Jah*, Tilly's girls attend a private Christian school that lets out earlier for the summer than most public schools in Rockport, so the family's comin' for a nice long visit. Oh, I can't wait to get my hands on their youngest! Tilly wrote in her last letter that he's growin' as fast as kudzu. It's past due for them to come see us." Sylvia set the dish on the counter. "Hope ya like homemade noodles and turkey with carrots and onions."

"*Wunderbaar*," Eva said. "*Denki*." She asked if Sylvia could visit awhile.

"For a little bit, I guess."

Frona was still ironing in the next room, but she came around to poke her head in to see who was there. "Did I hear something 'bout a turkey casserole?"

"I made a double batch." Sylvia sat down at the table and smiled at Frona, then Eva.

"Well, it ain't like we're in mourning," Frona said, startling Eva and obviously Sylvia, too.

"That is, we're putting on our bravest faces, waiting to hear—" Eva started to say, hoping to soften the blow of Frona's bad temper.

"It must be awful hard," Sylvia interrupted.

Frona frowned. "We're struggling . . . that's for sure." She sighed. "Eva and I are grateful for your thoughtfulness, Sylvia." Then she withdrew to the next room.

Sylvia motioned for Eva to join her at the table. "None of us knows what we'd say or do if we were put in the same circumstance as you and your family."

Eva smiled. "You're always so kind."

They talked about Menno's contact in Apple Creek, Ohio. "Let's pray he'll be able to find Lily and bring her home," Eva said, not surprised when Sylvia admitted she'd already heard a little about this from Menno's wife, Bena, just up the road.

"Something *gut* has to come of this." Sylvia touched the back of Eva's hand. "You believe it, too, don't ya?"

"I certainly try." She asked if Sylvia would like something to drink. "We have plenty of meadow tea in the fridge."

"I'll have a small glass," Sylvia replied. "What about you, Frona? Can you hear me . . . would you like something, too?"

Eva was pleased Sylvia had reached out to Frona, but Frona merely said she wasn't thirsty from the other side of the wall. *She must be embarrassed.*

While they sipped their cold tea, Eva asked if Sylvia might reintroduce her to Tilly. "If ya think it might suit sometime while they're visiting."

"I'll ask once they arrive," Sylvia assured her.

She didn't mind that Frona had probably heard what she was saying; Eva could just imagine her perpetual frown. "I'll look forward to meeting your daughter," she added.

"And Tilly will enjoy getting to know you, Eva."

Eva hoped she could manage without being too bashful. Oh, she wanted to pick Tilly's brain about ever so many things.

That evening, after they enjoyed Sylvia's hearty casserole meal, Eva and Frona each indulged in one of the delectable leftover truffles. Eva asked Frona's advice about letting Naomi see Lily's photograph. "I know she'll keep mum, if I ask her to."

"Show it to anyone you like," Frona said, wearing her oldest blue kerchief over her thick hair bun. She looked tired and was apparently still distressed over her rude response to Sylvia earlier. "It might be the last we see of Lily."

Eva sighed at Frona's dispirited remark. "Let's keep prayin'."

"Well, the bishop and I talked briefly yesterday before he went over to get you from your shop," Frona said. "According to him, the world can be more appealing than the Kingdom of God, 'specially to younger folks."

"That's one of the reasons we're praying."

Frona seemed to ignore this. "By the way, you never said how you ran across that photo."

Eva shrugged, not willing to admit to the sad affair. "You surely remember how Lily started backing away from the church after Mamma died."

"*Jah*, I do." Frona set her fork down. "But where'd you find the photo?"

I'll have to say eventually, Eva thought, not wanting to be impudent but still reluctant to talk about her final visit with Jed. *Not just yet.*

"Eva, ain't ya listenin' to me?"

"I don't think it matters, Frona. Honestly, I doubt Lily meant for us to see it."

"You and Lily, fully of secrets." Frona grimaced. "Guess I can't squeeze blood out of a turnip."

After the dishes were washed and put away, Eva headed across the road and straight to Naomi's side door. *How many times did we girls come over with Mamma for homemade ice cream?* she recalled. *Naomi's heart and home have always been open to us. . . .*

Inside, Naomi rose immediately from the table and led Eva into the front room while Abner stayed put with the coconut cream pie.

"Poor Abner," said Eva. "I've interrupted your dessert."

"*Ach*, I can tell by the looks of ya, you need to bend my ear, ain't so? Abner will understand."

"You know me well," Eva admitted and began to share about the surprising photograph of Lily. "Have a look if you want." She pulled it out of her pocket and showed Naomi.

For the longest time, Naomi held it out a ways from her face, her chin up as she stared at it. "Well, I've never seen Lily so dolled up before," she said softly, glancing now toward the doorway to the sitting room.

"What do ya mean?"

"Well, it looks to me like she's done something to make her eyes stand out." Naomi pointed to the photo, and Eva leaned closer to look. "See there?"

"I haven't the slightest idea where she would've gotten makeup," Eva said. "I never saw her wear it. And I can't figure out when she would've had this taken."

"Wait just a minute." Naomi put her hand to her mouth. "I was over at Ida Mae's the mornin' after Lily left, and Alan Yoder stopped by to deliver some biscuits from his mother. Evidently, a few weeks ago Lily asked him to take her to the mall—she was adamant that he wait for her in the parking lot."

"Wha-at?"

"*Jah*, he said Lily came out later clutching a flat paper sack."

"Maybe that was the day she had the picture taken." Eva was flummoxed. "Did ya read what's on the back?"

Naomi turned it over, and her lips moved as she read Lily's writing. "I wonder what was goin' through her mind. 'The best and worst day . . .'"

"It's awful peculiar."

"You haven't said how ya came across this." Naomi gave the photo back to her.

Eva leaned back in the chair, trying to relax—she felt too wound up. "You remember Jed Stutzman? He found it on the train comin' here."

"Well, I'll be. Must've been the same train Lily took to Ohio."

"I thought of that, but it also might've been that another traveler found it in a van or a cab and carried it onto the train. Without being able to ask Lily, how can we ever know for sure?"

Naomi reached for the settee pillow and pushed it behind her back. "We can't always know why things come our way. But we know this: 'All things work together for *gut* to them that love God, to them who are the called according to his purpose.' Remember?"

Eva was anxious to tell her more about Jed. "It was so nice of him to take me riding and walking. We had a wonderful time feeding the ducks at your pond, too. And then, before he left town, he stopped by The Sweet Tooth to see me."

Naomi was trying not to smile. "You're fond of him, and there's no doubt in my mind he likes you, Eva. Anyone who saw the two of you together would have to agree."

Eva felt confident enough now to reveal everything—how the minute Lily's picture had fallen out of his wallet, Jed's attitude had changed before her very eyes. "I can't explain it, but I know there's a link between that photograph and him seeking me out after we met by accident at the auction."

"Are ya sayin' you think he's enamored with the picture?" Naomi asked, eyes wide.

"I wondered at first, but I don't think it's that." She went on to tell Naomi about Jed's former fiancée. "It could be that he's just not ready to move on."

"Well, for pity's sake." Naomi put her hand on her chest. "Will you hear from him by letter, perhaps?"

"He said he'd write, but that was before I found out about the photo. Now I have my doubts." Eva thought of Alfred Dienner just then and told Naomi of the letter she'd received from him. "It surprised me, really."

"Why's that, my dear?"

Eva lowered her head.

"Listen here, these young fellas know a perty face when they see one." Naomi leaned forward. "And you've got a beautiful heart inside."

"Tellin' the truth, I've never been so confused." Eva poured out her angst over her uncertain future. "Menno's determined to take over the house as soon as possible, and there's really only room for one of us to stay. He seems to think—well, he *hopes*—we girls will be married by then." She sighed. "But now, with Lily gone, it just doesn't feel right to me. First Lily . . . and now Frona and I won't be able to stay together, either." She went on to tell Naomi that if things didn't work out for them to live with one of their other brothers, Frona supposed they might end up living in Berne, Indiana, with a great-aunt.

"So far away?" Naomi exclaimed.

Eva rose and went to stand next to the large window. "I'd miss ya something terrible."

"And I'd miss you, too. Yet when ya think 'bout it," Naomi said, coming over to stand beside her, "when you do marry, things will definitely change anyway—you won't be over here as often, of course."

"Even so, I don't want to rush into something with Alfred or anyone else just for the sake of stayin' put here."

"You don't have to cross that bridge yet." Naomi slipped her arm around Eva's waist. "I believe you have too many thoughts pushing round in your head for one evening, child."

Eva turned to clasp Naomi's hand. "You're prayin' for me, aren't ya? And Lily, too?"

"You know I am."

"Mamma always said prayer was ever so important."

Naomi nodded sweetly, and if Eva wasn't mistaken, there were tears in her eyes.

When Eva walked through the kitchen toward the back door, Abner was still sitting at the table, his old German *Biewel* open. His pointer finger was on the page, following the lines.

"Have yourself a restful night," he said, looking up at her.

"*Denki* for lendin' your wife's ear."

"Well, let's see once," he said, getting up to look at Naomi's ear. "Ah, it's still attached. *Des gut.*"

"I do love talkin' to her." Eva smiled at Naomi.

"Now, that's better. We like seein' our Eva smilin' again," Abner said before he returned to his reading.

"*Our Eva.*" The words were so dear and more comforting than the two of them could ever know. Best of all, Eva was grateful for Naomi's ongoing prayers for Lily . . . and for herself. *Only heaven knows what we're up against!*

CHAPTER TWENTY-FIVE

.... ✺ ....

BEFORE NAOMI AND ABNER FINISHED BREAKFAST the next morning, Lester Lantz dropped by. Abner waved him inside to join them, and Naomi greeted him, quickly excusing herself to pour Abner's brother-in-law some hot black coffee.

"Been hearin' some rumblings 'bout Omar," said Lester as he rested one elbow on the table. "Anything I might do to help?"

"Ain't sure what ya might've heard," Abner said, then went on to mention Omar's interest in voting.

"Wonder where he came up with that," Lester said. "Sure isn't like there's any leaning toward politics round here. That's the world's business."

Abner raised his coffee mug to take a sip. "'Tis the truth."

Naomi returned to the table, bringing some fresh fruit and another plate of sticky buns, which both men reached for the second she set it down. Taking a seat herself, she decided not to have anything more to eat, just slowly drink the rest of her apple juice, surprised and heartened that Sylvia's husband was this concerned for their Omar.

"We've tried to steer Omar in the right direction, but ultimately it's up to him to make his own decisions." Abner glanced at Naomi as though to cue her to say something.

"*Des gut*, really," Lester agreed. "I'll admit that I regret the way I pushed our Tilly away, when all was said and done. Honestly, if I could do it over, I'd be gentler with her." He drank some coffee; then, setting it down, he looked at first Naomi, then Abner. "I would caution you against using the same approach I did. It made Tilly even more determined to go her own way."

The room was still for a moment. Knowing Lester as she did, Naomi was glad to witness the softening in his face when he spoke of his daughter—many were the times young Tilly had sought comfort from her and Abner.

Lester continued. "Omar's mighty fortunate to have a father . . . and a mother who know how to talk to him 'bout something that other parents might take a hard line against. Some might even turn away from him, considerin' the controversy."

Naomi nodded as she listened. "We're hopin' he'll submit to the bishop's authority and consider fasting and praying 'bout his decision."

They talked further about the hardship of having Tilly and her younger sister, Ruth, out of the fold, yet wanting them to know they were welcome to visit anytime. "Sylvia and I wish the girls had made a different choice, but being they were never baptized into the church, we don't see any wisdom in shunning them. It's not going to bring them back."

Naomi voiced her agreement before going down to the cold cellar for some stewed tomatoes for the noon meal as the men settled in to talk of crops and livestock.

"I'll keep Omar in my thoughts," Lester said once he got up and made his way to their side door.

"*Denki*, means so much," Naomi said. Abner rose, as well, and walked with her out to the backyard as Lester headed to his waiting horse and carriage.

"Well, wasn't that nice?" Naomi said, wiggling her bare toes in the grass.

"He's been through more than we can imagine with Tilly and Ruth," Abner said. "A right *gut* man."

❧

Eva was pleased when Bena dropped by with two-year-old Katie Ann to provide Cousin Jeptha's mailing address for Lily's photograph. Bena hemmed and hawed, acting altogether curious to see the picture yet not coming right out to ask.

Frona's lips parted in a slight smile when Eva offered to show it to Bena, who quickly accepted.

Bena stared at it and shook her head. "I can't imagine what Lily was thinkin', can you?"

"Well, if nothin' else, this might help someone find her," Eva replied.

"Oh, an' before I forget, Menno mentioned that your brother Stephen thought you should have a copy made, in case this gets lost," Bena said, stroking Katie Ann's blond braids.

Frona spoke up from where she had returned to chopping carrots at the kitchen counter. "If it turns up missin', then so be it."

"Guess we'll take the chance and just mail it as is," Eva said, glancing at Frona, who clearly wanted to have the last say.

Bena seemed to accept that. She went to the pantry and got a box of blocks out for Katie Ann to play with. "I'm sorry I haven't been able to spend much time helping. What can I do?"

"There's always the mending," Frona grumbled, moving to the sink to wash her hands.

So Bena sat right down and helped mend for a good hour before she and little Katie Ann left for home.

"That was kind of her," Eva remarked to Frona. "'Specially when she has plenty to do at her place."

Frona smiled faintly. "I still can hardly believe she'll soon be in charge of this kitchen."

Eva went upstairs to address an envelope at her desk. She slipped the photograph carefully inside, wishing she were writing to Jed. *If he writes, what would I say?* she wondered, recalling their pleasant conversation while walking with him at the pond. But that sense of ease had come to an abrupt halt the moment Lily's photo fluttered to the candy counter.

"As open as Jed was about his fiancée and all he's suffered emotionally, why couldn't he be open with me about the picture?" she murmured, trying to suppress her feelings of missing him.

The more Eva contemplated this, the more she felt it signaled a lack of trust on his part. *Would Jed have withheld the truth from Lydiann, had she been in the same circumstance?*

Somehow, Eva doubted it.

Discouraged, she headed outdoors to mail Lily's photo. Back inside, she went to the small sewing area in the corner of the sitting room and stitched on the facing, then set in the sleeves for Frona's new dress. All the while, she prayed for Lily.

⚜

That night, after supper, Eva was determined to finish writing her letter to Alfred. She'd taken time to read through the few sentences of greeting she'd already penned, still wondering how she could be anything more than his friend. Truly, she wished she might hold on to her dream for a very special kind of love.

In light of what had happened with Jed, she wondered if it was wise to cling so tenaciously to her desire. Wasn't it time to abandon that hope and focus on her friendship with Alfred? *After all,* she thought, *he's the one pursuing me.*

Slowly, she began to write.

Honestly, Alfred, I'd feel better about all of this if we could talk directly. Letters can sometimes be confusing, so if you'd like to wait till you return this fall, that's all right with me.

Groaning inwardly, Eva hoped he wouldn't think she was impolite or putting him off. She really needed more time. Regardless of what it might mean for her immediate future, now wasn't the time to agree to court—at least not by mail. She folded her letter and placed it in the envelope, then picked up her Bible and read the first five chapters of Job before heading downstairs to hem Frona's dress.

"You really didn't have to do that," Frona said when Eva mentioned the dress was for her.

"I wanted to surprise ya, since you're feeling blue these days."

"Who's blue?" Frona looked about her comically.

"I just thought—"

"We're on pins and needles here. The whole family is." Frona sat down at the table and pressed her thick fingers into her neck. "Menno's tryin' to think of how else we can hunt for Lily."

"Well, that's why we sent the picture off to Ohio."

"*Jah,* but if nothin' comes of it, what then?" Frona's head covering drooped to one side, but she didn't seem to mind. "The bishop wants our brothers to take action—not let any grass grow under their feet. He says he'll be checking up from time to time."

Eva realized how difficult it must be for Frona to simply bide her time while they awaited word of Lily. Frona had always been somewhat in charge; Eva suddenly grasped that their parents had looked to her as a mother's helper since Frona was only eight or nine years old. *They molded her into being a fussy hen,* Eva thought. And in that moment, she wished with all of her heart she might lift the burdens poor Frona was expected to carry even now.

Admiring the newly sewn dress, even though it still needed pressing, Eva sighed—she had really hoped this gesture might go a little way toward cheering up Frona. Clearly, it would take far more than a new dress to do so.

❧

Early Saturday morning, Naomi hurried out the door to thank Abner for hitching up the horse and carriage. "You're always so helpful, dear," she said, patting his shoulder.

"It's the least I can do for ya," he said, then offered to drive her and Ida Mae down to Paradise and drop them off for the day.

"*Denki,* but I don't see us bein' there all day." Naomi laughed, adding, "Let's just say I'd rather not."

"Cousin Connie's not bothersome, is she?"

"Ain't that. But I can just imagine the grapevine's trailed down there by now, and who knows what she'll say 'bout Lily."

"Now, you can't expect the worse." Abner sounded like he was scolding.

Naomi headed for the carriage, and he helped her in. When she was seated on the right side and ready for the driving lines, she turned to him. "*Ach,* I forgot my walkin' stick."

"You gonna bop your cousin Connie to keep her in line?" Abner was chuckling as he went back into the house. A moment later, he returned and handed the stick to her. "Here ya be, my love. Now, watch yourself," he teased.

"I'll be home well before supper." She waved to him.

"Lord willin' and the creek don't rise." Abner grinned as she left.

Cousin Connie had two one-gallon jars of meadow tea brewing out on the back step when Naomi arrived with Ida Mae. Glad for her walking stick, Naomi hobbled up the stairs and was greeted warmly by Connie, whose plump cheeks were pink and moist with perspiration. "We've come to help with your sewin' projects," Naomi announced, to which Connie nodded and grinned.

After a refreshment of fruit and banana bread, Naomi and her daughter set to work, with Connie "directing traffic," as Abner might have said. Naomi smiled at the thought, glad to be sitting with the light from the window coming over her shoulder. *Best for my eyes.*

Ida Mae began to pin on the pattern for Connie's husband's new white shirt while Naomi worked on his black vest.

"Jacob will be mighty thankful," Cousin Connie told them. "He ripped his old Sunday clothes not long ago while out chasing down two of our mules after church."

"What's he been wearing to Preachin' since?" Ida Mae asked.

"*Ach*, he borrowed a shirt from his brother and is nearly swimmin' in it," Connie said, taking another sip of the tea. "And the vest he borrowed from his nephew is three sizes too small, so he has to keep it unbuttoned." She started to giggle, then covered her mouth. "Oh, if Jacob wasn't a sight last service!"

This got Ida Mae laughing, too. "Now, that's quite a picture, ain't?"

"And ya wouldn't believe how the mules escaped. Our watch dog let 'em out," Connie told them.

"Wha-at?" Naomi thought for sure she'd heard wrong.

"*Jah*, Buster jumped up and knocked the gate latch loose." Connie shook her head and laughed. "Have ya ever heard such a thing?"

"That's quite a story," Ida Mae agreed. "Dat would enjoy that one."

"Abner's had his fair share of *gut* stories, seems to me," Naomi said. "He's got a whole river of 'em, including one about the wintry day a snowbird spooked his driving horse and put the buggy into quite a spin. Round and round they went." Naomi bobbed her head. "Goodness, ain't?"

Connie's eyes widened. "Well, that *is* somethin'!"

Naomi nodded. "It would've been one rousing gathering today if Abner were here." She didn't reveal that he'd offered to bring them, and now she almost wished he had.

Later, when Naomi had finished sewing the vest seams and was hand stitching the facing, Connie said outright that she feared Lily Esch was setting a poor example for other young girls in the area.

"That story's not over yet," Naomi said softly yet firmly.

"But she's left the Plain life behind."

Ida Mae spoke up. "What Mamma means is we're all beseeching God for the outcome."

This quieted Connie down some, although it wasn't long before she brought up Jacob's encounter with Omar at the recent auction. "I'm tellin' ya, my husband got himself an earful from your Omar. He thinks it's important to vote for the next president of the United States, of all things. Makes me wonder where he's getting these ideas."

Naomi felt her face redden, and she wished Connie would calm her tongue. Ida Mae also looked embarrassed.

"You'd think Omar would listen to your head minister up there. Bishop Isaac, ain't? Such a wise man of God."

"That he is," Naomi said. "And he often preaches against the sin of gossiping."

This must have caught Connie off guard, because now *she* was red-faced. Right quick, she made an excuse that she needed to go and check on something upstairs.

"Is this what we get for comin' to help?" Ida Mae whispered.

"Now, don't fall into the same trap Connie's in."

"It's obvious she's upset with our family—and Lily Esch."

Naomi pursed her lips. "I believe she means well, I truly do." Privately, though, it was troubling that news of both Lily and Omar had traveled this far from Eden Valley—though the latter was Omar's own doing, speaking out as he had. And right then, Naomi was glad Abner had allowed her to come here on her own.

The minute the sewing's done, we'll head home.

CHAPTER TWENTY-SIX

EVA AND FRONA FINISHED WASHING WINDOWS at the schoolhouse frolic with the help of other Amish youth who were also involved with sweeping and scrubbing walls and floors, as well as doing repairs on swings and other playground equipment. The sisters had started at eight-thirty that Saturday morning as partners—Frona had practically refused to go unless Eva agreed to this. And stick together they had, scrubbing side by side until Eva's knuckles were pink and peeling.

But when it came time to break for a sack lunch, Sol Peachey came over to the two of them and sat down in a desk next to Frona, who looked so startled she practically bristled. Sol was an eligible young man from one of the Big Valley Amish communities nestled in the central Pennsylvania mountains. Eva knew he was a year younger than Frona and quite the cutup, too.

"Say, I noticed streaks on some of them windows," Sol mentioned offhandedly. "Saw 'em when I was tightening up the seesaw out yonder." He gestured in the direction of the playground, a humorous glint in his blue eyes.

211

"*Puh!* Couldn't have been the windows *I* washed," Frona said, reaching for her ham and cheese sandwich.

"Well, if you'd like, I could walk you around the building and show ya."

The brave fella wants to get her alone for a few minutes. Eva attempted to squash a smile.

Frona's eyes were wide. "And while we're at it, would ya like me to check on that seesaw you tightened?" she spouted back.

Sol's head went back with his laughter, but evidently he wasn't amused enough to stay put. Rather, he took his lunch and went over to sit near his cousins, in another aisle of desks.

Frona glanced at Eva and smiled mischievously. "That'll teach him, *jah?*" she whispered.

Sighing, Eva wondered if there was ever going to be *anyone* for Frona, for pity's sake!

Later, as they rode toward home, Eva talked of the fun she'd had seeing many of their own relatives at the frolic, as well as a few unfamiliar young men, although most of them were likely younger than Eva and Frona. *We're inching ourselves right out of the running,* Eva thought but said nothing about that to her decidedly prickly sister.

"No one breathed a word 'bout Lily's absence," Frona said as Prince turned into the driveway.

"Thankfully. 'Twas a relief."

"Well, I expected someone might." Frona shrugged and got out near the barn.

Max came running, wagging his furry white tail, begging for some attention.

Eva reached down to give him a nice hard rub around his neck. "*Gut* boy . . . glad we're home?"

She and Frona set to work unhitching the horse, quickly doing the task they'd learned as children, knowing who would accomplish what. After they had unhooked the tugs and pushed them into the *Hinnergscharr*—the harness on both sides around the back—they held the shafts and led out the horse. Eva volunteered to take their sleek black gelding to the stable, Max nipping at her heels. This was the graceful, swift horse their father had always doted upon, taking apples out to him in the stable, and sugar cubes, too.

"You want something to eat, don't ya?" She reached up and tousled Prince's shiny mane.

In the distance, she spotted the narrow path that led all the way out to a small patch of woods where Eva and Lily had, years ago, stumbled onto a tiny hut concealed by trees and brushwood. At the time, Eva had just started attending school, and Lily had followed her every step that late autumn day. Mamma had been busy with other womenfolk back at the house, making knotted comforters for a sunshine linen shower for two widows and a *Maidel* in need. The three elderly sisters shared a house up the road.

It had been Eva's idea to go exploring, and they'd followed a squirrel down the dirt trail while birds cried overhead, flashing from tree to tree.

The little wooden shack was locked that first day, but Eva managed to pry off the rickety catch and push open the door. The place was bare of furniture, too small for anything more than a table and a chair, if that . . . maybe a spot to count to one hundred while playing hide-and-seek. But Lily had insisted it was a playhouse, and it turned out she was right.

Eventually, they told Dat and Mamma about the enchanting discovery. Dat had forgotten about the cozy little place his own grandfather had built for his three young girls.

Eva recalled taking storybooks Mamma bought and pretending to be the characters, sometimes making up plays from *Little*

Women, their favorite. *It was the most fun when only Lily and I knew about it*, Eva thought.

With a flash, it occurred to Eva that Lily might feel the same way about her beau in Ohio. Now that she'd gone to pursue him and he was no longer secret, maybe it didn't seem so fun anymore. Eva dearly hoped so. *Does she miss us at all?*

"Eva!" Frona called, pulling her out of her reminiscing. "Sylvia Lantz is coming up the road, headin' this way. Are you expectin' her?"

Tilly and her family must be arriving. "I'll come right back to the house soon as I stable Prince," Eva told her.

By the time Eva was finished watering the horse and putting more feed into his trough, Sylvia was walking barefoot through the side yard, waving.

"*Wie geht's*, Sylvia?" Eva hurried her step.

Sylvia was beaming. "We'd like to invite you and Frona to come for dessert this evening. Tilly and Kris will be arrivin' in a couple more hours. Would ya like that?"

"If you're sure it won't put you out," Eva said and invited her inside for something to drink.

Sylvia shook her head, saying she had just a few things to do yet. "It's no trouble at all, and I know you'll enjoy meeting Tilly. Oh, and I'll remember to put a bug in her ear 'bout taking some time to talk with you, all right? Maybe a nice walk?"

"She might be tired from travelin'. So whatever works out is fine."

"Tilly's on the go a lot, and she'll be ready to stretch her legs." Sylvia smiled, then hurried down the driveway toward the road.

Sylvia's so thoughtful. Eva was curious to interact with the woman's *Englischer* daughter. She recalled hearing from Mamma that the former Amishwoman had been quite outgoing, and with a mind of her own even before leaving the community instead of joining church. But being thirteen years younger, Eva had never had reason to encounter Tilly one-on-one.

Eva headed into her quiet little shop and began to wipe down the counters and the empty display case. She swept the floor and got down on her hands and knees to scrub the wide planks till they gleamed.

Then she went around to the cupboard and found her favorite candy dish, a gift from Mamma on her sixteenth birthday. "The day Dat died," she whispered, carefully turning the pink bowl-like dish in her hands. She still remembered the delicious roast beef dinner Mamma had made for the noon meal that day. Dat had been smiling as he often did as he sat down to eat; then his kindly face turned solemn when he reverently bowed for the silent blessing.

If only they'd known he would not return to them alive, she would have asked him to linger long after the midnight chocolate cake was served and Lily had started up the birthday song, leading out in her pretty soprano voice. Eva would never have let him leave the house.

All was well with our family then. . . .

Gently sliding the lovely dish back into its spot, she turned and looked around her. She tried not to think of having to say good-bye to this special place when she married the man her heart yearned for, or if she was the one to go and live elsewhere. "It's in Thy hands, O Lord," she whispered into the air that usually held such an inviting aroma.

She moved to stand near the window, thankful for dear parents who had taught her and her siblings to love and revere their heavenly Father. And to trust always.

"Surely Lily hasn't forgotten so quickly. . . ."

"We prob'ly shouldn't rush the Lantzes' suppertime," Frona cautioned when she heard about Sylvia's invitation.

"*Jah*, we'll give Tilly and her family time to settle in and have a nice hot meal with Lester and Sylvia." Eva dried the plates carefully, remembering how Mamma loved to talk with them while cleaning up the kitchen, asking about their school day and what they'd learned. "Mamma really liked people, didn't she?" Eva asked, the question popping out.

"Like Lily, ya mean?"

"Well, not sure I meant that, but maybe."

"Mamm was a talker, for sure."

Eva nodded. "And Lily used to be."

"Wonder what made her change so."

Eva felt she knew, and if Frona thought more about it, she would, too. Lily had been just fifteen when their father died, and now she'd lost Mamma. And their younger sister was surely feeling pressured to join church, from Menno, especially. "Did Lily ever talk with Mamma 'bout taking baptismal instruction, do ya know?" Eva asked.

"Never heard."

Eva put away the dried dishes and tumblers. "Think what would've happened if she *had* been baptized and then ran off." She shuddered.

"Knowin' Bishop Isaac, she'd be under the temporary *Bann* already unless she came back and repented."

The shun, Eva thought. "Lily has a soft heart. Truly she does."

Frona reached for the soiled pans and slid one into the sudsy water. "But if a body's not careful, a heart can turn to stone."

"Mamma once said the Lord sometimes lets things happen to break the hardness . . . to make a heart pliable again."

Frona handed the clean pan to her to dry. "To be honest, I'm afraid to pray 'whatever it takes' for the Lord God to bring Lily home," Frona admitted.

Eva shivered again.

⟨~~⟩

On the long walk over to Lester Lantz's farm, Eva noticed a possum lying dead off to the side of the road. "I sure didn't see it on the way home earlier."

"A car must've got him," Frona said, scrunching up her face.

"Makes me wonder 'bout Lily. Do ya think she'd try driving? Not that she would be reckless."

Frona looked at her. "Driving already?"

"What'll stop her if she wants to be fancy? The longer she's gone, the more likely she'll fall into the world's grasp." Eva sighed. "I'd like to ask Tilly 'bout how long it took before she felt settled on the outside."

"I hope you're prepared to pry it out of her." Frona sounded adamant.

"Sylvia thinks Tilly will welcome my questions."

"Might depend on how nosy ya get."

Eva laughed nervously.

"I'd like someone to interview *me*," Frona said, then chortled.

"Oh, so you can say why you'll never leave the People and are very happy to just stay put here, *jah*?"

"How'd ya guess?"

They shared a laugh. Feeling relaxed with Frona for a change, since she was in such a pleasant mood, Eva decided now was as good a time as any to tell her about Jed's visit to the candy shop. "I know you're interested, so I'll just say it was Jed Stutzman who gave me Lily's photograph."

"*He* had it?" Frona's eyebrows rose suddenly. "Why?"

"He found it on the train, of all places." Eva admitted to not telling Frona this earlier because she wanted to keep mum that Jed had stopped by to see her. "Things were going so well till Lily's picture dropped out of his wallet. After that, things ended oddly between us. He seemed awfully uncomfortable."

Frona began to swing her arms. "So things with this Jed fella are kaput?"

"We didn't get to say much to each other. Bishop Isaac arrived and interrupted our conversation, so it's hard to know. Even so, I haven't heard from him since." *He hasn't bothered to write.*

Frona looked thoughtful. "Did ya load Jed up with plenty of sweets before he went?" she asked.

"I sent half a dozen Butterfinger truffles with him."

Frona clapped her hands. "Then I say there's a *gut* chance he'll come around."

Frona was doing her best to cheer Eva up, but no matter how addictive those truffles, Eva doubted she'd be seeing handsome Jed Stutzman again.

CHAPTER TWENTY-SEVEN

THE LIVESTOCK RUSTLED ABOUT, chomping on feed at the troughs as Jed helped his father sweep out the barn that evening. He worked quickly with the push broom, leaning into each long stride, thinking of Eva Esch all the while and wondering how she was doing. He recalled Perry asking yesterday if he felt ill, and Uncle Ervin mentioning that Jed hadn't been himself since returning from Lancaster County. Apparently Uncle Ervin was disappointed, because he'd meant the Pennsylvania trip for Jed's benefit.

If I could just talk to Eva, Jed thought. He'd started a letter several times but felt too embarrassed to finish. One thing was certain: He couldn't stop thinking about her. He finished sweeping and headed to the well pump to wash before making his way to the house.

Walking through the Lantzes' side yard, Eva noticed the white car parked in the drive alongside the main farmhouse where Sam and Josie lived with their children. A small black teddy bear peeked out the rear car window. *One of Tilly's children must have left it there,* Eva assumed, wanting to rescue it and carry it over to the *Dawdi Haus,* where Lester and Sylvia had moved two and a half years ago, when Sam took over the farm. "Should I?" she asked Frona, who immediately shook her head and encouraged Eva to stay focused on why they'd come.

In the kitchen, Lester and Sylvia warmly welcomed Eva and Frona and offered places at the table while Tilly's son played on the floor with wooden building blocks. In his colorful striped outfit, Baby Mel looked out of place to Eva—little Old Order boys wore black broadfall trousers and blue, green, violet, or white shirts. Even tiny Mel's golden blond hair had been cut to reveal his ears. She didn't know why, but it struck Eva as odd, and she realized she'd been hoping Tilly might have adopted something of the Plain way of dressing her children. Even Jenya and Tavani, Tilly's look-alike twin girls, seemed just like any other English children, except perhaps for their braided blond hair. The twins were taller than Eva had expected, and when Tilly's husband, Kris, came over to introduce himself, Eva saw where the girls must have gotten their genes for height. Kris was not only tall but also congenial, and Eva understood why Tilly had fallen for him.

They all sat down to enjoy some butterscotch pie, and Eva was impressed with the children's polite behavior at the table. They were as mild mannered as any Amish children she'd helped care for, including her young Esch nieces and nephews.

Tilly seemed eager to talk about the girls' interest in hand sewing, kindly including Frona and Eva in the conversation. "Jenya's making a quilted wall hanging right now—I have a snapshot of that and Tavani's embroidered pillowcases, too." Tilly went to get her purse and brought back two photos, which

were passed around amidst quite a lot of oohing and apprecia-
tive remarks. "I hope they'll be fine seamstresses one day," Tilly
added.

Both twins blushed and glanced shyly at each other, and
Sylvia's sweet face shone.

She's gotten her Tilly back, Eva thought. *But what is it like to
see her grandchildren only a few times a year?* This was so foreign
to the way of the People, whose very lives revolved around work
frolics, neighborhood gatherings, and worshiping together at
house church every other Sunday.

When all but a few crumbs of the delicious dessert had been
devoured, Frona offered to help Sylvia with the dishes, and as
if on cue, Tilly asked Kris if he'd get the stroller out, glancing at Eva. "Would ya like to walk with me?" she asked quietly
while the twins headed into the front room with their Dawdi
Lester.

"Sure," Eva said, feeling self-conscious and wondering what
Sylvia had revealed to Tilly. *I can't be shy,* Eva thought. *This might
be my only chance to talk to an Amishwoman turned* Englischer.

Frona glanced her way with a smile, and Eva hoped it was all
right to leave her and Sylvia with all the dishes. *Won't Jenya and
Tavani help dry?*

Outdoors, Tilly put little Mel into the stroller while Kris held
it steady. He kissed her cheek before heading into the house.

"It's nice of you to make time for me," Eva said right away. "I
wondered if ya might be tired after traveling."

"Actually, this is the best way for me to unwind." Tilly raised
her face to the sky briefly as they headed down the lane, past the
flower beds surrounding the birdbath. "Walking has always been
my favorite way to relax." Tilly looked about them. "Especially
back here at home . . . on a blue-sky day."

"Do ya miss Eden Valley?" Eva asked hesitantly.

"All the time."

Eva was a little surprised but glad Tilly seemed to feel comfortable telling her so.

"My mother says your younger sister has left the family," Tilly said softly.

"Seems like years already, but it's only been a couple weeks."

"This has to be hard for all of you."

Eva said it was. "Not to be snoopy, but was it during your *Rumschpringe* that you began to wonder 'bout the modern world? Was that when you first became curious?"

"There were other issues, personal ones . . . unresolved circumstances that compelled me to leave." Tilly stopped walking to check on her son, leaning down to talk gently to him in the stroller. "To be blunt, Eva, I never felt like I fit in with my family." She paused, then straightened. "Particularly with my father."

Eva chose not to reveal that it had been the exact opposite for her; she'd been exceptionally close to both her parents.

"I became bitter over time, and that led to my departure," Tilly added. "Thankfully, all of that has been talked through now."

Eva realized Tilly's reasons for leaving had to be much different than her sister's. "What are the chances of Lily changin' her mind and coming home, do ya think?"

Tilly pushed her shoulder-length hair over her shoulder. "I don't want to discourage you, but once I flipped on a light switch and experienced the other conveniences—and freedoms—of life on the outside, there was no turning back." She paused before continuing. "I eagerly embraced all of that. Even the different style of worship appealed to me. I discovered so many new opportunities . . . things I wouldn't have experienced here in Eden Valley."

Eva felt like the wind had been knocked out of her. "Quite a few here are prayin' for our Lily, though," she said softly.

Tilly nodded.

"So if the Lord God wants Lily back with the People, He'll lead her home, *jah?*"

Tilly agreed. "He can change her mind, of course. God is all powerful in every way, and we can trust Him with our hearts."

They talked more about Tilly's church, and Eva asked if she missed anything about the Amish way of worship. Tilly was surprisingly forthright, saying later that what she missed most was seeing her Amish family, including her aunt Naomi Mast. "And Uncle Abner, isn't he the most fun ever? And wise as King Solomon, too."

Eva felt a semblance of relief as the conversation changed direction. And the farther they walked, the more she enjoyed being with Tilly.

"Do you know if your sister has an English boyfriend?" Tilly asked.

"Supposedly so, but what little I know comes from her friend Fannie. But how long will the fella be interested?"

"Well, in my own experience, it's been a challenge to mesh my husband's and my backgrounds. I think it's hard enough when a couple has different church affiliations, let alone the enormous clash between the Plain and fancy ways of life. There are some pretty significant cultural differences to work through."

"I can only imagine," Eva said. "I have a few ideas of what my sister is up against."

They walked all the way down to Stoney Hill Road, then turned back onto Eden Road. The air was a bit chilly as they headed north, and Tilly stopped again to check on little Mel, saying he was "all tuckered out."

A buggy rumbled toward them from the opposite direction,

and the two young Amish fellows inside gawked as they went by, focusing especially on Tilly. Their stares weren't as pronounced as those of *Englischers* might have been had an Amishwoman been in the reverse setting. Eva couldn't help but wonder how Lily was managing out there in the world. Did she stick out like a sore thumb?

"I can't tell ya how *gut* it is to talk so openly," Eva said as the Lantz farm loomed into view.

"Hopefully it gives you a glimpse from the other side of the fence." Tilly looked at her and smiled. "Honestly, it's nearly impossible to remove the Plain life from a person's awareness. There were times I wept over my decision to leave, feeling constantly pulled back to my upbringing by strong cords. And it wasn't just missing the familiar life I'd abandoned. The Old Ways were ingrained in me, everything I'd come to know and understand. I was an odd puzzle piece in a world where my piece simply did not fit."

Yet she didn't feel like she fit in at home either, poor thing.

"For a while I leaned one way and then the other, even though I knew I'd closed the door on being Amish ever again when I married Kris." Tilly stopped pushing the stroller and turned toward Eva. "I know a number of former Amish who describe their leaving the same way. The Plain life doesn't just get under the skin; it runs deep into the soul. Being Amish isn't just what you do; it's who you are." Tilly wiped her eyes. "Lily will feel she's being ripped down the middle of her heart, wanting to live in both worlds. It could be excruciating for her."

If this proved true for Lily, Eva didn't see how her sister could stay fancy . . . unless she married her *Englischer* beau before she took time to think all of this through.

"Are *you* happy now?" Eva had to know.

"Very." Tilly said it convincingly enough. "Always remember: Embracing the Plain life is a choice."

Tilly's words played over in Eva's mind as they headed into the house, and later when Lester Lantz gave Eva and Frona a ride home after dark, following more fellowship and food. And Eva realized how unlikely it would be for Lily to return home, apart from divine help.

CHAPTER TWENTY-EIGHT

············· ❀ ·············

AS THE DAYS PROGRESSED and Lily was still missing, Eva sensed Frona was walking on eggshells, wondering when or if Menno or the bishop might come rushing over to say Lily had been found. But at the end of each day, when still no word came, both sisters prayed all the more fervently. Eva promised herself— and God—that she would never give up on Lily.

Candy sales were climbing ever higher, and Eva feared it was somehow tied to Lily's disappearance. Her loyal customers were anything but snoopy, yet nearly all offered their concern.

Ida Mae was one of them. "Lily must be markin' the days off on her calendar, figuring out a way to get home," she said with a heartwarming smile.

Others who were waiting in line overheard and glanced at each other, some nodding. One longtime English customer said she'd requested prayer for Lily at her ladies' Bible study group, and another mentioned asking for prayer for Lily at her monthly book club.

Naomi Mast was a frequent visitor, as well, although she was more focused on Frona and Eva, helping out with whatever they agreed to let her do in the house, given she had her own kitchen—and Abner—to look after.

"Word's getting out beyond Eden Valley's borders," Eva told Frona the evening of the first Saturday in June. "It's remarkable, the folks who care 'bout Lily."

"Can't believe we haven't heard a peep from my appeals to Ohio relatives," Frona said, putting a small basket with golden biscuits, nice and flaky, on the table. There was also raw honey straight from the bee-keeping neighbors up the road.

Eva tried to take what Frona said in stride. How was it possible that *none* of their Ohio cousins—and anyone they'd surely talked with by now—had heard anything about Lily?

Outdoors, the farmhands were heading for home. *If I married Alfred,* Eva thought, *I'd have a full table of workers to feed twice or more a day, like Mamma always did.* After their father died, Menno had stepped in and brought in new help. Now with Mamma gone, too, Frona only occasionally invited all of the menfolk to stay around for the noon meal—any more would have put a strain on the monthly budget. Several times a month, Bena cooked for the whole crew, since she and Menno lived only a short distance away.

Eva considered Alfred again and wondered what he'd thought of her letter. Not hearing back right away gave her some breathing room—time to ponder being courted by a man who was more like a friend than a possible mate. If it came to it, could she marry him and be content?

"Supper's ready," Frona said, and they sat down to a yellow tureen of corn chowder that had simmered all day.

Once Frona concluded the time of silent blessing, Eva chose a biscuit and waited for her sister to reach for the long ladle and dish up her own serving. The sight of Mamma's tureen brought back happy memories of days with many sets of feet under this big table, and dear Mamma dishing up Dat's bowl.

"Have ya heard anything from Jed Stutzman?" Frona said, reaching for the honey.

"I don't expect to."

"You had such a nice time while he was here. I'm really sorry for ya, sister."

Eva looked up, surprised at this from Frona, who rarely seemed so sympathetic. "Awful nice of you. *Denki.*"

Frona's cheeks reddened. "We need each other," she said softly. For a moment, Eva thought there might be a tear in her eye. "I did something today . . . something I never thought I'd do."

"Oh?"

"This morning I overheard Emmanuel talkin' with Rufus, and I spoke up," Frona admitted. "Evidently Menno had plans to knock down the playhouse out yonder, where you and Lily used to take your dollies and books."

Eva was horrified. "Why would he do that?"

"For firewood, Emmanuel said. Menno thinks the place has seen better days."

"Lily once told me she felt closest to God in that sweet little place. She could pray better there than kneeling at her bedside."

Frona grimaced. "You wanna know what I told our brothers? I interrupted and said they were *not* tearin' it down unless both you and Lily gave the say-so."

"You said that?"

"I've had it up to here." Frona tapped her forehead. "I'm beginning to feel like I might burst, all this fussin' over Lily, and no one able to find her."

"*Gut* for you, makin' a stand."

"I even went to see if Lily might have decided to hole up out there."

Eva hadn't thought of that.

"I didn't find her, of course, but I did see one of your shared books." Frona motioned to the sitting room. "I put it in there—a child's poetry book. Robert Louis Stevenson, remember?"

"Aw . . . Lily loved that book. I didn't know it was missin'."

"Maybe Bena's youngsters will enjoy it."

When they move in here and everything changes, Eva thought, looking pensively at Frona.

⟡

Naomi was out tending her flower beds and had just stood up to rest her aching back, thankful for the late-day sunshine. The first cutting of hay was at hand, and the air felt warmer. A breeze came up, cooling her brow, and with it the hush of the leaves high in the old trees that made up the northern windbreak.

She remembered being a little girl and pretending she could fly by riding on the crest of the wind, though she'd never told anyone. Not even her closest sister. Naomi wondered if Eva and Lily had ever shared those kinds of childish secrets. If so, wouldn't Lily feel like a lost soul wherever she'd taken herself off to?

The sun was sinking quickly now, and as Naomi made her way toward the house, stopping at the potting shed to put her hoe and trowel away, she noticed the bishop's horse and carriage coming up the road. Menno was riding inside with the man of God.

Oh, her heart leapt up, and she hoped this might be the good news they were all waiting for. Even though Lily had been gone for less than a month, it seemed like a long time coming.

⟡

Bishop Isaac stared at Menno as he sat across from him with Eva and her sister. "You'd think something would come of all the searching."

Eva sighed. Should she speak up . . . say what she was thinking?

Menno removed his straw hat and put it on the bench. "From what I was told, Cousin Jeptha King solicited help from a half-dozen other men and some women, too. They've gone to a good many small towns—rural, mostly—and talked to nearly all the local merchants, restaurant managers, and the like in each location, but not a soul has seen Lily or even heard of her."

"What if she's somewhere else?" the bishop asked. "Has anyone considered that?"

"Anything's possible," Menno said. "Which makes me wonder if we need to do more."

The bishop inhaled deeply. "You're not thinkin' of getting the authorities involved, are ya?"

"She can't really be classified as missing," Menno said, his eyes serious.

"*Nee* . . . since there's a note in her handwriting." Bishop Isaac glanced over at Eva. "Do you still have it?"

Eva nodded. "Would you like to see it?"

"If ya don't mind."

She was actually glad for the opportunity to leave the kitchen, tense as the atmosphere was. How was Frona managing? If she knew her sister, she would soon have coffee made and poured, and produce a plate of cookies, too.

Upstairs, Eva found the note, and while she didn't mind showing the bishop, she almost wished she hadn't offered it. Lily had written this only to Eva. "On this very desk." She ran her hand over the smooth surface—some of Dat's best handiwork.

How many times had their father sanded down this desk to make it extra smooth? She and Lily had watched him that day, years ago. Dat was perspiring and covered with sawdust from his work, yet he never would have considered stopping till the finished product was ready to be stained. She had been so delighted when he'd eventually placed it in this bedroom.

Drawing a sigh, Eva hoped the bishop wouldn't keep the note.

〜❦〜

Naomi wasn't expecting their son Omar that evening, but all the same, he walked right into her kitchen without so much as a knock on the side door. Unlike their other grown children, who knocked or rang the bell, he had never been one to do so, even once he'd left home to marry. Evidently Omar felt the most comfortable here. His light brown hair looked darker than usual tonight. *Oily from working in the fields all day,* Naomi thought, wishing he might have respected his father enough to clean up.

Abner invited him to sit at the table, where he and Naomi had been enjoying each other's company over a slice of snitz pie.

Naomi offered both men a cup of coffee, and Omar a piece of pie, which he politely declined, saying he'd already had dessert at home. Omar jokingly made a point of reminding her that he took his coffee black.

"Did ya think I'd forgotten?" she chuckled and opened the cupboard for one of her new coffee mugs.

Omar smiled as she poured him a cup before joining him on the wood bench. "I'd like to talk over my political leanings with ya, Daed."

"*Ach,* son." Naomi turned quickly, speaking out of turn.

Abner waved his hand and sent her a message with his eyes: *Let him get this out.*

Omar began again. "I know the Scripture verse from Romans the brethren like to quote: 'And be not conformed to this world . . .'"

"I read that one aloud quite a lot to you and your brothers and sisters while you were growin' up," Abner said.

Omar nodded. "That you did. And just so ya know where I stand on this, I don't believe that verse has anything to do with voting or performing jury duty, neither one."

"Jury duty?" Abner grimaced and took a slow sip of his coffee.

"*Jah*, I could be asked to serve once I'm a registered voter," Omar said, fiddling with the spoon near his coffee mug.

"Have ya talked this over with one of the ministerial brethren?" Naomi asked.

"I followed the bishop's urging and spent time fasting and prayin'," Omar said. "I really believe the Lord is directing me to vote."

Naomi was pleased to hear he had gone ahead and done this, but she was surprised, even disappointed, that he was still moving forward with registering. *We're citizens of heaven*, she thought.

Abner glanced at Naomi.

"For this election, at least," Omar continued, "I plan to vote on local ballot issues . . . and possibly in the presidential election."

Abner set down his coffee mug. "The outcome's not a'tall what I'd hoped for, but I'm glad you've taken time to consider this, Omar. It's important not to let the world direct our behavior . . . or the way we think. You've always been such an upstandin' church member."

Omar pushed his fingers through his bushy beard. "I know you and Mamm want me to be a *gut* testimony. Ya don't have to worry whatsoever. My wife and nine children are on my mind, as well as my baptismal vow."

Abner gave him a nod, and Naomi sighed.

"I'll be prayin' for ya," Naomi said gently. "Like always." She still didn't understand Omar's fascination with voting, but she was relieved that it seemed to be where his interest in the world ended. *If only the same were true for Lily Esch . . .*

CHAPTER TWENTY-NINE

PRIOR TO THE SHARED MEAL after Preaching, Jed encountered Bettina's young fiancé, Levi Hershberger, out near the stable while the courting-age men waited to be called indoors.

"My cousin Marilyn Halverston might show up ridin' with Bettina and me tonight after Singing, if you're interested," Levi said, his hands stuffed deep in his trouser pockets.

Marilyn Halverston? Jed was surprised. Marilyn was an exceptionally pretty girl, sweet spirited and soft-spoken, but her beau had gotten into some trouble, left the church, and been shunned.

"Marilyn doesn't have any expectations at all—she knows you've been through a rough patch, too," Levi continued. "It'd strictly be a favor to me and Bettina."

"A favor, you say?" Reluctantly, Jed agreed to the double date. "Just this once, though." He laughed a little. "Guess it's one way for me to keep an eye on you and my spunky sister."

Levi's eyes narrowed, and then he chuckled as he seemed to realize Jed was joking. "Tell Bettina for me, okay?"

Jed said he would. It wasn't long before *die Youngie* were called in to eat, and as Jed moved toward the house, he noticed Marilyn and three of her sisters walking together, all wearing pastel blue dresses with white organdy aprons. He caught Marilyn's eye. She gave him a demure smile before looking away.

I hope I haven't made a mistake, Jed thought.

A month ago he would have thought nothing of her innocent flirtation, but ever since his visit to Eden Valley, things were different. There was only one smile he longed to see now, and it wasn't Marilyn's.

⌑

Jed appreciated the thick shelter of trees as he and Bettina talked after the light meal that Sunday afternoon. They strolled through the well-manicured backyard, heading through the field lanes, where their father's six-mule team moved from one field to the next. Across the way, the neighbor's windmill turned slowly, creaking as the sun poured down on tall meadow grass.

"Daed talked to Levi first, then to his father," Bettina said with a glance back at the house. "He's convinced Levi is a *gut* man, Jed."

You're still too young, Jed thought, not wanting to lose his closest sister.

She poked his elbow. "So ya really don't have to worry 'bout me."

"Just sayin' it doesn't make it true." He watched the play of emotions on her face; Bettina wore her feelings on her sleeve. All the same, he was determined not to point out that just because Dat thought Levi Hershberger was a good man didn't mean she was ready to be a wife in charge of a farmhouse and, in time, a mother.

Bettina tugged on her white Sunday apron as they walked in the heat of the day. "Both Daed and Mamm are leanin' my way little by little."

"Like all parents, they want to see you happily married," he said, knowing she was thoroughly caught up in her love for Levi.

"I *am* happy! Why can't *you* be happy for me?"

They walked without speaking for a moment, and Jed picked up a brittle twig and tossed it.

Bettina folded her hands, keeping up with his pace. "Are you worried maybe because of Lydiann's passing?"

Her expression was soft and respectful. She'd loved Lydiann, too. Everyone had.

"Ain't fair for me to hold you back," he replied, "just because I've found it hard to move forward."

"Well, you are, though, whether you like it or not. Levi and I are prayin' for you."

He smiled. "Maybe it's working."

"What do ya mean?"

He hesitated. "Well . . ."

"Well?"

He plunged ahead. "If ya must know, I met a girl in Lancaster County."

"Honestly?" Bettina stopped walking, her face beaming. "What's her name?"

"Eva Esch."

"And you like her?"

He breathed deeply of the warm air. "I think so."

"You're not *sure*?"

"Well . . . she's compassionate and expressive, but not *too* chatty. She's really smart and—"

"And is she perty?"

He paused, embarrassed. "*Jah.*"

"You have to think about it?"

"*Nee.* Ain't that."

237

Her eyes were wide. "Jed, this is great news. And you know why, too."

"I s'pose it means I'm ready to let go of the past."

"So," she said, "I have to ask: Why'd you agree to double-date with Levi and me tonight? Aren't you goin' to court this Eva from afar . . . write to her?"

"I doubt she'd agree to it." He shook his head. "Things went sour between us right before I left to come home."

"Sour? What happened?"

"A misunderstanding." Jed shrugged.

"But still, if she's someone special . . ."

"*Jah,* she was."

"Was?" Bettina shook her head and turned to fall into step with him as they began walking again. "You can't just ignore this, can ya, Jed?"

He thought of the book and the photo, and of meeting Eva, who had been understandably distracted with Lily's disappearance. Even now, he recalled the look of heartache when Eva had realized the truth—when *he* had realized it—that he'd been carrying around a picture of her missing sister all along. Things had been so muddled up in his mind.

"Trust me, it's not fixable. Eva doesn't have a very high opinion of me anymore."

"Everything's fixable!" Bettina blew out a breath. "Honestly, sometimes it wonders me if some men are just *Dummkopps!*"

Jed laughed. "But you still love me, ain't?"

"You're my brother. I *have* to, according to Scripture."

"That's the only reason?"

"*Jah.*"

He folded his arms and puffed out his cheeks, and she giggled. He reached for a branch overhead and pulled off a leaf, tossing it at her.

"Seriously, Jed, is there anything I can do?"

"Prob'ly not."

"Well, you know that I'm here for ya. Besides, my prayers are like God's little arrows aimed right at your heart!"

He grinned.

"Maybe I could write to your Eva and beg her to forgive you."

Jed chuckled. "Don't you dare!"

"Well, try to have some fun tonight with us," Bettina said. "Who knows, maybe Marilyn will be the perfect match."

I had that once. . . .

Jed contemplated the evening ahead. *I can at least be friendly.*

<hr>

Jed's pent-up tension on the walk to the barn Singing dissolved as soon as he entered the upper level, where a long line of well-scrubbed young men in white shirts and black suspenders sat on one side of the long table. The young women, ages sixteen through about nineteen, sat on the opposite side, still wearing their best dresses and crisp white aprons from Preaching earlier.

He lifted his voice in unison with the other men. Catching Bettina's eye, he smiled. He envied her rosy glow—surely she looked forward to spending time with Levi, who was as polite to Jed tonight as he was admiring of Bettina.

Jed didn't dare look Marilyn's way, not wanting to make her feel self-conscious. *No pressure,* he thought while waiting for Perry's younger brother Abe to blow the pitch pipe and lead out in the next song, "Nearer My God to Thee."

<hr>

Eva hadn't planned to wander out to the old playhouse at dusk. It wasn't a place she and Lily had typically gone after daylight hours, but Eva needed some time alone. There were many thoughts in her head, and the steady chirp of crickets soothed her, as did the pretty pink still in the sky.

"Lily hasn't come home, dear Lord," she whispered, not accustomed to saying her prayers aloud. "Yet Thou art with her always. . . . I believe this with all my heart."

The truth was Lily's return home looked hopeless, apart from a miracle.

She noticed several white birch trees had been toppled by windstorms last winter. Seeing them felled made her even sadder, and she quickened her pace, carrying her father's large lantern. She had gone to check on the livestock after supper, especially the new calves. She recalled Dat's gentle way with the newborn animals. All her years growing up, she had witnessed his expert help and gentle care during difficult births for not only their cows, but also for one of their horses.

He was nurturing with us, too.

When Eva reached the little shack, she opened the door and stepped inside, having to duck now that she was all grown-up. It struck her as comical that their great-grandfather hadn't considered that his grown daughters might someday want to show their own little girls this place. No doubt they would have had to stoop just as Eva was now.

Looking around, she set down the lantern and felt the urge to sweep out the cobwebs and make the small window shiny and spotless. *In memory of Lily.*

"That's silly," she said right out. "My sister's not dead."

Just ferhoodled . . .

Eva leaned against the wall, still crouched lest her head bump the low ceiling. There was no need for tears. Even so, she was having one of those moments Dat used to talk about—when something sweet comes to mind, and you want to cherish it for as long as possible. *Till daily chores and other things push in, and you forget why your heart was so tender.*

She appreciated that her father's passing was a gift in a sense. His dying first had spared him the terrible pain of losing Mamma. *He loved her that much,* she thought. *Though poor Mamma had to bear the sting of Dat's passing.*

Moving toward the east-facing window, she slid her fingers along its frame, where she and Lily had long ago discovered a small piece of paper—a note their great-grandfather's little girls must have written and pressed into the wood frame, concealing it for posterity. Eva eyed the spot where she was sure the note had always been. The last time she and Lily played there, Lily had pulled it out and waved it around, chanting the quote from *Little Women: "Take some books and read; that's an immense help, and books are always good company if you have the right sort."*

Wondering if the note had fallen, perhaps, Eva brought the lantern closer and searched around the floor near the window, then carried it all around the small square of a room, bending low to look.

But the note seemed to be gone.

"At least I have my memories of it," Eva whispered, blue that the age-old paper was missing.

⚬⚬⚬

After the actual Singing, couples began to pair up—some were prearranged double dates, like Jed and Marilyn with Levi and Bettina, while others were known courting couples. The youth in their church district were not as secretive about their dating partners as were other districts in both Ohio and Pennsylvania. *A wise thing,* Jed thought, especially because it had given his parents the opportunity to discuss things sensibly with Bettina, airing their concerns about her marrying so young.

"Are ya comfortable?" he asked Marilyn as they got settled in the second bench seat, behind Levi and Bettina in the enclosed surrey. The details of the carriage interior weren't clear in the starlight, and Jed wondered who'd built it, then chastised himself for not paying attention to his date. *"Once a buggy maker, always a buggy maker,"* Uncle Ervin often said.

"It's a nice night for ridin'," Marilyn commented as she put on her black outer bonnet. Levi had mentioned there were several warm blankets in the back if they got chilly.

Levi and Bettina visited quietly up front, and Jed wished Bettina would turn around and address either him or Marilyn. But for the moment, her sister and fiancé were too caught up in each other.

"Which schoolhouse did you attend?" he asked Marilyn to break the ice.

She described the location, a few blocks north of the railroad tracks, evidently not realizing that had been the scene of Lydiann's fatal accident. It was all Jed could do not to visibly wince.

"You must've gone to the school close to your father's house," Marilyn said.

He told her where and quickly changed the subject, asking now if she was busy with the family garden, which got her talking about the many types of vegetables she and her sister had planted.

"We're out waterin' by hand a lot since we haven't gotten as much rain as usual for June."

"Not as *gut* as water from the sky."

"*Nee* . . . and hand carryin' water isn't the best use of my time, either. Though I'm not complainin', really."

A cloud passed over the moon, and suddenly the buggy was cloaked in shadows. He remembered taking Eva in Jonas Byler's carriage and feeling frustrated because he couldn't see her face in the darkness.

Marilyn continued to talk about her day, and Jed could detect his sister's soft giggles in front of him, but his mind was hundreds of miles away.

He had told Eva he would write but hadn't. The truth was, while he doubted she'd want to hear from him, he *was* curious if Lily had returned home, or if they'd gotten word of her whereabouts. Jed regretted again his final visit in Eva's beloved candy shop.

"It won't be mine much longer," she'd told him while showing him the shop, her eyes glistening with sadness, as if her whole purpose was about to be taken from her.

"Jed?"

He jerked to attention. Marilyn was talking to him, and he hadn't heard a word.

"Sorry?"

She smiled and repeated it. "What's your favorite ice cream?"

"Chocolate."

"Mine too," she replied. "And I say dark chocolate's best."

"Well, it's certainly much richer tasting than milk chocolate."

"For sure." She added that she also liked to make chocolate chip ice cream and chocolate-covered cherries. "And have you ever eaten chocolate bread custard?"

"Did I hear something 'bout chocolate back there?" Levi asked, turning his head toward them.

"It's chocolate everything," Marilyn answered, laughing softly.

"Since we're talkin' food, are we ready for sundaes?"

"Whenever you're hungry," Jed said, ready for a break from the confines of the buggy. *I shouldn't even be here. . . .*

Levi directed the horse to a trot, and as they drew closer to the ice cream shop, Jed knew without a doubt he must try to get in touch with Eva. And as far as he could see, there was only one way she might be willing to give him another chance. *Only one.*

CHAPTER THIRTY

························· ✿ ·························

THAT TUESDAY, EVA ironed all the pillowcases and top sheets, too, like Mamma had always done. Eva mentioned to Frona that she had gone out to the old playhouse to reminisce on Sunday evening. "I think maybe we're both tryin' to hang on to what's left of Lily," Eva said.

Frona looked up from her embroidery, eyes soft. "Sometimes I do that with Mamma." She sighed and laid the hoop on the table. "After the washing was out on the line yesterday, I went into the big bedroom while you were sellin' candy next door. I felt downright blue, so I headed upstairs and opened the door to our parents' bedroom and just stood there."

"I haven't looked in there for months."

"Prob'ly *schmaert*, really."

Eva folded the pillowcases on the warm ironing board. "I'd actually thought you should move in up there and make that room your own, but that was before Menno told us his plans."

"I'd feel out of place havin' Mamm and Dat's room."

"Well, since you're the oldest of us girls," Eva replied.

Frona's face broke into a sweet smile. "Awful nice of you."

Eva had noticed that Frona seemed different lately. Gentler, in some ways; less abrupt, too. It was such a lovely change, she wanted to go over and throw her arms around her, the way Lily used to do with Eva, but she didn't want to upset the fruit basket and scare Frona back into her grouchy shell.

When she'd put away the ironing, Eva walked out to the barnyard and groomed Prince, taking her time with him. She slipped him a sugar cube when she was done, then strolled out to the road to check the mail, breathing in the familiar farm smells. Across the road, back near his stable, Abner Mast took off his straw hat and waved it at her.

The day's as perfect a June day as they come, she thought, opening the mailbox. There, along with three circle letters for Frona, and one for her, was a thick envelope from Alfred Dienner.

She drew a quick breath and held the letter tentatively, like a soiled dishrag. Just then, a middle-aged *Englischer* came riding down the road on his bicycle, nodding as he passed. She'd never seen him around the area before and guessed he must be fit enough to pedal quite a long way. What must it feel like to ride so fast and free? She tried to imagine it as she watched the man disappear from view.

Turning toward the house, Eva decided to read Alfred's letter right away, instead of waiting till after chores were done. This way she could mull over whatever was on his mind.

⚬⚬⚬

The early robin's robust song had awakened Naomi around four o'clock that morning, making it difficult to return to sleep.

Thankfully, she'd felt reenergized after two cups of coffee and a hearty breakfast—three eggs for Abner and two for her, plus a half grapefruit each, and a generous portion of scrapple.

Omar had stopped in an hour or so later before going to work with Abner, telling them that he'd registered to vote. Why, oh why, couldn't Omar just settle down like the rest of their grown children?

Is this how Dottie Esch felt about Lily? she wondered.

Abner came inside looking for something to nibble on, hungry again. "Eva was out getting her mail just now," he said, making small talk. "She didn't seem her usual cheerful self."

"Well, no wonder," Naomi said. "They still haven't heard from Lily." She sliced two thick pieces of homemade wheat bread and slapped a good amount of peanut butter and strawberry jam on it to make a sandwich. "Maybe this will stick to your ribs till the noon meal."

"What'll it be today, love?"

She smiled. "Aren't you the bottomless pit?"

"Must seem like it to you." He grinned. "But I'm mighty blessed to be married to such a *gut* cook."

Naomi eyed his snack, nearly devoured already. "Want another?"

"Better not. I have to start liftin' hay bales with Omar and Elam right quick."

"Well, ain't you somethin'," she teased, waving him back out to the barn.

⟨⁓⁓⟩

Eva ran her thumbnail along the edge of Alfred's envelope. She'd excused herself to the barn, to Dat's former office, where Menno had set up file cabinets and altered the place to suit his needs. She closed the door and settled into the swivel desk chair.

Bracing herself, she began to read and quickly noticed that most of Alfred's letter was comprised of his daily schedule at the woodworking shop and of learning to use various saws and other

247

hydraulic tools. He'd also mentioned finding a candy store, but it didn't have offerings nearly as delectable as Eva's candies. *And I sampled quite a few,* he'd written.

In the final paragraph, he said he wanted to call her a week from today. *Will you be able to get away to the phone shanty at three o'clock in the afternoon?*

Eva knew talking had always been easier for him than writing. He'd admitted this some time ago, when he went with his family on vacation and hadn't bothered to send her even a postcard. She sighed. If he was more comfortable by phone, then so be it.

Eva had to decide how to reply; if she didn't hurry and do so, he'd have to postpone his anticipated phone call. Yet if she *did* agree, what would he say to her?

"What should my answer be, O Lord?"

She glanced at Tuesday, June 17, on the large farm seed calendar on the wall and found herself wishing Jed Stutzman had written instead.

CHAPTER THIRTY-ONE

EVA HURRIED OUT TO THE STRAWBERRY PATCH to help Frona pick the fresh crop, enjoying the warm day. There seemed to be less humidity than yesterday, and the birds were chirping merrily, competing with Max, who was barking as he raced through the meadow with the pony.

"I wonder what Lily's doin' today," Eva said, setting her large tin bucket down on the dirt near her bare feet.

Frona looked over at her, her blue bandanna keeping her hair bun secure. "Whatever she's doin' certainly doesn't include us."

"I'm sure she misses us as much as we miss her, though."

Frona moved to the next plant and stopped to get out a hankie to wipe her forehead. "I seriously doubt that."

Frona's old mood had made a reappearance, and Eva didn't think now was the time to share Alfred's request to call. Sure as the sunrise, when next Tuesday afternoon came, she'd have to explain why she was leaving to head across the field.

"*Gut* thing we're out here before the birds decided to make a *Fescht* of the strawberries," Frona said, then muttered something about nasty creatures.

When her pail was close to overflowing, Eva carried it to the house, careful not to spill a single berry. She drew some cold water and gently took handfuls of the bright red fruit and placed them in the sink, washing each one carefully before cutting out the stem.

By the time Frona came inside with her full pail, Eva was ready for that batch. They planned to make jam right away to lock in the freshness.

Later, as they were washing canning jars, Bena and little Katie Ann arrived with a casserole dish of tuna and noodles. Then, not ten minutes later, Naomi showed up with some pulled pork and scalloped potatoes.

"Well, isn't this somethin'?" said Frona, who thanked both women and invited them to stay for cold meadow tea.

"I thought you'd enjoy not having to cook with all those straw-berries comin' on fast," Bena said, setting Katie Ann on her lap at the table. "But I had no idea Naomi was thinkin' the selfsame way."

This brought a round of laughter.

"It does get busy round here," Eva said, realizing how much Lily had helped in the past. She took babbling Katie Ann from Bena and walked straight to the cookie jar to let Katie nibble on a treat.

"Not too many," Bena warned, looking like she could use a few minutes to sit and rest.

"*Ach*, we got caught," Eva whispered to her tiny niece. "Better just eat half, all right?"

Little Katie Ann frowned her disapproval, and Eva knew she was in a pickle, so she brought her niece back to Bena, who broke the cookie in half. The tot accepted the smaller portion and leaned her head on Eva's shoulder.

"She's such a dear," Eva said.

"What do ya expect? You offered her a sweet," Bena teased.

Eva asked Naomi, "Would ya like some more cold tea?"

"*Ach*, maybe so." Naomi fanned herself with the hem of her apron.

Eva gave Katie Ann back to her mother. "I'll pour some milk for her," Eva said, going to the fridge.

"As you can see, we're about to put up some strawberry jam," Frona was saying while Eva poured the milk. "Can hardly keep up with that berry patch!"

Bena mentioned they were trying to eat at least some of their fresh pickings. "We've plenty of little mouths to feed."

Katie Ann babbled in *Deitsch*, telling Bena she was ready for the other half of her cookie, and they all laughed about it.

"Sounds like she's got herself a mighty sweet tooth," Naomi said.

"Like her Mamma," Bena said, squeezing Katie Ann. "Ain't so, *Bobbli?*"

Katie Ann reached up a chubby hand, and Bena kissed it.

They talked of other things—an upcoming work frolic at the deacon's house, and another auction, too, this one a farm sale.

After a while, Bena said, as though she had been waiting for the right moment, "I have some news. Menno received another letter from Cousin Jeptha."

Eva swung around, all ears.

"He's heard rumors 'bout a runaway Amish teenager livin' somewhere outside of Kidron," Bena told them. "We're still lookin' into it. Not much to go on, really."

Eva took a seat next to Naomi. "*Jah*, not very reliable at all. But hopeful."

Bena nodded. "Jeptha assured Menno he's keepin' his eyes and ears open." She held the milk glass up to her little daughter's mouth, and Katie Ann put her dimpled hands on top of Bena's.

"Makes ya wonder how many *Youngie* run off lookin' for greener pastures," Frona said.

Or pastures that aren't so green, Eva thought.

Naomi's eyes welled up. "Perhaps this is the beginning of the miracle we've all been hopin' for."

Eva stared at Bena, not sure what to make of this news. Oh, she hoped Naomi was right.

⁕

It was unbearably warm and sticky in the buggy shop; the battery-powered fans hardly made a dent in the oppressiveness. Jed had been working all morning on the wooden dashboard for the two-seater surrey he was constructing.

His mind was occupied with several futile attempts to explore various leads about Lily Esch via the Amish grapevine, which could sometimes be so undependable. And he'd also placed phone calls from the carriage shop to Mennonite churches in the area, as well as to relatives. He even found the number for a halfway house for Amish runaways in Sugarcreek, and planned to call there, too.

Wouldn't someone, somewhere, have heard of a former Amish girl trying to go fancy? Perhaps one of the many scribes for The Budget *might write about it this coming week.* The thought spurred him on.

Needing something cold to drink, Jed walked the length of the shop to Uncle Ervin's office area, where there was a small refrigerator with chilled drinks. He reached for an orange soda and saw his uncle heading this way. "Say, I'm glad I caught ya." Jed stepped aside at the doorway.

"Something on your mind?"

Jed waited for him to lower himself into his comfortable chair near the handcrafted credenza. "I've been thinkin' a lot about joining church come September."

"Well, I'll be turkey feathers," his uncle declared, crossing his arms. "That-a boy. Mighty glad to hear it."

Jed smiled and nodded. "Ain't something I wanted to rush into, considering everything."

"You're wise to take your time—to know for certain this is the life you want. The baptismal vow is the most serious promise you'll ever make."

To God and to the church. "Later this summer, I'll begin my instruction with the deacon."

Uncle Ervin leaned back, his gnarled hands gripping the arms of the chair, and closed his eyes. He was silent for some time; then suddenly his eyelids fluttered open. "Such *gut* news . . . truly 'tis."

Due to the high humidity, the office room seemed cramped with the two of them, despite its being a decent-sized space. Jed took another long swig of his soda and said, "I'll get back to work now."

Uncle Ervin eyed him solemnly before Jed turned to exit. Over in Perry's work area, Jed strode past the partially built buggy and nodded cordially, then made his way to his own space.

As he worked, Jed recalled the latter part of his date with Marilyn Halverston. In all truth, Marilyn was just as pleasant as he'd expected, and things might have gone differently had Eva not been so heavily on his mind. He had felt so distracted that he wondered why he'd ever agreed to Levi's suggestion to double-date. Of course, the sundaes had been exceptionally tasty, given there were more than a dozen choices of toppings—various sliced nuts, miniature marshmallows, and chopped hard candies. Jed had chosen chocolate crumbles and walnut pieces, and Bettina had giggled as she pointed out the instability of the high mound atop his double dips, insisting it was all going to come rolling off.

Later that night, after returning home, he'd wandered out to the large pond overlooking the old ice house on his father's land, juggling his conflicted thoughts. He relived the long Sunday walk with Eva, when they'd fed the ducks. *When I held her hand . . .*

One thing was readily apparent: Not once since leaving Lancaster County had Jed longed for Lydiann, the woman he'd mourned a full year.

CHAPTER THIRTY-TWO

.... ✿ ....

EVA WORKED SIDE BY SIDE with Frona at Thursday market, where they'd put out dozens of pint jars of strawberry jam for sale, along with a selection of nut brittles, almond bark, and other candy—taffy, caramels, and toffee. She had written the labels with her best printing, something Lily had always enjoyed doing for Mamma, and then Frona. Presently, Eva cordially engaged their customers, all the while holding her breath for Cousin Jeptha's contact to discover more so that a trail might begin to open and lead them to Lily. This was Eva's constant hope and prayer. Since hearing from Bena two days ago, she had awakened in the night several times after dreaming about her sister.

Jed Stutzman had also shown up in one of her dreams. It was strangely vivid, and Jed and Lily had been walking through a large milking parlor in an Amish barn, smiling as they strolled along. Eva had awakened with a start, feeling dreadfully annoyed, as if they'd both abandoned their affections for her. *How odd*, thought Eva, wondering how her longing for Jed had become tangled up in thoughts of Lily.

255

Later, when there were fewer customers gathered about their table, Eva walked to the fudge display where Jed had purchased her surprise gift. She stared down at the colorful wrappings and remembered how her heart had fluttered at the sight of the box.

Jed felt something for me, she soothed herself.

"Can I help ya make your choice?" asked the clerk.

"Just lookin'."

"*Ach,* well, lookin's not tasting."

"Believe me, I know." She moved along the display case and admired how these candies were arranged, thinking of her own display.

She remembered again the last time she'd seen Jed. The tour she'd given him of her shop, his eyes so earnest, his smile infectious. "I'll have one of those," she said suddenly, pointing to the same type of fudge Jed had given her.

To relive that happy memory, she told herself as she reached for her purse.

⚜

It was Frona who noticed the flag down on the mailbox when they neared the turnoff to their driveway. "Looks like the mail's come."

"Are you expecting something?" Eva asked.

Frona shook her head and guided the horse to make the right-hand turn. "We're all caught up on circle letters, ain't?"

Eva said she was. "Your idea to spread the word to our Ohio cousins might be partly why Cousin Jeptha found out what he did. Have ya thought of that?"

"Like you, I'm leavin' it up to the Good Lord. Worryin' causes me an upset stomach anymore."

Frona said it so seriously, Eva's heart went out to her. "Aw, sister."

Then, halting Prince, Frona suggested Eva go and check the mail while Frona started to unhitch.

Eva hurried to the mailbox, since Frona could certainly use her help. It was no easy chore unhitching alone, and besides, it was beginning to rain.

She looked over at Masts' to see if either Abner or Naomi was in view. Abner was surely around someplace, given the work dairymen were required to do—sterilizing the milk house equipment, including scrubbing the bulk tank, and cleaning out the barn. All of it needed to pass muster with the milk inspector.

Eva opened the mailbox and pulled out a single letter with her name on the envelope. "Lily's handwriting," she whispered.

"Oh, praise be!" she said again and again, running now up the long driveway toward Frona, clutching the letter to her chest to protect it from what was now a downpour. "It's from Lily! Oh, Frona . . ."

Frona brightened but stated, "First things first," blinking through the deluge. The horse was still half in and half out of the harness and needed to be stabled and rubbed down and watered. Both girls were getting drenched as Eva returned from quickly putting the letter in the house for safekeeping.

Eva worked as fast and as efficiently as she could. With Frona's good help, they finally finished—the longest and soggiest twenty-five minutes ever.

Once Prince was settled in his stall and Dat's fine carriage was parked, Eva scurried into the house and washed her hands, waiting for Frona to do the same. "I'm soaked clear through to the skin," she said, shivering.

They took time to change into dry clothes before sitting down at the table. There, Eva opened Lily's letter with trembling hands and began to read aloud.

"June 9

Dear Frona and Eva,

If I know you, you're probably both very concerned about me.

But happily, I am safe and staying with a large family who runs a dairy farm, helping out as I can to earn my room and board. In my free time, I often get to see my boyfriend—an *Englischer.* He's one of the reasons I came here to live, and oh, it's been wonderful to have so much time with him!

I should have told you what I was planning, except I feared you'd try to stop me. It was wrong, and I pray you forgive me.

It's taking some real courage to be accepted by English folks, but I'm doing my best, and you mustn't worry about me. Promise?

I love you, sisters . . . and my whole family back there in Eden Valley.

Yours always,
Lily Esch"

"She sounds quite settled," Frona said, eyes misting. "Is there a return address?"

Eva showed her the front of the envelope. "The postmark is Wooster, for goodness' sake!"

"You don't see dairy farms in cities, so is she really where she says?"

Eva scanned the letter once more. "It's odd. I mean, if Lily was gonna write and tell us she's safe and happy, then why not reveal exactly where she is? I don't understand."

"She sounds too happy 'bout her beau, if ya ask me."

Eva nodded. "I hope she doesn't forget us."

Frona slipped her arm around Eva, and they sat that way for a moment, the letter before them.

At last they rose, and Frona laid out their money on the table and began to count it quietly. Eva set to work making a light supper, since they'd snacked here and there at market, what with the many vendors offering free samples.

Lily's letter stirred up a feeling of helplessness in Eva that she found hard to endure. How could she feel good knowing Lily was struggling? *"It's taking some real courage to be accepted."*

According to what she'd written, Lily might actually be living with Plain folks, Eva thought, considering the reference to a dairy farm. This was heartening, but it didn't line up with what Fannie had told them about Lily's plan to stay with her boyfriend's married sister.

Eva set to work chopping cabbage for slaw.

Frona looked up. "Still thinking 'bout Lily's letter?"

Eva admitted she was and set the knife down on the cutting board. "She's not interested in being found, is she?"

Frona shook her head. "She's made that clear."

Hearing Frona's opinion out in the open like that made it seem all the more certain.

During evening Bible reading and prayers, Eva sat quietly, respectfully, noting Lily's regular spot. Eva's emotions were emerging in a new way, and while on one hand she sensed a burden roll from her shoulders in relief at finally hearing something, she was equally troubled—even angry—over Lily's apparent apathy toward her and Frona. *And everyone else in our family, too.* Eva had expected more from the sister she'd known her whole life.

Is this what happens—the world changes who you are?

Her talk with Tilly had addressed numerous things but nothing like this, and Eva hardly knew what to make of Lily's letter as a whole. Still, she refused to doubt there was hope Lily might find her wits and come home.

259

CHAPTER THIRTY-THREE

THE NEXT FEW DAYS were dreary with rain, the thunder waking Eva in the night, then the steady downpour on the roof lulling her back to sleep.

Each morning, when Menno and Emmanuel came into the utility room to fill their thermoses with cold water at the sink, they seemed thankful to be in out of the rain, even taking a few minutes to visit with Frona and Eva. Emmanuel, especially, was interested in sampling Eva's new concoctions for The Sweet Tooth, more than happy to taste test.

Once the worst of the heavy rains had passed, Eva inspected the flower beds and saw that the delicate petunias had been beaten to the ground, and there were deep ruts in the soil of the vegetable garden.

At the designated time for Alfred's phone call Tuesday afternoon, Eva was pleased when Frona left the house for Ida Mae's to help make strawberry pies for several families, including the two preachers'. *She'll be gone long enough for me to talk to Alfred and return home*, Eva thought, calling for Max as she hurried across the backyard.

The grass was soggy, and she was glad they'd kept Mamma's old work boots so she could tromp through the meadow. Max kept running circles around her, looping forward, then back—the finest dog ever, and most companionable, too.

Glancing over her shoulder, Eva could see Menno and the other workers moving from the stable to the barn, where grain and hay were stored. She realized then how peculiar it would be to experience whatever adjustments might come once Menno and Bena moved in. *For whoever ends up staying on here as a mother's helper.*

Naomi Mast had once said that change was inevitable. *"It's one of the things you can always count on,"* she'd said. The observation had made Eva think.

She crossed a rise covered with wet maidenhair ferns; these volunteers had taken over the place since Dat's passing. Their roots were solidly placed, and unless they were mowed down or intentionally dug up, they were there to stay.

Transplants, like Lily? Oh, I hope not.

The old wooden telephone shed came into view, but because the preachers had deliberately placed it in the middle of a stand of fast-growing silver maples, a person had to know where it was positioned in order to find it.

Moving down the muddy path that led to the narrow shanty, Eva breathed in the thick scent of damp earth and bark. The meadow grass looked taller and deeper in hue because of recent rains.

Eva checked her wristwatch. *Six minutes before Alfred's call.*

For as long as she'd known him, Alfred had been prompt and a person of his word. But what he wanted to discuss today, she couldn't be sure, and she curled her toes in her Mamma's boots, shaky as a newborn calf.

Eva remained just outside the door of the phone shed. She

disliked standing inside, too aware of the cobwebs she often bat-
ted down with her hand in an attempt to dismantle any evidence
of spiders—her least favorite insect in God's collection of bugs.

The last time Eva had come here was cloaked with sadness,
for it was the day she'd run headlong through the deep snow to
dial 9-1-1. Mamma was near death's door, and the ambulance had
arrived too late for the paramedics to revive her.

Max wagged his tail and panted as he looked up at Eva. A
butterfly caught his attention, and he turned and bolted after it.
Saturday is Naomi's surprise birthday party, Eva thought, looking
forward to making a pretty card to take to Ida Mae's when the
rest of the womenfolk arrived after noon with cake and ice cream.
We'll have us a nice time. . . .

The phone rang loudly, and she stepped inside the shed.
"Hullo?" she answered, suddenly feeling bashful.

"Eva, it's Alfred. *Wie bischt?*"

"Fine . . . and you?" Truthfully, she wasn't feeling altogether
fine just then. He sounded different to her, or maybe it was the
long-distance connection.

"I've been looking forward to callin'," Alfred said, then went
on to mention the weather, one of his favorite topics. "Heard it's
been raining quite a lot there."

"The fields are like sponges."

He laughed a little. "Hope ya wore your boots."

She told him she had. "Is it nice out there?"

"Not too hot, which is always helpful when you're workin'
inside a woodshop."

She let him talk about his work, noting his obvious enthusiasm.

"The more I learn, the more I believe I'm cut out for woodworking."

She smiled at the clever quip and wondered if he was aware
of what he'd said.

"I really enjoy handling different types of woods and such, Eva—each job brings something new. It's far more creative than farming, of course. Less reliant on the elements, too."

This was a surprise. Never had she expected to hear Alfred say a word against farming.

"There's plenty to learn, of course, but it seems I've got a knack for it, or so my boss tells me."

"I'm happy for ya," she said.

"But that's not the only reason I called. I have a terrific idea, and I hope you'll agree."

She listened, unsure what was on his mind.

"You might have noticed I've written about the young people here and some of the places I enjoy. The countryside is beautiful, too. It's a growing area for *gut* reason."

Where's he going with this? Eva wondered.

"It's happened awful fast, but I've been offered a job as a shop assistant. I'll continue to learn the trade as I go, like an apprentice, but with decent pay." He stopped for a second. "Enough for me to settle here."

Alfred's not coming back?

He went on. "So I got to thinkin', instead of waiting till we marry, I'd like for you to come here for our courtship."

She was stunned.

"What would ya think of that, Eva? I've already found a nice place for you to stay."

Well, she didn't think much of it at all. No, she could just envision poor Frona living all alone, bouncing around in their parents' large house until Menno and his family moved in. Or maybe he'd move in all the sooner, Eva didn't know.

"This is so sudden," she said. "I hardly know what to say."

"I miss seein' you, Eva. It'd be *wunnerbaar-gut* to have ya out here with me."

How could she say she'd think about it when she just wanted to hang up the phone?

"*Ach*, Alfred, I didn't envision our courtship progressing quite this fast . . . 'specially with Lily gone an' all." Feeling cornered, she wanted to still her racing heart.

"*Jah*, I wondered how you were holding up when Mamm said there'd been no news."

Eva nodded into the phone. "It's one of the worst things to happen to my family."

"I wish I could comfort you in person, Eva," he said softly. Then, going on, he said, "I could easily arrange for you to be here within a few weeks."

She considered his remarkable offer, but things were moving much too quickly. "If you're willing to wait, Alfred, I'd like to think about it. And meanwhile, we could discuss this further by mail, all right?"

"I'll wait, *jah*." His voice brightened considerably. "I'll be glad to."

After they said good-bye and hung up, she walked back over the waterlogged pasture toward home. "'Tis unbelievable," she whispered.

Their spitz sprinted up behind her, then slowed to walk along-side. "I'd miss *you*, dear Max," she said, running her hand across the length of his white back. "And everyone here in Eden Valley." Just then Eva realized how happy she might be feeling about such an unusual proposal if it were coming from Jed.

But that door appears to be closed, she thought regretfully.

During a short break that afternoon, Jed slipped away to Uncle Ervin's office area to use the phone. Searching the yellow pages, he found the number for the Ohio Chamber of Commerce.

Immediately, Jed was encouraged when he spoke with a woman

who seemed eager to help. "I live here in Ohio," he explained, "but I'd like to request a listing for tourist accommodations in Plain communities." He told her that he'd heard there was such a list, which included Mennonite and Amish guest housing.

"I can mail it to you, sir." The woman asked for his name and address.

Jed gave her the information, then thanked her and said goodbye, his spirits rising.

CHAPTER THIRTY-FOUR

FRIDAYS WERE TYPICALLY FRENZIED at the carriage shop, and this one was no different as Jed worked on his assigned surrey. He and Perry had to have their six-day workweek wrapped up before the Lord's Day—from the earliest time of their apprenticeship, Uncle Ervin had nudged them to be as productive as possible.

Jed was meticulous while finishing the flooring of the large family carriage. All the while, he could hear Uncle Ervin making small talk with Perry, who was building a two-wheeled cart, the simplest type of buggy.

Perry was describing a recent visit to Charm, where he'd run into some old school chums, one of whom was leaving the Amish life behind. Uncle Ervin wagged his head at that, then said something that caught Jed's attention.

"Speaking of Amish going to the world, I ran into a farmer friend, Abram Kurtz, who grew up in Lancaster County but now lives in Kidron," Uncle Ervin was saying. "Abram was in line at Lehman's Hardware behind an *Englischer* girl, who was all dolled up in earrings and makeup, short skirt, fancy hairdo, but—get this—she had an Amish accent a mile wide and kept mixin' up her Dutch with English."

"Not fancy a'tall, I'm thinkin'," Perry interjected. "You can take the girl out of the Amish, but you can't take the *Amish* out of the girl!"

Ervin nodded. "Abram was convinced she wasn't from anywhere in Ohio!"

"Why's that?"

"He could tell by her accent she was from his old stompin' grounds back in Pennsylvania."

Jed turned to get a better listen, very curious.

Perry slapped his knee, fully engaged, and Ervin kept going. "So Abram decided to have some fun with her and said right out loud, 'What part of Lancaster County are you from?'"

Ervin continued his story. "Well, I guess the young woman turned as white as a sheet in the wind. And Abram took it even further and said he had some friends who lived south of Strasburg—asked if she knew 'em."

Perry howled with laughter.

"Her mouth dropped, and right quick, he offered a handshake and introduced himself all proper-like. She played along, it seemed, told her name, but it wasn't *Amish*, let me tell you. Then suddenly, she excused herself like she'd forgotten something, and rushed out of the store, leaving her things behind."

Perry shook his head. "Guess it ain't funny after all."

Ervin agreed. "If ya leave the People, son, you'll spend the rest of your life pretending to be what you're not."

Perry nodded and glanced at Jed.

Unable to keep quiet any longer, Jed asked, "So, what was the young woman's name?"

Ervin thought for a moment. "Well now, I don't recall." He was frowning, apparently still trying to remember. "Wait a minute. *Jah*, I believe 'twas something like . . . Lillian."

Perry harrumphed and stepped back to use the level on the buggy box he was constructing. "Doesn't sound very Amish, does it?"

Ervin agreed. "But the Pennsylvania Amish do use some different first names than round here."

Lillian? An Amish girl from Lancaster County?

"What're the chances?" Jed murmured, going over to Perry's fine-looking two-wheeler. He commented on the well-built base, hoping his uncle might say more about the conversation with his friend. Finally Jed asked, "So this was at Lehman's Hardware, ya say?"

Ervin gave him a quizzical look. "*Jah*, in Kidron."

"Small town," Jed added casually.

"Sure is," Ervin said.

Too small to hide in, Jed thought. A sudden idea presented itself, and Jed knew right where he was going to be tomorrow—if he could work fast enough. *And if I can hire a driver, too.*

❦

After supper that evening, while his father and the neighboring farmer were nailing together beehive frames, Jed offered to help Bettina groom the horses. The stable smelled of fresh bedding straw, and he drank in the scent—he missed some aspects of daily farm life after spending nearly all of his daylight hours at the carriage shop.

"I need to pick your brain," he told his sister with a glance over the horse's mane.

"Sounds painful." She smirked in the horse stall next to Jed.

"I'm serious."

"What's on your mind?" she asked, grooming brush in hand.

"It might sound peculiar, but let's say you decided to go fancy and wanted to hide from your family in the outside world—"

"What on earth?" Bettina blinked, her eyebrows rising. "Somethin' you're not telling me, Jed?"

He shook his head. "It's not about me, *Simbel*—silly."

"Who, then?"

"Just put your thinkin' cap on for a minute and help me out."

"Well, I wouldn't dress Plain, that's for sure."

Obviously, Jed thought. "So how would I spot you if you looked like every other *Englischer*?"

"Oh, I see." Bettina stopped her brushing and placed her hand on the chestnut mare. "You must be lookin' for a girl who's gone a little overboard. She wouldn't have a very *gut* fashion sense—for an *Englischer*, that is. She'd look fancy but a little off."

"How do ya mean?"

"If it was me, I'd be the one trying too hard to fit in. First, I'd cut my hair real short and maybe color it, too." Bettina touched her auburn hair where it was visible outside the white bandanna. "How would I look as a brunette?"

Jed pondered her response.

"Most of all, I wouldn't *sound* Amish, if I could help it," she continued.

Jed nodded. According to Uncle Ervin's friend, it was the woman's accent that gave her away.

"I'd also spend nearly all my time with Amish folk, since I'd be awfully homesick," Bettina said, clinching his plan.

Of course! Jed thought. *There are oodles of Amish at Lehman's Hardware.* "I guess I just need to check with the locals . . . ask if there are any fancy folk hanging round Amish."

"*Ach*, Jed." She stared at him, frowning. "Is this a *real* girl we're talkin' about?"

"She's very real, and she's a runaway."

"Well then, I'm sure someone will know *exactly* who you're looking for. But, Jed . . . most likely, even if ya could track down a girl like this, she might not have a thing to do with you. Runaways are fed up with bein' told what to do and how to be."

Lillian, he thought. *If Lily's changed her name, what else has she changed?*

"Tell me more." His sister stepped out of the horse stall and came to the door where Jed was working. Leaning on the door, she was clearly curious. "This doesn't have anything to do with the girl you liked in Lancaster County, does it?"

"There's nothin' to tell, frankly."

Bettina gave him a look. "I'll keep mum, I promise."

He thought of Eva's sisterly concern for Lily, and of Uncle Ervin's comments—if they panned out. "I'll let you know when or if I find out. How's that?"

Turning back, she slipped inside the other stall again and picked up the grooming brush once more. "It'll be your fault if I don't sleep tonight, ya know, wonderin' what you're up to."

"I'm just spinning my wheels. Prob'ly nothin' will come of it." He fluffed the bedding straw with a pitchfork. If Lily wanted to be fancy, that was her right, since she was old enough to make her own decisions. Even so, it was Eva he was concerned about, and he couldn't help but wonder if she had heard from Lily by now.

And if not . . .

What if I could bring Eva at least some measure of relief? But do I dare interfere in her life after messing up so badly?

Yet Jed felt he had little hope of another chance with Eva if he did nothing about Lily. It wasn't a perfect plan, but it was *something.*

Later, when he and Bettina had finished with the horses, his sister headed to the house to help their mother with some

271

hemming, and Jed made his way to the woodshed to split a pile of dry logs with his father.

Right away, Jed brought up the idea of an Old Order Amish person trying to go English. Typically, he and Daed didn't talk much when they worked together, but he wanted to hear what insight his father might have.

"What's this about going fancy?" His poor father looked *ferhoodled.*

"Ain't me, so don't worry."

"'Tis *gut.* Thought I heard from the deacon you were planning to take baptismal classes this summer."

"Right." Jed knew he'd better come up with something to shed a bit of light on what he was planning. "Someone I met in Pennsylvania has a relative who left the Amish community back there."

"And you'd like to locate him?"

"Well, it's a young woman, actually."

"I see."

Jed didn't feel obliged to tell more. "I just thought you might've heard accounts of some Amish youth tryin' to fit in with the outside world . . . and if they're ever persuaded to return to their families. What helps them want to stay put once they're back home?"

Daed leaned his axe against the woodpile and scratched his neck. "You don't hear of this a lot round here. Does the girl have a good church family to keep her from backsliding? Because none of us is immune to temptation, son."

"I know very little about her or the church district."

"Well, given the right—or wrong—circumstance, any of us is capable of sin." His father quoted 1 Corinthians 10, verse 12. "'Wherefore let him that thinketh he standeth take heed lest he fall.'"

272

Jed had heard that very verse during Sunday sermons.

"The Lord gives us the responsibility to keep track of each other." Daed stopped to wipe his brow with the back of his shirt sleeve. "Makes me wonder where the young woman's family is in all this."

"Sadly, her parents are deceased—her mother passed just recently."

"So then someone else needed to come alongside the girl to encourage her in the faith, ain't so?"

Jed wondered, now that his father had said this, if Lily's brothers had been too caught up with their own families, perhaps, or if they weren't even aware of Lily's struggles. Surely the latter was true. Yet with a loving, caring sister like Eva, how could Lily have been enticed by the world?

Daed had more to say. "The Deceiver of souls looks for discouraged and disconnected believers—'specially those isolated because of grief or disappointment. Such folks are cut off from the church body as a whole by their own doin'." Daed looked off in the distance like he was remembering someone in particular. "You've known people like this, Jed. They tend to drift away like chaff in the wind."

Jed nodded, keenly listening. "I'd like to help this young woman, if I can find her."

"Be careful, son. You might not like what you discover. Satan's trickery abounds." Daed picked up his axe and began chopping again, and Jed worked, too, glad to help his wise father.

May the Lord be with me, Jed prayed, wanting to do this for the right reason . . . though he could almost imagine Eva's lovely face when she learned that Lily had been found.

CHAPTER THIRTY-FIVE

·························· ❖ ··························

AT THE BREAKFAST TABLE the next morning, Jed's father opened his big Bible to the book of Proverbs. Mamm and Bettina were scrambling eggs and making waffles when Daed slid the Good Book under Jed's nose. "Here's another helpful verse to consider, son, concerning our conversation last night."

Jed read it silently. *Where no counsel is, the people fall: but in the multitude of counselors there is safety.*

He thanked Daed, and during the silent table grace, Jed asked God for direction in his search. *Please let me find some answers, O Lord.*

Following family worship after the meal, Bettina caught up with Jed as he was hitching up for work extra early so he could take off for Kidron at three o'clock that afternoon. "You must've talked to Daed 'bout what you told me," she said as she held the horse steady for him.

"It's always a *gut* thing to get our father's perspective."

Bettina agreed, smiling. "You said you'd let me know, remember?"

He assured her he wouldn't forget, if he even had anything to relay once all was said and done. The more he thought about Lily Esch, the more saddened he was that she'd allowed herself to become disconnected from her church . . . and, obviously, from her family. It just didn't make sense—how could a wayward girl have such profound thoughts and ideas about life . . . and love?

⌘

After a noon meal in which Menno, Emmanuel, and three farmhands had enjoyed Frona and Eva's cooking, Eva slipped her homemade card for Naomi into an envelope she'd found in Mamma's old writing desk. Eva and Frona then headed down Eden Road to Ida Mae's house for Naomi's birthday gathering. "Do ya think she'll be surprised?" she asked.

"Don't know why not," Frona replied. Like Eva, she wore her best blue dress and matching long apron.

"I'd thought of giving Naomi something from Mamma's dresser drawer—a pretty embroidered hankie or something like that, as a keepsake."

"Ain't a normal sort of birthday gift, is it?"

Eva glanced at Frona, who was apparently in a blue mood. "Would it be all right with you . . . when the time is right?"

"Don't we have more important things to think about today, Eva?"

Without saying more, she matched her pace with Frona's and kept quiet for the duration.

When they turned into Ida Mae's lane, several neighbors had already arrived, including Sylvia and Josie, as well as Naomi's daughters-in-law, Marian and Laura.

"*Ach*, I never thought my birthday was somethin' to celebrate much," Naomi said, cheeks pink as she sat in the kitchen. "Not at my age, anyway."

"You ain't that old, Mamma," Ida Mae said, taking a dish of nuts to the table.

Eva noticed the beautiful two-layer chocolate cake with two dishes of mints on either side. There was also a large glass pitcher of fruit punch. *She deserves a nice celebration*, Eva thought, glad Sylvia and Ida Mae had put their heads together and managed to get Naomi here without suspecting anything.

The party commenced with a fast game of Dutch Blitz, which got as loud and lively as Eva had ever experienced. When things calmed down a bit, Ida Mae wanted Naomi to open her cards and small gifts—a stationery set and a large-print leather New Testament several of the women had gone together to purchase.

Later, while they were enjoying birthday cake and ice cream, Naomi's older daughter-in-law, Marian, began to share about a young Amish couple from New Holland who'd purchased the farm next to them. "I'm not sure if they're kidding or not," Marian said, "but they said they'd removed the fire alarms, sayin' alls they need is a big bag of popcorn taped outside their bedroom door."

Marian had everyone's attention round the table. "According to her, if the house catches fire while they're asleep, the poppin' corn will wake them up."

Eva was amused and looked over at Frona, who muttered under her breath and shook her head.

"'Tis a joke, right?" Sylvia asked, her face reddening as soon as she'd spoken. "Surely that wouldn't work."

Eva kept waiting to see if Marian's expression changed, making it clear it was just a funny tale. But Marian took a bite of her cake and denied the other women's comments that this must have been something she'd read in *The Budget*.

"I wouldn't lie," Marian insisted. "You know well enough there are conservative Plain groups that prohibit fire alarms."

Naomi acknowledged this with a nod. "It's comforting to know you can wholly trust our heavenly Father no matter what you do—install a fire alarm or not, or put slow-movin' vehicle signs on your buggy. The Lord's will is highest and best."

We can depend on God's sovereign will, Eva agreed silently.

Afterward, while Frona and Ida Mae cleaned up the kitchen, Eva and Naomi went to sit in the front room, the sunlight pouring in around them. "Are ya sayin' that Alfred's declared himself to you?" Naomi asked.

Eva decided to tell her about the letters, the phone call, and the surprising invitation to move to Wisconsin. "The thing is, I'm not ready to take the serious step of relocating to allow him to court me."

"Did you let him know this?"

"I've been praying 'bout it, just as I told him I would. Honestly, though, I'm not leaning in that direction a'tall."

"If your heart's clearly against it, then you must say so." Naomi crossed her legs at the ankles, her feet bare. She studied Eva. "But can ya live with that decision?"

Eva sighed. "Maybe someday I might have feelings for him. Shouldn't I just be patient? Give things more time?" She looked toward the window, still feeling Naomi's gaze.

"Are ya concerned you'll end up a *Maidel?* Is that it, my dear?"

"Maybe so." Eva sighed. "I do want a loving husband and a family of my own someday."

Naomi rose and walked the length of the room, her hands clutched behind her back. Then, turning, she went to the tall, ornate grandfather clock and pulled the chain, watching first one weight rise, then the other. "You know what I believe?" She ambled back to sit again. "If the Good Lord wanted you married to Alfred, you'd find that kind of love in your heart right here and now, not hope it would blossom someday."

The wise, gentle words sounded like something Mamma might have said—Naomi cared so deeply about Eva's future.

"I daresay you can trust that your feelings aren't there for this young man. Nor your commitment."

Eva's mind was racing. "*Denki* for takin' time to chat, 'specially on your birthday."

Naomi laughed a little and folded her hands in her ample lap. "I'm doin' what I enjoy . . . spending time with one of Dottie's dear girls."

Eva began to feel better as she clung to Naomi's words on the way back to the house, where she and Frona set to shining their black church shoes for tomorrow's visiting Sunday.

"Did Naomi get you all straightened out?" Frona said, not looking up from where they were working out on the back porch. She dabbed more polish on one shoe at a time.

"*Jah* . . . guess I have a letter to write," Eva said.

"Poor Alfred."

Eva ignored her. "Naomi was so pleased over the party. Makes me think we oughta do this more often."

"Well, not on *my* birthday."

Eva disregarded that comment, as well. When she'd buffed her shoes to a shine and left them to dry, Eva excused herself and went upstairs, feeling all in.

Sitting on her bed with a sigh, she began to pray in earnest. When she was spent, Eva gave in to her mental exhaustion and leaned back on a pillow, promptly falling asleep.

The sound of a horse neighing woke her, and Eva discovered she'd rolled over onto her side during her nap. She stretched and yawned. The small clock on the bedside table showed that a half hour had already passed, and so deep her sleep had been, she must have dreamed, although she didn't recall the details.

Even so, she was all the more certain that she could *not* marry Alfred. She'd had a taste of how it felt to really connect with someone, and even if she never heard from Jed again, it would not change the truth.

I won't settle for less than what God's put in my heart. A lasting and meaningful love.

Getting up, Eva walked to the writing desk and sat down with renewed resolve. She opened the narrow middle drawer and removed a single piece of stationery, then began to write.

Saturday, June 21

Dear Alfred,

I hope you are doing well.

I've given your invitation some thought, and after praying about it, I know I cannot accept.

From what you've told me, it sounds like you're enjoying your work in Wisconsin, and the church district there, too. I don't doubt you'll make many new friends and sooner or later meet someone who loves you the way you deserve to be loved.

Thank you for being so kind to me. You're a very fine man.

> *Your friend,*
> *Eva Esch*

CHAPTER THIRTY-SIX

ONCE NOONTIME CAME AND WENT, Jed had caught himself glancing at the black wall clock every half hour at work. He had paced himself so that at three o'clock, he would be ready to meet his driver out front. Since Kidron was only twenty miles or so away, Jed knew he'd have ample time to look around there, pick up the items on his mother's shopping list, and nose around for information about the young woman named Lillian. Even so, he really had no game plan. *I'm looking to the Lord for that,* he thought as he hung up his work apron and called good-bye to Perry and his uncle, then hurried out the door.

"If you've never been to Lehman's Hardware, you'll be astonished at all there is to look at," the driver, George Garver, told him. George had been driving the Amish for decades, according to Uncle Ervin, and came highly recommended.

"I've been there a good number of times," Jed said, opening his mother's list. "I have a few things to locate while I'm there."

"Well, you'll have no trouble, believe me. They've got just about everything."

"High on my mother's priorities is an antique brass shopkeeper's bell."

"Oh? Is she setting up shop out back?"

"Hard to say." Jed chuckled. "But she's real eager for some of Troyer's trail bologna. Daed'll like that, too."

"Ah, smoked over hickory wood—nothin' like it," George said, smacking his lips. "It really pays to buy in bulk, ya know. I'll bet she wants some canning dome lids, too, and sugar. My wife gets all of her canning supplies at Lehman's."

Nodding, Jed tuned out the driver, becoming lost in his own thoughts. Was it even conceivable to think he could find Eva's younger sister? And if so, could he talk Lily, a girl he'd never met, into returning home to Eden Valley?

⟨⤳⤳⟩

Just as Jed remembered, Lehman's Hardware was flawlessly organized into sections—hardware, kitchen wares, canning supplies, handcrafted items, wicker baskets of all shapes and sizes, and large appliances, such as wood-burning cookstoves and gas-powered ranges, too. There were clocks, radios, and batteries of all manner of type and voltage, and books such as *Baer's Almanac*, *The Foxfire Books*, and a book demonstrating how to build your own root cellar. He was drawn to the home and farming tools and spent several minutes perusing the shelves.

Then he wandered over to the maple-sugaring supplies, vegetable and herb seed packets, and old-timey poplar fruit baskets, fruit harvesters, and food grinders.

I sure could lose track of time here, he thought, going to get some help from a nearby clerk, a Mennonite woman around his mother's age who welcomed him, then proceeded to share that she'd worked at many different retail outlets, and Lehman's was the best of all. With her assistance, in short order, he managed to gather up all of the items for his mother.

At the checkout, when Jed finally asked his question, the cheery woman said she'd never heard of a Lillian from Lancaster County or anywhere else. "Are ya sure that's the name?" the clerk asked as she searched for the price on the brass shopkeeper's bell.

"It's quite possible she goes by Lily." It was a long shot, but it was all he had.

"If she's going English, maybe she's gone south, where there's a nondenominational ministry for runaway Plain youth . . . helps them get acclimated to the outside."

Jed drew a deep breath. "Are there other Amish folk I might talk to 'bout this?"

"Well, there's ol' Joseph over yonder." She pointed behind Jed as she rang up the total. "If anyone has an ear for that sort of news, it's him or his wife."

Jed hadn't seen the older gentleman whom he now spotted sitting near the cookstoves, arms crossed, a piece of straw between his teeth.

Cautiously hopeful, Jed took his purchases and went to dilly-dally by the barrels, kegs, and crocks, feeling a bit awkward as he moseyed over to the aforementioned Joseph.

"May I help ya?" the friendly Amishman asked, leaning forward as Jed approached.

Jed glanced down at his large bag. "I found what I came for, but I'm wonderin' if you might've heard tell of a young newly fancy gal by the name of Lillian."

Joseph pinched up his round face and removed the piece of straw. "*Newly* fancy, ya say?"

"Within a month or so," Jed added quickly, then recounted the snippet of information he'd overheard his uncle telling Perry. "Have you heard anything along those lines?"

The old man paused a moment, then nodded. "Honestly, I don't miss much of anything. And *jah*, I have seen a newly minted gal in here quite a bit, and it looks a little strange 'cause she's not the kind of young woman you see in a hardware store." He paused again. "At least not dressed like she was. Lillian, you say?"

Jed nodded, hopes rising again.

"Hmm." The older man gestured toward the door. "Can't place the name, but I've seen a fancy girl walkin' down the street, usually by herself, so I'm gonna say she lives no more than a few blocks or so from here."

"Which direction?"

"East," Joseph said, pointing. "Likely right off Emerson." Then he cleared his throat. "Well, I can't rule out Jericho." He shuffled a bit. "Well, no, prob'ly Emerson."

Jed sighed. *A lot of homes along Emerson.* But it was a place to start, if only he had more time. He thanked Joseph, then was headed for the main entrance when he heard the old man bellowing across the store, "Why don't ya try the machine auction over yonder? Somebody there might help ya get closer."

Jed thanked him again and headed out the door, making his way to the van parked in front of the store. There, he unloaded his purchases and told George he was going to wander about the auction. "Would ya mind waitin', say an hour or so?"

"Take your time." George smiled and waved his hand. He'd gotten himself a Coke somewhere and had the radio going.

Jed walked across Kidron Road, where town workers were applying a patch of asphalt. A few black carriages were coming this way, and on his side of the street, a fatherly looking Amishman was pulling a small red wagon with two young boys inside. The bearded man nodded and said, "Hullo," pulling off to the side of the road. *Probably headed to the auction, too.*

More Amish, two teen boys and a girl, came strolling along, the boys wearing black Preaching clothes and the girl in a pale violet dress and black apron. The girl ceased talking when she spotted Jed. Then, as they passed, she let out a hushed giggle.

Like Bettina might.

Jed decided to head to the auction, too, and started asking a few folks outside the building. Once inside, feeling nervous, he approached the first Amishwoman he saw and explained his mission, but she only shook her head, so Jed went on to the next woman. For the next forty minutes, and feeling increasingly foolish, Jed asked one person after another, but no one could recall an Amish teenager recently turned English living in the vicinity. "Could be anyone, really," one woman said. "There's a bunch of former Amish living round here."

And Jed began to wonder if Joseph was imagining things.

It wasn't long before the hour was up, and Jed had nothing to show for it. He headed across the street, ready to throw in the towel for today.

Deep in thought, he glanced up and saw a young couple, both *Englischers*, heading this way. The woman was especially pretty in navy walking shorts and a white sleeveless top, her short blond hair in soft waves as she talked to the man in jeans and a black T-shirt.

Jed nodded as they approached, then passed. He lifted his gaze toward the sky, taking in the warm air and wondering if he'd done the right thing, coming here.

He felt frustrated that he didn't know where to turn, or what to do next, so he prayed for God's help as the late afternoon sun played on the trees, dappling the leaves and casting shadows on the ground as he walked. Was the gate slamming shut on his hope of finding Eva's sister?

When he'd gone clear to the outskirts of town, Jed hurried back to the van, not wanting to keep his driver any longer. "Thanks for your patience," he said as he got back into the front passenger seat, realizing he'd met his dead end. On top of that, he'd missed supper back home. *I'll be eating warmed-up leftovers tonight.*

CHAPTER THIRTY-SEVEN

JED'S DRIVER TURNED CAUTIOUSLY onto Kidron Road, mindful of the many cars and buggies. And as they crept along, Jed felt reluctant to leave the area for home, though he couldn't put a finger on why.

A few blocks up, Jed noticed the same blond girl he'd seen earlier walking alone wearing sunglasses, barefoot now as she dangled her white sandals. Oddly, her young man was hurrying down the street in the opposite direction with a determined gait, as if angry.

Wait a minute, Jed thought.

"Could ya pull over and park here, George?" he blurted.

The driver looked askance at him.

"This shouldn't take long." Jed opened the van door and got out. He waved to the young woman, feeling mighty awkward as he tried to catch her attention.

She glanced toward him and then turned away, heading up the sidewalk.

Jed continued briskly and did the only thing that made sense. He called her name, hoping she'd respond. "Lily!"

287

The young woman stopped walking and turned to face him, clearly startled.

Jed was a few yards away, hoping not to spook her any more than he already had, when she removed her sunglasses and squinted. "Lily Esch?" he called to her. He suppressed his smile, having stared at her photograph long enough to know this was, in fact, Eva's sister. "It *is* you."

Her mouth dropped open. "How do ya know me?"

Jed was close enough to smell her perfume. Her face was made up, her lips bright red. Jed had already mentally rehearsed what to say to her, aware that he had only so long to win her over. "I know your sister Eva," he said hastily.

A worried look crossed her countenance. "Did something happen to her? Is that why you're—"

Jed shook his head. "Eva's fine."

Lily seemed relieved, then scowled again. "Did she send you here to look for me?"

"*Nee*, but she's very worried."

Lily's eyes suddenly clouded.

"Can we talk?" Jed asked.

She glanced back at the retreating man, now more than a block away. "I'm not sure, I . . ." Fidgeting with the hem of her top, she stared at her feet.

Jed sensed his moment slipping away. "It's not too late to go home, Lily, if that's what you want."

Her head came up at the suggestion, and for a moment, he expected her to laugh at the notion, or to become angry at his presumption that she would *want* to return home.

He waited for her reply as she stared back at him, as though debating her reply. Once again, she glanced up the street, then back at Jed, her expression riddled with indecision.

I spoke too soon. "Listen, you don't have to decide this minute," he said now. "You can think about it."

"*Ach*, what a dumb thing I've done." Tears began to roll down her cheeks.

"Are you okay?"

"Not at all." She brushed away her tears, smearing her makeup so that she had dark smudges under her eyes. She looked at him curiously. "I'm sorry . . . who did ya say you are?" she asked in *Deitsch*.

"Jed Stutzman, from Berlin . . . not far from here."

"And you know Eva?"

She's not convinced.

"Eva gave me a look around her candy shop after we met at an auction near Quarryville a few weeks ago." He described the glass case filled with candies, naming some of Eva's favorites. "She loaded me up with her famous truffles for my trip home."

"How are they doin'—my sisters?" Lily struggled to ask.

"They're terribly concerned. Eva was distracted the whole time we were together, frettin' over you."

"And I'm stuck out here, trying to be something I'm not." She groaned as she fiddled with a heart-shaped necklace. "I could kick myself."

"There's only one way to fix a mistake," Jed said gently, looking back at George in the van. "Just don't keep goin' forward with it."

"Poor, dear Eva, what I've put her through! How can my family forgive me?"

The sight of this fragile yet beautiful girl crying right there on the street made him want to take care of her somehow. *But I'm a stranger to her. . . .*

"I guarantee they'll welcome you with open arms," he said quickly.

Lily shook her head. "I can't just go home as if nothin' happened."

"They love you. You're their sister."

"But I have no money, not even to make a phone call."

He saw his chance and took it. "Leave that to me. I'll get ya home, Lily."

At first, Lily was hesitant to get into the van with two men she didn't know.

George saved the day when Lily gave him the address of the Mennonite family with whom she had been staying. He lit up, saying they were his relatives. "That's one of my father's many brothers. You can call him if you want to double-check," he offered Lily.

Everyone's related round here, Jed thought, grateful for another divinely ordered facet to his search. *And to think I nearly gave up looking!*

Clearly reassured by this happenstance, Lily wasted no time in getting into the van. George drove them directly to the redbrick farmhouse surrounded by cornfields, where Lily quickly gathered up the few articles of clothing she'd brought, as well as thanked her kind host and hostess. It was time to say good-bye.

As they neared Jed's parents' farmhouse in Berlin, George pointed out the neighbors, who were putting on a new roof. A half-dozen Amishmen were crawling around high on the pitch of the roof, nailing down shingles. "A fine day for such a big chore," George said.

It was so quiet behind Jed that he wondered if Lily had fallen asleep. She'd said very little once they'd left Hank Garver's place.

By the time they were turning into the familiar lane, Jed had decided how he would tell his family about Lily's need to spend the night. He hoped to leave for Lancaster before dawn tomorrow, a visiting day for Jed's church district. *We'll arrive in Eden Valley a little after noon, perfect for a surprise reunion with the Esch girls.*

Jed hadn't thought much farther ahead than that. The whole thing was in God's hands—He alone had arranged Jed's every step thus far.

George had already consented to drive Jed and Lily to Lancaster County. *I'll run up quite the bill with this driver,* he thought.

He paid George in cash, then helped carry Lily's small suitcase to the back porch, where he asked if she'd mind waiting in one of the hickory chairs there. "Don't worry," he assured her. "You'll like my family."

This is a first, he thought. *I've never brought home a fancy-looking girl before!*

"I'm sorry to put you out like this, Jed," said Lily, sounding chagrined.

"Believe me, no bother."

His mother was kindly accommodating when he mentioned he was helping a young woman return to her Amish community.

"Your father mentioned this to me last evening," Mamm said, her dish towel slung over her left arm. "I'll warm up some supper for the two of yous, all right?"

Just then, Bettina walked downstairs and into the kitchen. "There's a girl in shorts sittin' out on the porch," she said quietly. "Is this—"

"*Jah,* her name's Lily Esch," Jed said. "I'm taking her home to Pennsylvania tomorrow."

"You found her that quick?"

"It's a long story, and it all started with finding a photo of her in a book on the train. She's a sister of the girl I met back in Lancaster," Jed explained. "And I don't know what happened to change Lily's mind, but something definitely has. I guess I was in the right place at the right time—glory be." He wondered how ridiculous this must sound. "Honestly, I was ready to give up and head home when I felt prompted to stay the course."

"Kinda like a miracle?" Bettina asked.

"*Jah*, I'd say so." *Beginning with the book and the photograph.*

Bettina grinned at Jed. "Surely George can get Lily home without you tagging along, ain't so?"

"Why, sure, but . . ." Jed stammered. "I just want to make sure . . ."

Bettina's face shone with delight. "And you say she's the *sister* of the girl back in Lancaster?"

Jed sighed. Bettina was going to have fun with this. "*Jah*," he confirmed, crossing his arms, waiting for further grilling.

"You're gonna look like quite the hero, I'll say."

Jed nodded. "That's the goal."

"Plus, you'll see your friend again . . . uh . . . what's her name?"

Mamm spoke up at last, eyeing Bettina. "All right, young lady. Leave your brother be."

She laughed, and Jed couldn't help laughing with her.

Eyes dancing with humor, Mamm snapped her fingers at Bettina. "Hurry now. Go up an' make sure there's fresh bedding on the spare bed, won't ya, and stop being such a troublemaker!"

Bettina nodded, but before she left, she grabbed her mother's tea towel and snapped Jed's knee.

"Daughter!" Mamm exclaimed. "Behave yourself!"

But Bettina was already gone, scampering upstairs to finish her chore, leaving an echo of giggles trailing behind her.

Jed smiled at Mamm and headed outside to get Lily, who looked quite relaxed in her chair.

Lily glanced up and smiled. "I'll need to do something 'bout these clothes."

Jed pulled up another chair and sat, appreciating her concern. "Did ya bring along a change?" he asked, thinking also about tomorrow. Her attire would disappoint her sisters.

"Unfortunately, I got rid of everything Plain." Lily pulled on her hair and looked glum. "And this curly mop." She moaned. "How will I ever get it under a *Kapp*?" She confided in him, saying that the first thing she'd done upon arriving in Kidron was to get her waist-length hair cut. "Got a permanent wave in it, too, but it turned out too curly."

Jed smiled encouragingly. She looked beautiful to him, but he could see how it would be mighty tricky to get her hair into a bun. *Nee*, he thought, *impossible for many months. She must've been determined to be English.*

"Why am I tellin' you all this?" she laughed, blushing.

"It's okay, really. I have a sister who tells me strange things. Well, a few sisters, actually."

She smiled and covered her legs with her hands. "I wonder if one of your sisters might have a dress I could borrow. I look so, um, worldly."

To her credit, her shorts weren't short shorts like some fancy women strutted around in, but Daed wouldn't know what to think. Such attire simply wasn't respectful.

"It's just Mamm and my youngest sister inside, so now's a *gut* time to meet them and find out if Bettina has something for you."

Lily offered a relieved smile and gushed her thanks.

He picked up her suitcase and held the screen door for her. Tomorrow was another day, and hopefully it, too, would prove to be providential.

CHAPTER THIRTY-EIGHT

.... ❀ ....

BETTINA JOINED JED AND LILY when they sat down to the
reheated leftovers, something Jed assumed Mamm had privately
asked his sister to do. Bettina had managed to work wonders
with Lily upstairs. With the help of many bobby pins, Bettina
had plastered Lily's hair down on both sides around her middle
part. Bettina's lavender dress and black apron were equally trans-
forming on Lily, who'd washed the makeup from her face, as well
scrubbed as any rosy-cheeked Amish teenager.

While they enjoyed Mamm's leftover pork chops and onions,
and mashed potatoes and gravy, Bettina kept the conversation
going, and it appeared that Lily liked her rather well. *She spared
Lily further embarrassment,* Jed thought, watching the two of
them interact so comfortably across the table.

Lily glanced over her shoulder and must have noticed that
Jed's mother had slipped outdoors. Leaning forward, Lily lowered
her voice. "I've never known any fella to be so *ferhoodled* as my
boyfriend," she said, eyes sad.

Bettina covered Lily's hand, her manner warm and gentle. "How did you meet him, Lily?"

Lily took a small breath and sighed. "I met him a year ago, when I was in Kidron with my friend Fannie Ebersol and her family. Mark was at the Thursday hay and cattle auction, where Fannie and I had gone for fun. Mark came right over while I was looking at some of the craftware. He said he was a horse trainer, and a very *gut* one. I guess I should've picked up on his bluster even then." She went on, reliving the relationship aloud, explaining how Mark had been eager to seek her out despite her Plain appearance. He'd even urged her to give a mailing address where he could write to her. "With Fannie's permission, I gave him her address, and he began writing to me there twice a week. For nearly a year, he never missed."

Jed couldn't get over how trusting Lily had been of an outsider, and as she described their quickly developing romance, she admitted that reading Mark's expressive letters had made her yearn for modern life.

"I mistakenly believed that if I could just live closer to Mark, I'd learn how to put my Plainness behind me," Lily told them. "But as it turned out, he became upset, even angry—that's what happened again earlier today, when he stormed away—and denied that I was givin' my all to be English, like him. 'You're more Amish than you know!' he hollered at me." Her chin trembled, and she bowed her head.

Bettina put her arm around Lily's shoulders. "Aw, Lily, it seems to me it was a *gut* thing he lost control of his temper and left ya. Don't you?"

"I never dreamed things would go downhill so quick." Lily was crying now.

Hearing Eva's sister talk about the futile relationship, Jed recalled her notes in the book. *More than anything, I long for a love that makes my heart sing,* she'd written on one of its final pages. He felt truly sorry for Lily. Her dreams and romantic wishes, all thought to have been found in Mark, had not been fulfilled in the least. *A young woman who was sadly misguided in looking for true love—enough to give up her family and faith.*

Jed made a call to Uncle Ervin's shop phone and left a message on the answering machine about his sudden trip to Lancaster County tomorrow. "Depending on how it goes, I may not be back till sometime Monday."

Later, alone in his room, Jed reread one of the highlighted passages that had popped out at him earlier in *Little Women*: *"Love will make you show your heart someday. . . ."*

He let the words flow through his mind, knowing he must return the novel to Lily tomorrow. It had been an enlightening journey in many ways, but it was winding down and coming to an end.

⌁

That Lord's Day morning, Eva read aloud the first half of Psalm 139. "'O Lord, thou hast searched me, and known me. Thou knowest my downsitting and mine uprising; thou understandest my thought afar off.'" She continued through verse twelve, then passed the Bible to Frona, after which they had their silent prayers. Following their family worship, they discussed which relatives to visit today, an off-Sunday from Preaching service.

Frona mentioned two aunts they hadn't seen in some time. "But I'd like to be home for the noon meal, even if it's a bit later than usual," she said. "Honestly, I'm tired, and some peace and quiet might be in order."

Eva agreed, thinking Frona looked a bit peaked. *Being apart from Lily makes us both feel off beam.*

"I wouldn't mind if we just stayed put at home resting and reading," she said, her heart going out to Frona.

"Well, what if we made just one stop to Mamm's aunt Rose Anna down on Groff Road? In fact," Frona said, rising from her spot on the front room settee, "what if we took our time and walked over there?"

Eva liked the idea, considering the amount of time it would take to hitch up the horse and all. The sunshine and fresh air would feel ever so good.

"We'll leave midmornin', then," Frona said.

"And I'll take along some candies to spread cheer."

❧

Naomi sat outside with Abner on the front porch that late June Lord's Day, rocking on their chairs and enjoying each other's company. As was sometimes the case, neither said much, content as they were.

They'd had their devotions together after breakfast, and presently Naomi took her rest in the words of their Lord in the Gospel of Luke. *Take heed to yourselves: If thy brother trespass against thee, rebuke him; and if he repent, forgive him. And if he trespass against thee seven times in a day, and seven times in a day turn again to thee, saying, I repent; thou shalt forgive him.*

Closing her eyes, she prayed again for Omar. *May he find his peace in Thee, O Lord.*

She breathed the fragrance of nearby honeysuckle blossoms. *Sweet as Eva's candies.* And, lo and behold, across the way, Frona and Eva herself were strolling down their driveway toward the road. Eva was carrying a small white box with a pretty pink bow perched on top. *Must be some of her delicious concoctions,* Naomi assumed, waving to them.

Abner called, "A blessed Lord's Day to ya both!"

Frona merely nodded, but Eva smiled. "Same to you," she answered.

"Such a thorny road they must walk," said Naomi. "I pray the Lord God comforts their dear hearts."

Abner reached for her hand. "'Tis my constant prayer."

"Just look at them," she said.

"Last year at this time, they seemed so happy, remember?" Abner remarked. "All of them . . ."

Naomi refrained from saying what was on her mind. Seeing the Esch girls, just two of them now, made her heart ache so.

"Ain't possible to put a price tag on the love of family, *jah*?" Abner raised her hand to his lips and kissed it.

❦

The van was heading into the populated retail and restaurant sector of Route 30, approaching the turnoff onto Route 896 to Strasburg. Jed's pulse beat a little faster as he recalled his first trip there by train. He reached behind him for the novel packed in his duffel bag on the seat opposite Lily but couldn't quite get it.

"Would ya mind handing that bag to me?" he asked, leaning around the front seat. "There's something I've been meaning to return."

Lily lifted the bag forward.

"I found this book on the train to Lancaster." He removed it from the bag and handed it to her. "It was stuck between the wall and the seat."

She accepted it with a puzzled frown. "You *found* this?"

"I was on the same train you must've taken to Ohio."

Lily's eyes widened.

"You left your picture in it," he added.

"*Ach* no," she muttered.

"Far as I know, Eva has the photograph now."

Lily shook her head, clearly embarrassed. "I'm sure she destroyed it, which is all right with me."

Jed recalled the words on the back of the picture but didn't want to open old wounds, considering all she'd been through. But his curiosity got the best of him. "Lily, I couldn't help noticing what you wrote: 'The best and worst day . . .'"

Lily smiled wistfully. She was quiet for a moment, as if gathering courage. "*Jah*, I was giddy with happiness, eager to please Mark. . . . I thought I loved him," Lily said softly, glancing at their driver, who didn't flinch. "I had a strip of pictures made for my boyfriend and kept one for myself. It was an impulsive thing to do . . . and terribly wrong."

Jed waited for her to say something about what she meant by the worst day, but he guessed it meant all that she was giving up for Mark in Ohio—her Amish life, her family, too. Besides, he didn't want to make her feel any more self-conscious than she already was.

"You must've thought I was shameless to have a picture made while wearing my *Kapp*."

"It was a bold move."

She reclined against her seat with a sigh. "I have so much to make up for."

They were deep into farmland now, whizzing past bank barns and giant silos and herds of grazing cattle. Often, Amishmen waved to them at the yield signs on the road. *Everyone waves*, Jed thought.

He was about to turn back in his seat when Lily spoke again. "So now *I'm* curious. How'd ya happen to meet Eva?" She was thumbing through the front pages of the novel. "There's certainly no address in here."

Jed considered that and told his story, leaving out the part about his fascination with the margin notes and underlined passages. "It was while I was in town to meet Jonas Byler that I ran into Eva at an auction. I thought she was *you*."

Lily laughed a little. "Honestly? So you and Eva obviously became friends in a very short time. Have you kept in touch . . . written, perhaps?"

He hesitated, then figured she'd eventually hear the full account from Eva anyway. "Unfortunately things ended on a sour note between us. You see, I didn't tell her about the photograph right away like I should have." He shook his head at the memory of Eva's shocked and befuddled expression that day. "Guess maybe she thought I was a little too taken with your photograph."

"That's silly." Lily laughed again.

Jed shifted in his seat, wishing he'd sat back there so they could talk more privately. This had become a very open conversation, considering George was hearing everything. "Actually, I was impressed . . . but not by your picture, Lily."

She placed her hand on her chin. "What do ya mean?"

"I paged through your book."

"Not exactly male reading material, *jah*?" she said.

Jed chuckled. "You've got that right. But honestly, I was taken with your notes and what you chose to underline."

She grimaced. "Jed—"

"What I'm sayin' is . . ." He paused. "Okay, I understand how foolish this might sound to you."

"You felt a connection with the person who wrote the notes?" Lily interrupted.

"Like minds, I guess you could say."

Lily smiled and looked at *Little Women*. "My sister Eva is the dearest person to me, so I'm not surprised you would be impressed with her notes. Her thoughts are all over these pages."

Jed frowned. "What?"

Lily's smile widened. "It's not my book, Jed. I only brought it along so I'd have something to remind me of Eva."

The book isn't Lily's? Jed could not have imagined this.

Their driver, George, burst out with a chuckle. "Well, Jed, ain't that something?"

Jed and Lily joined in laughing at his unexpected interjection.

Moments later, Lily's smile disappeared as she glanced out the window, wringing her hands. "Thanks for takin' me home, Jed. But I'm so nervous."

"They'll be excited to see you, so don't be," Jed said.

Lily sighed again. "I hope so."

Still amazed at Lily's revelation, Jed turned to watch for the turnoff to Eden Road as they headed south through rolling hills and pastureland. "Is this the quickest way?" he asked George.

"You seem anxious, too, Jed," said Lily with a titter.

He glanced over his shoulder. There was a mischievous glint in her eyes now that they'd shared each other's secrets. "Do I, now?"

"After what you've told me, I'm not sure which of us is more keyed up."

He chuckled. She was right. "Will ya put in a *gut* word for me with Eva?"

"I think you'll do fine without my help, honestly."

He asked to see the book again one last time. Opening at random, Jed noticed one of his favorite notes: *Yearning for true love points us to the all-lovely one—the great Lover of our hearts, the Lord Jesus.*

He wholeheartedly agreed. *To think it was Eva all along . . . from the very start,* he thought, closing the book.

The driver slowed to heed the speed limit on Eden Road, and as they gradually moved west, Jed spotted a line of lake willows set back beside a broad meadow covered in wild daisies—and then his eye caught something more. *Can it be?*

"Let's stop here," he instructed George. "Look there, Lily," he said, opening his door, then getting out and opening Lily's. "Your sisters are sittin' over on a fence. See them?"

"I can't believe this. It's Eva's and my spot," Lily said, her eyes dancing. Then, just as suddenly, she shrank back. "What if . . ."

"Follow me," Jed said, leading her.

Eva must have seen them; she was already running this way, her skirt tail flying. Frona was hurrying behind her, waving.

"Lily!" Eva called. "Oh, Lily, you've come home!"

Jed didn't have to look to know there were happy tears; he could hear Lily's sniffles. And then she took off toward her sisters.

Observing the heartwarming scene unfold, Jed hung back, letting Lily have the promised reunion in the grassy meadow.

"I don't have to introduce you to Jed, do I?" he heard Lily say.

Grinning, he reached down to pick one of the daisies.

Eva hugged Lily repeatedly—this was so unbelievable. Yet she'd longed for this moment every single day of Lily's absence. "God answered our prayers," she said, reaching for Lily's hand. "He obviously wanted you home, where you belong."

Frona started to laugh, though she was trying to smother it as she stared at Lily. "Your hair is, well, very different, sister."

Another curl sprung loose as Lily reached up to touch it. "It's the worst thing I've ever done to myself."

"*Ach*, it'll grow back," Eva said with a tug on Lily's hand.

Lily glanced back at Jed, standing yards away. "Someone came a long way . . . and not just to accompany me home," she whispered.

Eva's glance followed her sister's, and she was struck again by how handsome Jed was. But she wasn't surprised to see him with

Lily. "I'm so glad Jed finally found you." The thought was bitter-sweet, but she was too happy to see Lily again to let anything interfere with her joy. "He must've been awfully determined to manage to track ya down once he got back to Ohio."

Lily broke free, her eyes alight with mischief. "*Jah*, I'll say he's determined. But the girl he was searchin' for was right here all along."

Eva was confused. "I don't understand."

Lily gazed earnestly into her face and gently held her by the shoulders. "Jed only came back with me to see you, Eva."

"Are ya ever so sure?" she whispered, guarding her heart.

"Come, Frona, let's head for the van," Lily said with a grin back at Eva. "We should leave the two lovebirds alone."

Looking toward Jed, Eva walked to him, her heart in her throat. *Does Lily know what she's talking about?*

"Hullo again," Jed said, offering a yellow daisy.

"*Denki* for bringin' my sister back to us. I don't know how to thank you."

"It was the Lord's doing, but I have to admit I asked Him for a hand. S'pose you didn't expect to see me again so soon."

She sniffed the flower, then looked up—his eyes were fixed on hers. "Seein' you is sure a welcome surprise, Jed." She couldn't help but recall the times she'd prayed for peace in the midst of her bewilderment. And to think Lily was home again, and here Jed was, standing before her, too.

Frona said he'd be back for more of my truffles, she thought, letting a smile take over her face.

They went to the van, where Jed asked George to take Frona and Lily home. "We're going to walk awhile."

George nodded. "At your service."

Lily let out a little giggle, and Frona shushed her before Jed closed their door.

"I want to tell you a little story," Jed said as he fell into step with Eva on the dirt shoulder.

"Sounds nice. I like a *gut* story." *Especially love stories,* she thought, wondering what was up his sleeve.

"This one's about a fella who was a little sweet on a girl he'd never met," Jed began. "And then when he naïvely thought he'd met her, he knew he was a goner—she was better than he'd imagined." He stooped to pick another flower and gave it to Eva. "Of course, he really confused things by not being straightforward with the girl—a mistake he's regretted ever since," he added. "But then there was a twist he wasn't expecting."

"Sounds like a mystery." Eva liked this.

"One with a startling surprise at the end."

"*Jah?*"

Jed nodded. "When the fella finally figures it all out."

"And does the story end happily?"

"Well, that part's unfinished," Jed said, catching her eye.

"Maybe we could finish it together," Eva suggested.

They walked along slowly, the breeze warm on their faces. Birds twittered high overhead, flapping their wings as they soared against the wind. Eva noticed the run-in shed the neighbors had recently built for their horses, and the way the trees moved gracefully, as if somehow swaying to a heavenly melody.

At last Jed said, "I was wondering if I could borrow your copy of *Little Women.*"

Startled, Eva turned her head quickly but saw the twinkle in his eye. She played along. "I'm afraid that book's just for women, Jed."

He chuckled. "Well, I've already read a good portion of it. Besides, it's where I found Lily's photograph."

Jed told her the full story, and her eyes widened.

"So you've been reading my secrets, have ya?"

Jed slowed his stride. "Can you forgive me?"

"Absolutely not." Then she began to laugh.

He was grinning now and stopped walking to face her. "I said it before: I want to get to know you, Eva."

She smiled. "Honestly, I think you already do."

Eva couldn't help it—her heart sang as Jed reached for her hand and raised it slowly to his lips this shining Lord's Day afternoon.

Epilogue

IF SOMEONE HAD SAID even a month ago that I'd be courted long-distance by a serious beau, I wouldn't have believed it. In addition to Jed's frequent letters, he visits me every other weekend. Abner and Naomi have opened their home to him when he's here, welcoming him as warmly as Dat and Mamma would have—they're sure Jed Stutzman was hand-picked by God for me. It's hard not to blush when Naomi privately tells me such things.

As for Lily, her longing for the fancy world is a thing of the past, and she has been cheerfully received back by the People. Our neighbors have gone out of their way to drop by to visit, some bearing red and pink bleeding hearts picked from their flower beds. Lily has fully embraced the Old Ways and even plans to join church come mid-September. She revealed this recently when we wandered out to our old playhouse together, where she confessed to having taken the *Little Women* quote jotted down decades ago.

"*When I left home, I needed something of my early roots,*" Lily explained. "*That's why I took your book, too.*" While we were there,

Lily also made a point of explaining why she hadn't written for so long after her disappearance. *"And even then, I had someone mail my one and only letter from Wooster, in case ya noticed the postmark. I was awful selfish, not wanting you to come lookin' for me."*

Together, we slipped the quote back into its narrow quarters along the window frame. It was a meaningful moment, and we decided that, perhaps in the future, one of our own little girls might discover the words hidden in the playhouse, since Menno has promised not to turn it into firewood. Thanks to Frona!

When I think of leaving Eden Valley behind someday, I know how much I'll miss my family, and our dear neighbors, too. But being Jed's bride will be worth the parting many times over— should he ask me.

I'm so thankful to have met a man who shares my heart. Nice as Alfred is, I could never have settled for him. Here lately Miriam Dienner told Naomi Mast that Alfred has met someone in Wisconsin. It's comforting to know, because Alfred deserves someone to love him, too.

❦

During blistering August, when the cornstalks towered high over us and the humid days stretched longer than the nights, Jed came to Eden Valley for another visit and borrowed Abner's family carriage to take me riding.

He eased back in the seat and slipped his arm around me. "I've been talkin' with Jonas Byler about renting his carriage shop, and all the tools and equipment, too, just till I can afford to officially take over his business. My time with him and his many connections will be awful handy once I relocate to Lancaster County."

"Oh, Jed." Happy tears welled up. "You're movin' *here*."

We talked further about his plans, including Perry Hostetler's eagerness to run Uncle Ervin's buggy shop. Jed also wanted me

308

to attend his sister Bettina's wedding in Ohio. "My family can meet you at last."

"Are ya sure you want to move away from them?"

"Why wouldn't I?" He cupped my face with his hands and looked deep into my eyes. "My heart's right here, Eva . . . with you."

❧

The following May, when the lily-flowered tulips painted the beds yellow along my parents' former front porch, Jed dropped by to see me at Abner Masts'. I had accepted their kind offer to stay with them once Menno and his family settled into my childhood home last October.

Jed wanted to walk around "our" pond, and I felt sure something was up. The willow grove behind the Masts' house was bursting with new foliage, and there beneath the heavenly green canopy, Jed bent down and kissed my cheek. "I've been thinking 'bout something," he said furtively. "But everything hinges on one thing." He paused and smiled tenderly. "Only one."

I felt nearly breathless. "What is it?"

He rubbed his smooth chin. "I'm wonderin' if ya still have that recipe for those tasty truffles," he said solemnly.

"Believe me, I would never think of losin' that top-secret recipe!"

"*Des gut*, 'cause if you'll have me as your husband this wedding season, those truffles would be perfect at the feast."

I started laughing so hard I could hardly stop.

"Well, I hope *that's* not your answer," he said, feigning horror. "I mean, a hearty laugh instead of: '*Jah, Jed, I'll be happy to marry ya.*'"

"Oh, you!" I tried to regain my poise, taking a deep breath. "I would be honored to make irresistible sweets for ya all the days of your life."

309

Jed made a big show of wiping his brow. "*Ach*, you had me worried."

"Don't be silly." I rose up on my tiptoes to kiss his chin.

"My whole family will want to come for our wedding," Jed said. "That is, once I inform them that you've agreed to marry me."

"And I surely have." My heart was as full as a cream-filled bonbon.

"By the way, I've got an idea. My uncle, a few years older than Frona, might be her ideal match."

"Really? Surely not a *perfect* match?"

"Considering he's nearly as tetchy as Frona can be, they might be cheerfully prickly together."

I smiled. "And just when do ya plan to introduce this relative of yours?"

"At our wedding, of course."

"If it's a match," I said, the wheels turning in my mind, "Frona won't have much reason to worry anymore."

"And Lily?"

"Oh, I assume she'll continue being a mother's helper for Bena, at least for the time being. Or do you have more unmarried kin up your sleeve?"

Jed's laughter rang out. "I'll see what I can do."

Later, the sun beat hard on the gray vinyl roof of Jonas's buggy as we rode, coming upon Ida Mae's roadside vegetable stand down the way. We waved and she motioned for us to stop and have some ice-cold lemonade. "Freshly made," she said, bringing two tumblers to the buggy.

"What do ya know? A lemonade drive-in," Jed joked as he reached into his pocket.

Ida Mae refused his payment. "It's the least I can do for you two."

The word's out. I glanced lovingly at Jed.

Thanking her, we headed onward, and it was a joy to see this verdant area through his eyes, especially when he stopped in front of a modest clapboard house on the east end of Eden Road and pointed to the *For Sale* sign out front.

"Lookee there." He leaned forward. "I wonder how hard it would be for someone to build a candy shop in back." Jed turned to wink at me.

"Are you kiddin'?" I whispered, searching his dear face.

He admired the house again. "Seems solidly built—perfect, too, for tourists comin' in and out of the lane."

My smile was so big, I could feel it stretch clear across my face. "When can we see it?" I paused, realizing I was jumping ahead of Jed. "I mean . . ."

He pulled into the lane and checked his wristwatch. "The real estate agent should be arriving right about now."

My heart was beating wildly. To think I'd worried about having to someday leave my family and Eden Valley!

Later, after seeing every inch of the lovely house, we took our time while driving back toward Abner Mast's place. And as we turned into the drive, I noticed the front porch swing moving in the breeze.

"I know my parents would've liked you," I said when Jed came around to offer a hand.

"Somehow, I hope they know how happy you are, Eva."

"Oh, I trust so." I could hear Abner calling his lead cow in his down-to-earth way, ready to bring the herd home for afternoon milking.

"I'll water the horse," Jed told me. "You go in and talk to Naomi. I'm sure you want to."

With all of my heart, I did. I hurried across the yard, past Naomi's rainbow of peonies in mature bloom, a gift from Mamma years ago. Standing on the side porch, I took in the rich array of pinks, whites, and crimsons. *Gifts of love live on and on.* I thought of these flowers appearing every springtime . . . and of Dat and Mamma's sweet love for each other and for all of us.

Jah, they would rejoice in my love for Jed. *The man I was born to love.*

Author's Note

THIS PARTICULAR STORY is sweet to my writer-heart for many reasons. I admit to being drawn to the Amish farmland around which I grew up, and the return to the setting of Eden Valley from *The River*—and the glimpses of Tilly Lantz Barrows and her growing family—are a result of my desire to step back into this rural area not far from my own childhood home. It was there that my sister and I read *Little Women* and acted out plays, just as the four celebrated March sisters did. I share Eva's love for that classic novel, as well as her yearning for a love that makes her heart sing.

Speaking of love, I am grateful to my own dear husband for his superb help with the first edit of the initial manuscript, as well as the appetizing breakfasts and lunches he so cheerfully makes when I'm on deadline. A thousand thanks and more, Dave!

To my faithful prayer partners—Jim and Ann Parrish, David and Janet Buchwalter, Aleta Hirschberg, Iris Jones, Donna DeFor, Judy Verhage, Amy Green, and my immediate family: God bless you abundantly for your care and faithfulness.

To my astute and very supportive editors—David Horton, Rochelle Glöege, Ann Parrish, and Helen Motter: I am in awe of your expertise, encouragement, and the way you seek to enhance my work.

To my research assistants, fact-checkers, and proofreaders— Hank and Ruth Hershberger, Fred Jones, Barbara Birch, Dave Lewis, Rhonda Abbott, Teresa Lang-Tsingine, Jolene Steffer, Cheri Hanson, and dozens of Amish and Mennonite readers and consultants: You continue to play such a vital role. Thank you!

To my lovely readers: Thanks for your cheery cards, gifts, emails, snail mail, and Facebook posts and messages. You are the dearest reader-friends ever!

Also, I am indebted to the writings of Louisa May Alcott, whose endearing letters and journals I have read and relished for decades, along with her renowned novel *Little Women*.

Researching my stories is part of the fun of writing, and while I strive for accuracy, sometimes it is necessary to fictionalize certain details. For the sake of this story, I devised a common passenger coach between Alliance, Ohio, and Lancaster, Pennsylvania. After all, Jed needed somewhere to discover that intriguing photograph!

My magnificent Eskimo spitz, Maxie, makes his debut in this story, brought to life again on the page as a reminder of happy childhood days in Lancaster County. And one of my favorite sweets is here too—peanut butter balls like Eva's own.

As I close this note, I think again of Dottie Esch's instruction to young Lily. May we all remember that the footprints made on life's journey can either lead others astray or lead them aright. Thankfully God is ever near to guide when we ask.

Soli Deo Gloria!

Beverly Lewis, born in the heart of Pennsylvania Dutch country, is the *New York Times* bestselling author of more than ninety books. Her stories have been published in eleven languages worldwide. A keen interest in her mother's Plain heritage has inspired Beverly to write many Amish-related novels, beginning with *The Shunning,* which has sold more than one million copies and is an Original Hallmark Channel movie. In 2007 *The Brethren* was honored with a Christy Award.

Beverly has been interviewed by both national and international media, including *Time* magazine, the Associated Press, and the BBC. She lives with her husband, David, in Colorado.

Visit her website at www.beverlylewis.com or www.facebook.com/officialbeverlylewis for more information.

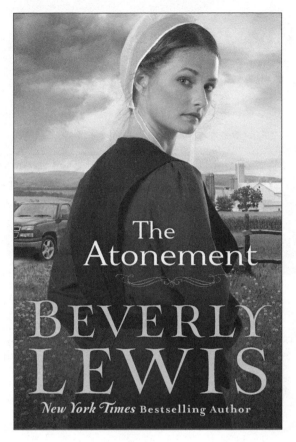

More From Bestselling Author
Beverly Lewis

Visit beverlylewis.com or find Beverly on Facebook to learn more.

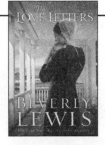

When Marlena Wenger is faced with a difficult decision—raising her sister's baby or marrying her longtime beau—what will she choose?

The Love Letters

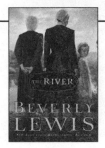

When two formerly Amish sisters return home for their parents' landmark anniversary, both are troubled by the past and the unresolved relationships they left behind.

The River

More From Bestselling Author
Beverly Lewis

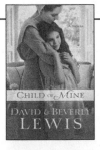

Kelly Maines has never stopped searching for the daughter who was taken from her. Eight years later, will she find her at last?

Child of Mine (with David Lewis)

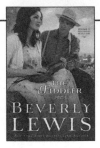

Journey home to Hickory Hollow, the setting where Beverly's celebrated Amish novels began in *The Shunning*! With her trademark style, this series of independent books features unforgettable heroines and the gentle romances her readers have come to love.

HOME TO HICKORY HOLLOW: *The Fiddler, The Bridesmaid, The Guardian, The Secret Keeper, The Last Bride*

◊ BETHANYHOUSE